PATRICIA H. RUSHFORD

S0-ASN-975

Sins of the Mother

Our purpose at Howard Publishing is to:

- *Increase faith* in the hearts of growing Christians
- *Inspire holiness* in the lives of believers
- *Instill hope* in the hearts of struggling people everywhere

Because He's coming again!

Sins of the Mother © 2003 by Patricia H. Rushford
All rights reserved. Printed in the United States of America
Previously published under the title *Morningsong*

Published by Howard Publishing Co., Inc.
3117 North 7th Street, West Monroe, Louisiana 71291-2227
In association with the literary agency of Alive Communications, Inc.
7680 Goddard Street, Suite 200, Colorado Springs, CO 80920

03 04 05 06 07 08 09 10 11 12 10 9 8 7 6 5 4 3 2

Interior design by John Luke
Cover design by The Resource Agency

Library of Congress Cataloging-in-Publication Data

Rushford, Patricia H.
[Morningsong]
Sins of the mother / Patricia H. Rushford.
p. cm.
Previously published as: Morningsong. Minneapolis : Bethany House Publishers, c1998.
ISBN 1-58229-342-2
1. Women country musicians—Fiction. 2. Sound recording industry—Fiction. 3. Mothers—Death—Fiction. 4. Divorced women—Fiction. I. Title.

PS3568.U7274M67 2003
813'.54—dc22

2003056616

To my husband,

Ron,

for thirty-nine years of enduring love.

About the Author

Patricia Rushford, internationally known author and speaker, has written more than forty books that have gained her a reputable spot in both the adult and youth fiction markets. With more than a million copies sold, her books are enjoying overwhelming success with readers of all ages.

She has numerous awards to her credit, such as an Edgar nomination, and a Silver Angel Award for Excellence in Media. Patricia has appeared on numerous radio and television talk shows throughout the U.S. and Canada, including *Prime Time America* and *Focus on the Family.* She also conducts writer's workshops and retreats across the country and is codirector of Writer's Weekend at the Beach.

Patricia is a registered nurse and holds an M.A. degree in counseling. She and her husband, Ron, reside near Portland, Oregon. Visit Patricia's Web site at www.patriciarushford.com.

Prologue

A lone figure lingered in the shadows behind Elizabeth O'Brian's modest home on the Morningsong Estate, listening to the purr of Elizabeth's black Porsche—and waiting while it filled the garage and her bedroom above with its noxious fumes. She'd be dead soon. He'd wait a few days, then come back and search for the evidence Elizabeth claimed to have against them.

Come morning, Elizabeth's daughter, Shanna, would come home from her concert tour and find her mother had died in her sleep—a tragic accident…or maybe suicide.

Elizabeth O'Brian woke out of a deep sleep. Had she heard something? A car running somewhere nearby? She turned onto her back, taking a deep breath. *Air. Need air. Get out of bed. Open window.* She willed her body to move, but it failed to respond.

Elizabeth closed her eyes. So tired. Her mind, restless and churning, dragged up a seventeen-year-old memory. Elizabeth, who avoided the past at all costs, suddenly had no energy to fight against it. Her daughter had been so small and innocent then. Such a long time ago, yet the memory hung in her mind as clear as the full moon in the midnight sky.

"Come on, Shanna. Hurry!" Elizabeth called from the front porch of their miserable excuse for a home. "We don't want to be late for your appointment."

"Can I take Libby, Mama?"

Her seven-year-old daughter hugged a bedraggled rag doll as she jumped over the threshold. Elizabeth cringed. The doll had been a

Christmas gift from Shanna's father, shiftless so-and-so that he was. She hated that doll—hated all it represented. It was as threadbare as their furniture and most of their clothes. But this wasn't the time or the place to argue. She couldn't afford to have her little girl tearful and upset, not now.

"All right—as long as you promise to leave her in the car when we go in to see Mr. Morgan."

"Do we have to go, Mama?"

"Of course. He's a very nice man, darling. I wouldn't take you there if he wasn't. All you have to do is sing your best. You can do that for Mommy, can't you?"

"Yes."

"Good." Elizabeth had pulled a lot of strings for the opportunity to have Shanna audition for the great Andrew Morgan. If she could sign Shanna up with Morningsong Productions, they would be set for life. If she didn't...well, Elizabeth wouldn't entertain that possibility. She'd spent all of her savings, along with that month's food money, on their new outfits.

Elizabeth gripped her daughter's hand and pulled her down the stairs toward the waiting limousine and climbed inside. Mr. Morgan had insisted on picking them up. That was a good sign. She just wished the house and neighborhood they'd been living in weren't in such disrepair. well, no matter. If all went according to plan, they'd be living high on the hog in a few months. The driver closed the door, shutting them safely inside. A very good sign. Elizabeth smiled and leaned against the cushy leather seat.

Driving away, Elizabeth felt a twinge of guilt, then quickly extinguished its flame. Though she'd been accused of it by her ex-husband and his friends, she wasn't taking advantage of her little girl. She was merely seeing to it that Shanna's talents didn't go to waste as hers had. Patting Shanna's golden red halo of curls, Elizabeth made a vow. "You'll be a big star one day, darling," she whispered. "I'll see to that."

Even now, seventeen years later, that first meeting with Andrew Morgan brought bittersweet memories. Andrew had immediately recognized the potential in Shanna. While he and his entire family had come to embrace Shanna as one of their own, they merely tolerated Elizabeth. That was fine with her. She didn't need the approval of the rich and powerful Morgan clan.

Under Elizabeth's stern and watchful eye, Shanna had gone on to become a superstar. Elizabeth, acting as her manager, reaped the monetary benefits and a certain amount of power. In recent years she'd fought hard to maintain control over her daughter. There had been some heartbreaking moments, but as Elizabeth reminded Shanna time and again, it was for her own good.

Now Elizabeth controlled the Morgans, as well. They didn't like it one bit, but what could they do? It never occurred to her until that very moment she may have gone too far. Demanded too much.

She thought again of Shanna, but this time of the baby boy Shanna had given birth to five years ago. Elizabeth had gotten rid of the infant. She couldn't let anyone or anything hinder Shanna's rise to the top of the charts. Elizabeth clung to the assurance she'd done the right thing. Hadn't she?

Why these thoughts and memories passed through her mind at this moment she wasn't certain. Perhaps God wanted her to make amends. Lord knew she had a lot of them to make. Somehow she knew there wouldn't be time to seek forgiveness for all of them, and Elizabeth wasn't certain she wanted to.

She drew in a ragged breath. A sudden grief passed over her, so strong and heavy she thought it would smother her. She'd been wrong. Oh, so terribly wrong. "I'm sorry, Shanna. I never should have..."

The air felt oppressive. She strained to lift her head. It lolled back and forth as if it had somehow become detached. Elizabeth O'Brian's voice fell silent. Her breathing grew more and more shallow...until it stopped altogether.

Chapter One

"Five minutes, Miss O'Brian." The stagehand rapped on Shanna's dressing-room door.

"Thanks!" Shanna called out, then turned back to the light-framed mirror. "I need more blush. I'm still too pale."

"You look fine." Beth Watson, her longtime makeup artist and assistant, tipped her head to one side, appraising her work. Beth's Caribbean tan and short, dark hair contrasted sharply with Shanna's pale, freckled skin.

"You're a miracle worker, Beth. I don't know what I'd do without you." Shanna had arrived in Denver that afternoon looking like a corpse—the aftereffect of that morning's shattering news. Her hand shook as she rearranged several of the flaming red curls that framed her face.

She could still hear the anguish in her ex-husband's voice when he'd called to tell her about his grandfather's death. Shanna still couldn't believe it. Andrew Morgan, president of Morningsong Productions, dead of a heart attack. Andrew had given Shanna her start in country music and had made her a star.

"The funeral is tomorrow," Joshua had said. "You're planning on coming, aren't you?"

"I'll be there," Shanna replied, then added, "I'll have Max make the plane reservations. We'll leave right after the show tonight."

"Skip the show, Shanna," Joshua insisted. "You don't have to go on tonight. I'm sure they'll understand."

"No, I can't do that. Andrew would have wanted me to go on."

"You still don't get it, do you?"

Shanna winced at the sudden hardness in his voice. "What are you talking about?"

"Some things are more important than…never mind." He paused, then added, "Have Max call me when he has your flight schedule."

More important than what—music? You're a fine one to talk about priorities, Joshua Morgan. Shanna choked back her acidic response. This wasn't the time for arguments. "Fine," she responded with a finality that surprised even her. "I'll see you tomorrow, then."

Their conversation that morning had been nearly as brief as their marriage. But hearing his voice again opened old wounds that should have healed long ago.

"You don't have to go on, you know," Beth said, interrupting Shanna's thoughts. "Max can still cancel."

Max Montgomery, Shanna's manager, had offered to do just that. However, Shanna wouldn't hear of it. "I don't want to cancel." Her response came out more harshly than she'd intended.

Beth took a step back and raised her hands in mock surrender. "OK, OK. It was just a suggestion. I mean, you've been through a lot lately with your mother dying and now Andrew."

"I'm sorry, it's—" Shanna clasped her hands in her lap. "These people have paid good money to see me perform, and I don't intend to let them down." Her gaze locked with Beth's in the mirror.

"Sure. I can understand that, but you seem…" Beth shrugged. "I don't know…scared. You haven't been back to Morningsong since your mother died."

Shanna rubbed her neck. "Well, maybe I am afraid. The police still haven't ruled out murder. Guess I just feel safer on the road."

"If you think you might be next, I wouldn't worry. Unlike your mother, you don't have an enemy in the world. Besides, you are very well protected. Max has seen to that."

Shanna smiled. "You're right about the protection. I don't know about the enemies. I'm sure I've made a few."

What Shanna didn't tell Beth—and hadn't told anyone—was that her reluctance to cut her tour short and head back to Morningsong had more to do with seeing Joshua again than it did her mother's death. While she often worried that a deranged killer might still be on the loose, her real fears were based on coming face-to-face with her ex-husband.

The last time she'd seen him had been at her mother's funeral. She'd ignored him then—or tried to. She thought she'd gotten past the hurts. His phone call had brought with it not only the grief of Andrew's passing but a flood of unpleasant memories. Memories she had no intention of reliving.

Shanna took a deep breath and closed her eyes to prepare herself for the concert. The queasiness she felt might have been stage fright, but she doubted it.

"Are you sure you're going to be OK, honey?" Beth's question scattered Shanna's thoughts.

"I'll be fine." She tossed Beth what she hoped was a reassuring look and with an exaggerated Western drawl said, "Jist give me mah gee-tar."

A smile firmly planted on her face, Shanna rose and turned her back on both the anxious image in the mirror and on the memories, then made her way to the stage entrance. Shanna loved performing, and tonight, as they had so many nights before, the lights, the people, and the songs would chase away the ghosts and, for a time, numb the pain.

The announcer's voice boomed over the loudspeakers as he introduced her. He went on forever it seemed about Andrew Morgan's life and how the recording magnate had developed some of the world's greatest entertainers. He talked about how Shanna had been part of Morningsong Productions since the tender age of seven. "And now, ladies and gentlemen, let's welcome country music's leading lady...Shanna O'Brian!"

When the applause died, an expectant hush settled over the auditorium. In the silence Shanna could hear the swish of her acoustic rhinestone-studded guitar as it brushed against her sequined turquoise gown. Someone in the audience whistled. Another hooted approval. Shanna waved.

Not trusting herself to speak, she greeted her fans with a nod and a smile. After signaling the band, Shanna slipped the guitar strap over her head and played a progression of chords leading into her first number.

In a moment she would have herself together. She would set aside the lingering effects of Joshua's phone call and Andrew's death. Shanna drew in a long breath, then tucked away the past and the fears and began to sing. Her words came out surprisingly clear, only hinting of the aching emptiness she felt inside.

The pure, haunting melody of the classic "Yesterday When I Was Young" seemed to please the audience and gave her a heady sense of power. The song was one of Shanna's favorites. Andrew hadn't wanted her to include it in her latest album. *"You're much too young to be reminiscing about the pangs of growing old,"* he'd said, his gentle blue eyes crinkling at the corners when he smiled. *"You're still a child."*

Maybe in some ways she was. Elizabeth had certainly gone to great lengths to keep her that way. But in other ways she'd grown up too fast.

Shanna was only five when her father abandoned them. By age eighteen she had lost a husband and a child. More recently there had been her mother's mysterious death and now Andrew. She was qualified to sing about yesterdays, all right. Outside she still looked young and innocent—at least that's what people said. Inside she felt used, old, and weary.

But yesterday doesn't matter anymore, she told herself as she had so many times before. Nothing mattered now except her career—her beloved music and her fans. The auditorium was packed with people who had come to be entertained, and Shanna Elizabeth O'Brian was not about to let them down.

For an hour she sang the songs they'd come to hear—classics, contemporary, gospel, and country favorites. Into the songs Shanna poured her strength, her love, her joy, and her sorrow. She finished the program with the lead song from her new album, "Winter Roses." She'd written it years ago when she'd received her first roses from Joshua. It was a love song about the perfect gift of roses on a cold winter day. For years the song lay unfinished. Recently she'd found it in an old journal and added a verse about the roses dying—withering away—like the petals of the fragile love two people once shared. Shanna ended the song with tears in her eyes and a catch in her voice. "My love once brought me winter roses."

They gave her a standing ovation and demanded more.

"Thank you," she called above the applause. "Thank you so much." Their appreciation coursed through her veins like new blood. She renewed her vow to keep going—to keep singing no matter what the cost.

Finally, the giving and taking complete, Shanna blew the audience a farewell kiss. Clutching the bouquet of white roses someone had given her, she backed slowly out of the spotlight.

Shanna hesitated at the edge of the light and shivered at the thought of stepping into the shadows. She had an odd sense that the darkness harbored an insidious evil that would descend on her the moment the lights dimmed. If she could just stay in the spotlight—sing her songs—then everything would be all right. She couldn't stay, of course. Life went on…and death.

"You were great as usual, darlin'." Max draped a lean, muscular arm across her shoulder. "I wasn't sure there for a while, but as always, you came through."

"I told you not to worry." She smiled at the man who had become indispensable to her over the month since her mother's death.

"I still think we should have canceled and headed for home this morning. Joshua wanted us to come right away."

"Joshua may run Morningsong now that Andrew is dead, but he doesn't run me." Shanna bit the inside of her cheek. The irony of what she'd said was almost laughable. Who was she kidding? In a way, Joshua, or at least thoughts of him, seemed to control every aspect of her life. Not a day went by when she didn't think of him and wonder what might have happened if she'd been stronger—if she'd taken charge of her own life. *Stop it,* she told herself. *It does no good at all to dwell on what might have been.*

Max looked away, stuffing his graying hair into a battered Stetson. In a voice more raspy than usual, he added, "We'd better get a move on. We leave in less than an hour, and it would be just our luck for the flight to be on time." Placing a hand at her back, he guided her off the stage.

"You really are a dreamer." She buried her nose in a fragrant blossom. "By the way, Max, thanks for the roses."

"What—?" He frowned and glanced at the flowers. "Oh, those are from Joshua. Should be a card with them."

Max turned from Shanna to bark last-minute orders to the crew and other musicians who traveled with Shanna's band. A few of them, including Beth and Max, would be returning to Morningsong for the funeral. The others would drive the buses to Oregon, where they'd rendezvous in a week and continue the last half of their six-week tour.

Max ushered her toward the rear exit and limo, where Beth waited with their luggage.

"Shanna! Shanna, wait!" Three young girls about thirteen years old rushed up to the car. "Could we have your autograph, please?" "You're our favorite singer." They all spoke at once.

"I'm sorry," Max said, "We—"

"It's OK," Shanna interrupted. She turned to the girls and signed the photos they'd purchased. Pulling the card free of the green paper holding the roses, Shanna crumpled it up and tucked it into her pocket, then handed the bouquet to one of the girls. "You can have these too."

Their eyes danced. "Oh wow…thanks," one said.

"I can't believe it," squealed another. "It's really you."

The third pumped Shanna's hand. "I will never, ever forget this. I want to be a singer just like you."

"No, no, you don't," Shanna murmured as she turned and ducked into the car. "Not like me."

Max climbed in beside her. Moments later they were on their way. "I wonder how those kids slipped through the barricade. I'm going to have to beef up security."

"Oh, Max. They're harmless fans. One of them probably has a dad or brother who's working as a guard."

"Humph. Can't be too careful these days. After what happened to your mother…"

"That was an accident," Shanna said quickly. At least that's what she wanted to believe.

"Stop being such a worrywart." Beth, who was sitting in the rear-facing seat, leaned toward Shanna. "That was a sweet and generous gesture. I think you've made three lifelong fans."

Sweet? Generous? Hardly. Shanna shrugged. "They're beautiful flowers. Seemed a shame to take them with us on the plane. They need water and someone who'll appreciate them." What she wouldn't admit to Beth or Max or anyone else was that she wanted nothing from Joshua. He hadn't sent her flowers since… Shanna canceled the memory, tossing it away as she had the roses.

Chapter Two

"Why?" Joshua sank into his grandfather's large leather chair, burying his face in his hands. "Oh, Grandad." He shook his head. "You couldn't have picked a worse time to die." Hauling in a deep breath, Joshua straightened and lifted his gaze to the portrait on the far wall. "But then, you didn't have much choice in the matter, did you?"

Andrew Morgan had ruled his empire from that chair for half a century. Never had Joshua felt at such a loss. He'd been primed for taking over the business since he was a kid, but not for the shocking news Andrew had delivered just prior to his death—or for the death itself. Andrew was seventy-five and nowhere near retiring. The dying man's confession had turned Joshua's world upside down. Now, somehow, he'd have to relate that news to Shanna.

Ever since he'd learned the truth about the phony papers, Joshua had been practicing what he would say and wondering how she'd react. Their phone conversation hadn't gone well. No one could bring out his temper or stir his emotions like Shanna O'Brian. Of course, except for watching her television specials and videos and staring at her picture on occasion, he hadn't had much to do with her for the last six years. He realized now that had been a big mistake.

"There's a call for you on line one." Laurie Daniels made the announcement in person rather than using the intercom. "It's Max."

The attractive brunette had been his secretary since his move to

California six years ago. He hadn't expected her to accompany him back to Nashville, but she'd insisted on coming, at least until things settled—or so she'd said. That had been a little over a week ago, and Laurie, as always, had things running smoothly.

"Thanks." He waited for her to close the door, and when she didn't, he asked, "Did you need something?"

"Ryan's on the phone—wants to know when you're taking him swimming."

Joshua grinned at the thought of his five-year-old son pacing the floor at Nan's. "In about ten minutes."

"I'll tell him." Laura started to close the door, then stepped back in. "I'll be leaving now. Unless you need me for something."

Joshua ignored the innuendo and the shapely woman in the low-cut silk blouse. Laurie Daniels clearly wanted more than friendship. Joshua had been tempted more than once to comply. She'd been invaluable to him all these years not only as a secretary, but as a friend. He owed her big time, but how could he give his heart to another woman when Shanna still held it?

"No. Um…on second thought, would you mind stopping at the house and checking on Nan? She's supposed to be resting, but knowing her…"

"Not at all." Laurie sent him a knowing look with just the right amount of compassion.

When she'd gone, Joshua picked up the phone. "Max, hi. When are you coming in?"

"We're taking a red-eye out of Denver after the show," Max said. "Should be in Nashville around 3 A.M."

"I'll be there." Joshua picked up a paper clip, turning it over and over between his fingers.

"Uh, Josh, not that it's any of my concern, but it might be better if you didn't come to the airport. Shanna doesn't seem too happy about meeting up with you again."

Joshua didn't answer at first. Max's remark caught him square in the gut. "I see."

Max cleared his throat.

"What am I gonna do, Max? I want her back. None of this crazy business should have happened in the first place, and now that Elizabeth is gone, Shanna is free to do what she wants."

The pause on the other end made Joshua wish he'd kept his mouth shut. Max knew too much already.

"I'm sorry, Josh. I don't know what to say. I think it would be a mistake to rush into anything. Give her some time to get used to you being in charge. Shanna's a reasonable woman. When the time is right, I'm sure she'll be willing to at least talk to you about a reconciliation."

Joshua bent the paper clip back and forth. "All right. I'll wait. But order a dozen roses for her—make sure she knows they're from me."

"You got it."

They made the final arrangements, then hung up. The paper clip he'd been playing with broke, and he tossed it in the wastebasket.

Max had a point. Now was not the time to try to talk to her about the changes he planned to make. She'd be tired. Joshua raked his hands through his coarse, sandy hair. He didn't really blame her for not wanting to see him, but still it was disappointing. He'd been thinking about their reunion all day. He imagined her walking off the plane and searching the crowd for him. Shanna would break into a run and throw her arms around him, nearly crushing the roses he'd sent. He'd tip her face up and kiss her.

Joshua shook his head at the fantasy. No matter how much he wanted to see her, he wouldn't be there. Shanna might not want to see him now, but she'd soon change her mind—he'd see to that. Maybe he'd have to keep his distance for a couple of days, but then—after the funeral—he'd make his move.

"Be patient with her, Joshua," his grandmother had cautioned him that morning over breakfast. *"Tell her how sorry you are—ask her forgiveness for your part in all of this. I'm sure that when she realizes you still love her, she'll come around."*

He seemed to remember Nan encouraging patience once before when he'd first talked to her about marrying Shanna.

"Wish I'd listened to you then," he said aloud. Patience had never been his forte—certainly not back then when most of his brain cells were swimming in testosterone. If he'd waited until they were older and more mature, maybe he and Shanna would still be together.

Grabbing his jacket, Joshua headed out the door, down the hall, and through the double glass doors. Within moments he was on the concrete walk that led to the house. In fact, there were several houses on the grounds now, along with an apartment complex, a recording studio, and the corporate offices he'd just come from.

The Morgan home sat at the highest point on the estate and consisted of two wings separated by a large marble entry and a palatial ballroom. One wing was for entertaining guests; the other less ostentatious wing housed the Morgan family. Joshua walked up the wide floral-bordered path, admiring the columns and arches, the fountain courtyard, and the curved drive where the royalty of country music arrived in their finery. His grandfather had loved entertaining, and at least once a month he and Nan would throw a formal dinner party. Guests were met at the door by an elegantly attired doorman. A butler escorted them through the massive marble entry, where Nan and Andrew welcomed them. From there they entered the ballroom. For a typical party Nan hired as many as twenty staff. Joshua supposed he'd continue the tradition, though he didn't look forward to playing the host without Shanna at his side. Face it, he didn't look forward to entertaining, period.

He walked past the columns and wide double doors to the side entrance and the family wing where elegant became ordinary once you stepped inside. This portion of the house had been the Morgan family ancestral home since before the Civil War. The original three-thousand-square-foot farmhouse had grown to twenty thousand.

When he opened the door, a small whirlwind blew out and landed in his arms.

"Whoa. Slow down, boy. Where are you going in such a rush?"

"You promised to take me swimming, Dad."

"And I will. Give me a minute to change."

"Can I wait for you by the pool?" Ryan's sky-blue eyes widened. "I promise I won't go in till you come."

"You know the rules, Ryan. Under no circumstances do you go near the pool without an adult."

"Why don't you come help me in the kitchen, darling." Nan approached wearing a starched white apron over the same black dress she'd worn to the funeral home. Only now it was almost gray from flour dust. They'd gone early that morning to view Andrew's body. The minute they got home, she'd put on her apron and headed for the kitchen.

"You talking to Ryan or me?" Joshua set Ryan down and kissed his grandmother's cheek.

"You both can come. I made three pies and two batches of cookies, and I need someone to eat them."

"You work too hard, Nan." Joshua followed her through the large entry, past the formal dining room. "Why didn't you call Inga or one of the other cooks? You should be taking it easy—especially today."

"Nonsense. I needed something to do besides cry and sit around feeling sorry for myself. What would you like? Peach, apple, or rhubarb?"

Joshua breathed deeply, savoring the familiar scent of Nan's pies. "How about a little of each."

"Dad." Ryan pulled on the sleeve of his jacket. "You promised."

Joshua shrugged. "You heard the man. I'd better get changed. How about dishing me up some, and I'll take it out to the pool."

For the next few hours, Joshua relaxed by the pool and swam with Ryan, then ate a light supper. After an evening ritual of reading several of Ryan's favorite books with him, Joshua almost succeeded in taking his mind off Shanna. He'd have done just fine if Ryan hadn't handed him the *Mama, Do You Love Me?* book.

It featured whimsical drawings of an Eskimo woman with her child. The child would think of outrageous and naughty things to do, then ask, "Would you love me if I…?" No matter what the child did or said, the mother emphatically declared her love. Joshua could understand why Ryan loved that book so. He missed having a real mother. Of course, he had Nan and Laurie, but it wasn't the same.

Joshua seldom talked to Ryan about his mother. How do you tell a kid his mother gave him up for adoption?

No, that wasn't quite fair. Joshua knew better now. According to Andrew, Shanna hadn't wanted their marriage to end any more than he had. She hadn't wanted to give up their baby, but Elizabeth had insisted—and Elizabeth almost always got her way.

Joshua had never told Ryan about Shanna. He wouldn't, either—not until he was sure she would love and accept the boy. All Ryan knew about his mother was that she had to go away right after he was born. As far as Ryan was concerned, the pretty lady with the nice voice whose picture hung in his daddy's office was just one of Morningsong's many recording artists. Ryan had never met Shanna in person. Joshua had gone to great lengths to protect his son and keep the details of his birth a secret from everyone except Nan and Andrew. The secret hadn't been difficult to keep while he was in California and Shanna was based here in Tennessee.

And Shanna didn't know he had their son. Shortly after he moved to California, the gossip rags spread lies about his supposed involvement with Laurie and their having a child. Joshua never bothered to correct them.

Maybe he'd been wrong to hide the truth all these years. It wasn't fair to Shanna or Ryan. He hoped to rectify that soon. He just didn't want Ryan hurt in the process.

Joshua set the book aside when he'd finished. "That's it for tonight, son."

"Dad, could you say prayers with me?"

"Sure." Hand in hand they prayed the familiar old verse, "Now I lay me down to sleep." At the end, Ryan added, "And please, God, bless my great-grandpa Andrew up in heaven. And my daddy and Nan." He sighed. "And could you please bless my mommy and help her find her way back home. Daddy and me need her to take care of us. Amen."

Unable to find his voice, Joshua bent over to gather Ryan in his arms, letting the pillow catch his unexpected tears. He kissed Ryan good night, then hurried downstairs, grabbing his jacket on the way out.

"Joshua?" Nan joined him in the tiled entry.

He paused, his hand on the doorknob. "I'm going for a walk."

"Are you all right?"

Joshua rubbed his forehead. "Not exactly. Ryan's asking about his mother again. I wish I could tell him."

Nan reached up and grasped his shoulder. "Darling, I'm so sorry."

"It's not your fault."

"Isn't it? I knew something wasn't right with Elizabeth. I just couldn't believe she could be so cruel." Nan, no longer wearing the apron, clasped the ends of her sweater and wrapped them around her, warding off the chill from the open door. "But—never mind about that. I shouldn't be speaking ill of the dead."

"Hmm. You'd best go back inside where it's warm. I'll be down at the lake if you need me."

Nan nodded and headed back into the living room, where a fire burned in the hearth.

Joshua stood in the doorway for several long moments, torn between needing to be alone and wanting to comfort his grandmother. She and Andrew would have celebrated their fiftieth anniversary this year. She now sat in her favorite rocker, eyes closed, listening to music from another time.

Not wanting to intrude, Joshua made his way through the gardens and turned down the familiar path that led to Morningsong's three-acre lake. As he walked, distant memories filtered through his mind like moonlight through the trees. Six years ago he and Shanna had walked along this same path, ready to spend a lifetime together. How, he wondered, could such a perfect beginning come to such a disastrous end?

Chapter Three

Due to the lateness of the hour and what Shanna considered a miracle, they had only a twenty-minute delay before the plane finally lifted off.

While her companions dozed, Beth in the window seat behind her and Max on her left, Shanna glanced through the newspaper. In her usual postconcert high, she was too wired to sleep. The headline story drew her attention: "Recording Magnate Dies."

Andrew Morgan, founder and president of Morningsong Productions, died Friday of a massive heart attack. Morgan was seventy-five and is succeeded by his wife, Mary, and their grandsons, Joshua and Tom Morgan.

Shanna folded the paper. She didn't need to read any more. The Morgans had built the largest conglomerate in the music industry. Andrew had been her mentor as well as her employer, and while she hadn't always agreed with his methods, she loved him.

Shanna stuffed the paper into the seat pocket in front of her, then turned to stare into the black, starless night outside the 747's tiny window.

It would be 3 A.M. before they reached Nashville. Once on the ground, they'd drive another hour to the Morningsong Estate, catch a few winks, then attend the memorial service at eleven. Shanna released the seat and leaned back. If she could sleep, she wouldn't have to think too much about Morningsong or Andrew or Joshua.

Shanna startled when she felt a callused hand on hers.

"You OK, darlin'?" Max leaned forward in his seat and fixed his concerned gaze on her.

No, I'm not OK. I'm angry, I'm afraid, and I want to go back to Colorado and then on to the West Coast. I want to get as far away from Joshua as possible. In spite of her thoughts, she smiled and said, "I'm just tired." There would be no turning back. Besides, she wanted to pay her last respects to Andrew. Even in the worst of times, he'd offered his support.

Max lifted his hat and combed his fingers through his unruly black and silver hair. "It's going to be a long trip."

After several minutes passed he spoke again. "Hard to imagine Morningsong without old Andrew. 'Course, I doubt things will change much. Joshua will step in and fill his granddaddy's shoes just fine."

"I'm sure he will."

Max must have felt her stiffen, seen the look of panic in her eyes. He stared at her for a moment, fingering the band of the hat that seemed as much an appendage as his ears. "What's troubling you, sugar? And don't tell me it's Andrew's death. Losing him is a terrible thing, but I know it's something more."

Shanna clenched her teeth. "I know it sounds crazy, but I can't work with Joshua. I…I'm going to have to leave Morningsong."

"Sure you can. It won't be so bad. Joshua's a great guy." Max leaned back against the seat and settled the hat back on his head.

"To you, maybe." She swallowed past the lump in her throat. How could she explain her feelings to Max? She hardly understood them herself. All she knew was that being with Joshua again would tear her apart. She'd worked too hard to overcome the past to have her life disrupted all over again.

"Look, Shanna, I know working with your ex won't be easy, but you don't have much choice. You signed an ironclad contract with Morningsong Productions. You can't leave for at least another year."

"Don't remind me. I'd never have signed on again if I'd known Andrew would die on us." Shanna's voice broke. The tears she'd held in for what seemed like an eternity slipped down her cheeks. She accepted the hankie Max offered, as well as his sympathy and advice to have a good cry.

When the tears diminished she chided herself for being so weak. *Somehow you'll make it through this,* she told herself with renewed certainty. *You'll go to the funeral, finish the tour, and get on with your life.* She'd start by moving away. With Joshua at Morningsong Estate, it wouldn't do to stay on the grounds. She'd find an apartment or house in another city or state. Then she'd see about getting out of her contract.

"There has to be a way out, Max. I'll hire a lawyer." Shanna put words to her thoughts. She was beginning to sound desperate. In a way she was.

"Suit yourself, but I wouldn't hold my breath. Even with Andrew dead, Morningsong's got the power. If I were you, I'd hang loose for a while. See how things shape up. Who knows, maybe Joshua has changed. Maybe he still loves you and wants to work things out. When I talked to him on the phone, he seemed pretty anxious to see you." He poked a finger at the brim of his hat, lifting it so he could look her full in the eyes. "That is what you want, isn't it? For the two of you to get back together?"

Shanna's face warmed. "It most certainly is not!"

Max gave her an empathetic look. "You might say so, but I know better. I've seen your face when someone mentions his name."

"My face… If you see anything, it's contempt."

"Oh, I don't think so. Trust me, darlin'. What you're feeling for Joshua is not contempt."

Flustered, Shanna took a deep breath. "Look, just forget I said anything."

"OK, no need to get huffy. Just trying to tell you not to worry about what might happen. Relax and deal with things as they come. I learned long ago to leave my problems in God's hands."

"Well, God may have handled your life all right, but He's made a mess of mine. Still, maybe you're right—about waiting to see what happens. It doesn't do much good to get all worked up." She tipped her head back and massaged the muscles in her shoulders. "Do you think he'll make many changes, Max? If he runs things like Andrew did, I won't have to worry. I don't spend much time at Morningsong, anyway. Maybe I won't have to see Joshua at all. You could do all the negotiating for me. I suppose you think I'm being childish, but I don't know if I can take being around him." She was rambling now and couldn't seem to stop.

Max sat up and caught his hat in his hands. "Everything will work out fine. No need to work yourself into a frenzy."

"I'm trying, Max. I really am. It's just that I have this feeling—you know, like everything is coming apart." *Come on, Shanna,* she scolded herself. *Get a grip. You've had plenty of time to get over him.*

"It's been six years, hasn't it? I never did learn the whole story about your breakup, but I should think you'd have had long enough to sort out your problems—you know, forgive and forget. I figure it's about time you two resolved your differences. Andrew mentioned awhile back that he'd like to see the two of you get back together."

Shanna shook her head. "That's impossible. Even if Josh loved me and I loved him—which I don't—I could never go back. There is no way I'd subject myself to that kind of hurt again. Even if I could trust Joshua, a marriage could never survive my career."

"Humph," Max snorted. "That's a bunch of hogwash."

Of course he couldn't understand. No one could, except maybe Elizabeth and the few members of the band who had tried and failed to make their marriages work. When you're on the road performing at two hundred concerts a year and shuffling recording sessions and television appearances in-between, there's little room left for a husband or wife. While Elizabeth may have colored Shanna's opinion of marriage and men, Shanna knew from experience how pointless it would be to try again.

"Max, look around you. Every one of the band members that ever tried marriage is divorced. The rest are smart enough to know it can't work—at least not for long."

"I could point to several couples in this business whose marriages are still going strong after fifteen years. Take Jess and Margaret, for instance. She travels with him whenever possible, and when she can't—well, I think that's where the difference comes in. Jess is as faithful then as when she's around."

Max was right about that. Jess, their lead guitarist, and his wife seemed to be doing fine; but that was only one success in who knew how many failures. "Unfortunately, Joshua isn't like Jess." Shanna stroked her forehead with the tips of her fingers to ease the beginnings of a headache. "Anyway, I don't want to talk about Joshua anymore."

Just as Shanna closed her eyes, the flight attendant offered them drinks. She asked for a Perrier. Max declined.

"Sure you don't want to tell me about it?" Max asked, handing Shanna's drink over to her.

"No. But I suppose I should. It might explain my position." Shanna took a sip. "Joshua and I were very close growing up. I suppose part of me always knew we'd be together someday. We fell in love. Maybe if Elizabeth hadn't worked so hard to keep us apart, things might have been different."

"I'm not sure I understand. Why would she want to keep you apart?"

"She was afraid, I think. She never liked Joshua—I'm not sure why. She rarely let me out of her sight. Whenever Joshua came around, she'd find some excuse for me to do something or go somewhere. After a while we started sneaking off and meeting secretly. As I look back on it, Joshua and Mother always seemed to be fighting over me."

"Fighting, huh. Who won?"

"I don't think anyone did, really. I suppose that sounds strange—the fighting part. There weren't any knock-down-drag-outs. Mostly it was like a mental tug of war.

"Joshua finally convinced me to marry him. We eloped. It was just two weeks before my eighteenth birthday—a big mistake. When we got home, Andrew and my mother were furious. Mother insisted on an annulment. Andrew sent Joshua to Los Angeles to head up

Morningsong West. A week later the tabloids printed a picture of Joshua and one of his *singers* in a magazine. The article said Laurie Daniels was his new flame."

"And you believed those gossip rags?"

"I may have been young and gullible, but I wasn't stupid. Joshua didn't have to go to L.A. And he certainly didn't have to play around."

"That doesn't sound like the Joshua I know."

"Pictures don't lie, Max. Besides, when Laurie gave up her career to have his baby, I knew."

"Humph. Don't believe everything you hear."

"It was true, all right. He never spoke to me after he moved to L.A.—not even when I wrote to tell him I was pregnant. But then, why would he care about me—he had Laurie."

"You had a baby?" Max frowned. "I…I didn't know."

"I gave him up for adoption. I didn't want to, but what choice did I have? Joshua was gone and apparently wasn't coming back. I was eighteen and…what kind of life would a child have with a playboy father and me for a mother? Elizabeth and Andrew helped me make the right choice. And this way, my little boy has a chance at a normal life."

A strange sadness filled Max's dark eyes. "Ever regret it?"

"Sometimes." *All the time.* Every time she saw a little boy, she wondered what her baby was like. Did he have a good home? Was his hair blond like Joshua's or red like hers? Did he have his daddy's smile? Or her dimples? "It was for the best." Shanna took another sip of sparkling water.

"You're a hard one to understand, Shanna. Looks to me like you'd be a great wife and mother. Don't know why you're so bent on denying it."

"You wouldn't say that if you knew my background. My parents had a miserable marriage. Of course, I'm mostly to blame for that."

Shanna licked her lips. The memories of her parents' bitter quarrels still haunted her. She'd been too young to remember much, but Elizabeth's hateful words still burned in her memory like a brand on cowhide. *"My marriage wasn't worth the paper it was written on. We're better off without him, Shanna."* Michael O'Brian had been an alcoholic and a womanizer, and after countless separations, her parents finally divorced. He'd never bothered to contact them and died a few years later.

"You're being kind of hard on yourself, aren't you?"

"Am I?"

"Well, I don't know. Why don't you tell me about it? Sometimes it helps to talk things out."

"Maybe some other time." Shanna folded her arms and turned her face to the window. She suddenly missed her father very much. Maybe it was something Max said or the way he said it. *"It helps to talk things out."* Shanna remembered her father wanting to do that the last time she'd seen him. He'd been drunk and crying and begging them not to leave.

Oh, Daddy, I wanted to stay, a small voice inside of her struggled to be heard. *I wanted to take you with us. But Mama said you didn't love us anymore. And the music... Mama said we couldn't give up the music.*

"Suit yourself." Max's voice broke through her reverie. "Better get some shuteye. Morning's gonna come mighty quick."

Shanna didn't answer. Out of the corner of her eye she saw Max shrug his shoulders and retreat under his weathered hat.

She was thankful for Max's comments, but she needed to force the unwanted memories back where they belonged. Years ago she had boxed up those hurts, sealed them tight, and buried them in a distant corner of her mind. Sometimes a thought or two would slip out when she let herself get too tired, but she had always been able to deal with them—forcing them back to where they didn't hurt anymore. But Andrew's passing seemed to have undone all her hard work and triggered a landslide of feelings and memories.

No, not now. Definitely not now. She had enough to think about with having to go back to Morningsong. Max was right, of course. She'd have to face Joshua eventually. Somehow she needed to gain the courage.

Chapter Four

"Maybe he still loves you." Max's words hovered over Shanna like a promise of rain on a thirsty day. Her skin flushed warm and her heart lurched.

Ridiculous. Even if he still cared, there would be no purpose. For her, there could be no marriage, no children. She'd made her decision years ago—or had Elizabeth made the decision for her? She couldn't remember.

"Maybe he still loves you." Max's comment persisted.

No. *"You're a drifter, Shanna, remember?"* Shanna could almost hear her mother's voice. *"You've been on the road since you were six years old. You couldn't settle down now if you wanted to. And look what marriage did to your father and me. Look what happened between you and Joshua."*

"Maybe he still loves you." The thought stampeded into her mind again like a wild stallion. Powerless to stop it, Shanna let the memory of their first meeting play through her mind.

Shanna and Elizabeth had first come to Morningsong shortly after Shanna's seventh birthday. She remembered how awestruck and frightened she'd been. Andrew Morgan had been a big man—not only in stature but in the music industry. Her mother had spent weeks instructing Shanna how to act and what to say. It had been the most important step in her career. Signing on with Morningsong meant national coverage, records, videos, radio, and television.

"Hello, Mr. Morgan. It's a pleasure to meet you at last," Elizabeth said in a smooth stage voice as she stepped forward to shake the man's hand. She turned and nudged Shanna forward. "I'd like you to meet my daughter, Shanna."

"Shanna." The man knelt down beside her and smiled. "What a beautiful name. Welcome to Morningsong."

"Thank you, Mr. Morgan." Shanna, normally shy of strangers, felt an odd sense of familiarity—as though she had met this man before. She thought for a moment of leaning forward and wrapping her arms around his neck and calling him Grandpa. She didn't, of course. Her mother would not approve of such behavior. Shanna stepped back and thought for a moment she'd seen a flash of disappointment in the older man's eyes.

Andrew rose and called over his shoulder, "Joshua, come on over here. I'd like you to meet Shanna and her mother. Shanna will be auditioning for us this afternoon. We'll cut a demo and see how it goes."

A sandy-haired boy popped out of the sound room in front of them and came to stand beside Mr. Morgan.

"Hi." He glanced up at Elizabeth, shook her hand, then turned to Shanna.

"This is my grandson," Andrew said, making the appropriate introductions. "Joshua will be running the sound booth this morning. Elizabeth, if you'll just come with me, we'll watch from the back."

"But…," Elizabeth stammered, "he's so young. Are you sure he can—shouldn't I stay with her?"

"Relax. Joshua may only be twelve, but he's a pro. Knows this side of the business better than I do. Shanna's in good hands."

"I'll take good care of her, Mrs. O'Brian," Joshua assured her. He looked back at Shanna again, a warm smile curving his lips. "Don't be nervous," he said, as though he knew how frightened she felt and wanted to put her at ease. He motioned for her to follow him.

Shanna glanced up at her mother for permission, and Elizabeth nodded, tight-lipped. Even then she must have sensed Joshua would bring trouble. At the time, all Shanna could see was his kindness.

Once inside one of the cubicles, he pulled a headset from a cupboard and placed it on her head. "All you have to do is sing; I'll take care of everything else."

"I've never sung in a studio before," she whispered. "I'm not sure I can sing if I don't have people to sing to."

His soft blue gaze captured her fearful brown one as if to measure her sincerity. After a moment, he grinned. "We usually keep it dark in here, but I'll turn the light on over my head and you can sing to me."

Shanna didn't mind singing to Joshua. In fact, she adored it—and soon came to adore him. They worked well together. The singer and the recorder. At the end of each song, he'd give her a high-five and tell her how great she'd been.

Over the years, Morningsong became Shanna's home. Andrew had a house built for her and Elizabeth on the grounds so they'd have a home base between tours. Shanna loved being part of the Morningsong family. Having lost her own father and never knowing her grandparents, it gave her a sense of security she'd never felt before. The Morgans made certain Shanna was included in many of the family's activities.

Elizabeth would have preferred that Shanna spend less time with Joshua and his younger brother, Tom, but she bowed to Andrew's insistence that children needed time to socialize. "It isn't normal for a child to be around adults so much," he reminded Elizabeth on more than one occasion. "What harm can there be in having friends her own age?"

In the world of music and entertaining, her life took on a magical quality, and Shanna felt as though all the fairy tales she'd ever dreamed had come true at Morningsong. Her career blossomed, as did her admiration for Joshua. He and Tom did their best to make her feel at home when she was there—which, unfortunately, wasn't very often.

Most of her days were spent on the road with Elizabeth, riding from one town to the next in a specially equipped bus. She studied on the road, with at least a dozen different tutors, all of whom Elizabeth deemed incompetent after only a few months. Elizabeth finally took over Shanna's education herself. Somehow, through it all, Shanna managed to attain an education equivalent to a college degree in music in less time than it took most students to graduate from high school.

Although there was little time for fun—what with studies, recording sessions, and personal appearances—not once did Shanna feel deprived...at least not at first. She loved singing more than life itself and couldn't imagine herself without the stage and the spotlight and the fans.

Being part of the Morgan family between tours was an added bonus. Shanna had fond memories of picnics by the lake, skipping rocks, horseback riding, walking in the woods, and sneaking out of boring and endless dinner parties in the Morningsong ballroom to swim in the lake with Joshua and Tom.

Not all the memories of her times at Morningsong were happy ones—especially as Shanna grew older. Joshua had become like an older brother by then. Eighteen and doing what normal young men do, he began to develop other interests, like girls and cars. Her young adolescent heart ached at the thought of him dating other girls.

She saw very little of Joshua after he left for college. Thinking back on it now, she suspected that her mother had made a deliberate effort to keep them apart. Except for the holidays, their schedules were as far apart as the sun and the moon. Not that Shanna pined away for him. Her own career and studies kept her too busy to think much about him. By age sixteen she'd resigned herself to the fact that she and Joshua were never meant to be anything more than friends. He'd taken an executive position with Morningsong right out of college and was fast becoming a multimillionaire. Newsmagazines touted him as one of the world's most eligible bachelors. Though he'd never been an actor or singer, he achieved movie-star status. That he should even look at her amazed Shanna. Maybe that was why she'd been so gullible and eager when he began taking more than a passing interest.

On her seventeenth birthday Joshua showed up at Morningsong Estate to help her celebrate. Her heart raced even now with the excitement she'd felt when he asked her to dance. "Dance?" She stared up at him. "You want to dance with me?"

The look in his eyes turned her insides to mush. "Why would that surprise you?"

Shanna shrugged her shoulders, struggling not to make a fool of herself. *It doesn't mean anything to him,* she told herself. *He's just doing his duty.* After all, she had become one of Morningsong's biggest stars. She moved into the circle of his arms and never wanted to leave.

Nearly one year later, he asked her to marry him. At first she'd said no. She'd known from the start it would never work. Romances like theirs seldom did. But Joshua convinced her that their love would get them through, and she was gullible and starry-eyed enough to believe it.

They never dated; Elizabeth would never have allowed it. But they did manage to meet in secret from time to time.

In the heat of August, they eloped, escaping to Joshua's yacht off the Gulf of Mexico. For one glorious week they sailed toward the edge of the world in each other's arms. So in love and caught up in the idea of a marriage made in heaven that nothing else mattered.

"Forever," he'd promised. "I'll love you forever."

But forever ended when they arrived back at Morningsong.

Furious, Andrew and Elizabeth had the marriage annulled. As Shanna looked back on the scene now, she could still feel the pain of being ripped away from her best friend and the only man she'd ever loved.

Elizabeth lashed into them the moment they arrived home from their honeymoon. "How dare you," she yelled at Joshua. "Andrew, I expect you to handle your grandson. In the meantime, my daughter and I are going to have a little talk."

"Talking won't do any good." Joshua settled a protective arm around Shanna's shoulder. "She's my wife, and nothing is going to change that."

Elizabeth laughed and leveled a hateful gaze at him. "We'll see about that. Shanna is underage. Need I say more? She'll do as I say. And you, you..." She glared at Andrew. "Get him out of my sight."

"You're the one who should leave." Joshua's hold on Shanna's shoulder tightened to the point of hurting. "Shanna doesn't need you or anyone else telling her what to do."

"Joshua, don't." Shanna winced. "It won't help to get angry."

"Come on, son." Andrew placed a restraining hand on Joshua's arm. "Shanna's right. Arguing isn't going to get us anywhere. We need to discuss this rationally."

Joshua loosened his grip. "I'm sorry. I didn't mean to hurt you. It'll be all right, honey," he whispered, kissing her cheek. "We'll fight this thing together. I'll be back in an hour or so. Just don't let her bully you."

No, don't go. Don't leave me alone with her, she wanted to scream but couldn't. All she could do was stand, dumbfounded, while her mother showed Andrew and Joshua to the door and locked it behind them.

Elizabeth turned back to her daughter. "How could you? Do you have any idea what you've done?"

"Of...of course I do," Shanna stammered. "We love each other." She dropped onto the couch and wrapped her arms around a pillow.

"Love. What do you know about love?" Elizabeth softened, then came to sit beside Shanna. "I suppose this is as much my fault as anyone's. I should have been more aware of what was going on. I had a feeling he might try to force you...poor baby. Did he hurt you? This was all his idea, wasn't it? He talked you into it."

"Mama, don't. It was as much my decision as his. I...we love each other."

"You don't know your own mind," she snapped. "Joshua is a womanizer—just like your father was. You know how vulnerable and easily persuaded you are. Sometimes I wish you weren't quite so compliant." Elizabeth patted Shanna's hand. "Well, fortunately, the tabloids haven't gotten wind of this. At least Joshua did that much right. I think we can fix things. You leave everything to Andrew and me."

"What do you mean? Mother, what are you planning to do?"

"End the marriage—as simple as that. It was never meant to be. You know as well as I do that it would never work. Can you see yourself keeping house and being pregnant and...diapering some bratty kid? You'd have to give up your career—your music, Shanna. Is that what you want?"

"I..." Shanna didn't know what to say. The idea of having Joshua's baby appealed to her on one level, but she couldn't imagine not singing. "Joshua said I wouldn't have to give it up."

"Of course he did. And how long do you think that would last? Believe me, sooner or later you'd have to make the choice—him or your career. Believe me, it's better to put an end to it now before you have children."

The following morning, Shanna had left on a concert tour and Joshua left for Los Angeles, where he promptly discovered Laurie Daniels. Laurie was a singer looking for a chance at the big time. Joshua offered her that and more. Shanna, the foolish teenager, learned a painful lesson: Love is a pointless, overrated emotion—full of pain and broken promises.

Staring at the seat in front of her, Shanna shoved the memories aside. She couldn't afford to let her thoughts linger on Joshua, for no matter how hard she tried, she could never hate him. It might have been easier if she could. Part of the blame fell on her shoulders. Maybe she should have said no to his proposal in the first place. Or at the very least, she could have stood up to her mother and refused to go on tour, then made her place beside him in Los Angeles. She could have refused to give up their baby. Maybe then...but, no, she couldn't allow herself to think about what might have been. Joshua, as her mother pointed out far too often, wasn't worth the effort.

"Can't you see, Shanna," Elizabeth had said after showing her the photos of Joshua and Laurie in the gossip rag, *"you were just another notch on his belt. He wanted you, and after he made his conquest, he tossed you aside. That's the way men are. They want you to give up*

everything for them, and for what?" She ripped the photo in two. *"You're lucky to be rid of him, darling."*

It all worked out for the best, Shanna reminded herself now. And if she were tempted to renew their relationship—if Joshua still loved her, which she doubted—she would have to think of the pain that their misplaced love had brought both of them. Perhaps that would be enough to keep her from making a tragic mistake all over again. It never would have worked. She needed to remember that above all.

To pull her mind away from memories, Shanna glanced at Max. He had come into her life shortly after her mother's death, when Andrew recommended hiring him as her manager. After the way she'd treated him at first, it was a wonder he stayed with her. She was used to having her every move planned by Elizabeth—especially after the annulment and the baby. Shanna didn't have the strength or desire to run anyone's life, including her own. It was much easier to let Elizabeth take care of everything. Though she hadn't realized it at the time, Shanna had been suffering from chronic depression and still had not fully recovered.

Max had urged her to see a counselor and forced her to make decisions on her own. No matter how much she argued and stewed, Max held his ground, telling her it was time she grew up and took control of her life.

Shanna smiled in his direction, glad he'd accomplished his goal—or at least come close. Maybe she'd swung too far in the other direction; she'd been accused of it often enough. Max often called her bullheaded. At times she was sure Max regretted his attempts to make her independent.

Now at twenty-four, Shanna found herself far removed from the compliant young girl who'd let Morningsong, her mother, and Andrew dictate her every move. After her mother died, Shanna had been confused and frightened, like a top spinning out of control. Then Max came along and righted her. He'd taken her out of her sheltered life and shown her at least a part of the real world.

I'm in control of my life now, and I intend to keep it that way. Shanna leaned back into her seat for a much-needed rest. With her eyes closed she envisioned herself once again in the spotlight, singing to her fans—the only place where the dark thoughts of her past couldn't penetrate.

What she couldn't think about and refused to consider was what would happen to her when the lights went out.

Chapter Five

Shanna stepped into the airport terminal and let her gaze drift over the handful of people coming in or taking flights. Feeling partly fearful, partly hopeful at the prospect of seeing Joshua again, she held an expectant breath until she realized he wasn't there.

"Joshua isn't coming?" She tried to sound nonchalant, as if she didn't care.

"Nope. I told him it wasn't necessary. He needs his rest. It's been a tough week for him." Max placed a hand at her back and nudged her ahead toward the baggage-claim area. His lips curved in a crooked grin. "You disappointed?"

"Of course not. Just surprised, that's all. After what you told me about him being anxious for me to get here, I thought he'd be here with an armed guard to escort us to the estate." After spending the last few hours thinking of Joshua and what they'd meant to each other, she didn't need a psychiatrist to tell her she still loved him.

It's better that he didn't come, Shanna told herself. *If he had, you might have run right into his arms and made a complete fool of yourself. The fact that he isn't here shows the feelings aren't mutual. And even if they were, it would be better not to start something you're incapable of finishing.*

After a few hours of restless sleep, Shanna spent fifteen minutes in a hot, steamy shower, which warmed her but made her more lethargic. Finishing a cup of tea, Shanna slipped her funeral dress from the hanger—the same dress she'd worn to her mother's funeral and probably the same one she'd wear to her own.

Shanna sighed and shook her head. Funerals always seemed to bring such morbid thoughts. "Natural, I suppose," she muttered to her mirrored image. She so seldom wore black. It washed her out and gave her a ghoulish look.

When she was younger, Shanna had wondered what it would be like to wear white to a funeral. After all, if the dead person really was going to heaven, wouldn't it be more appropriate? She'd never acted on her impulse, though. Elizabeth would have taken her to task. Black was the proper attire for a funeral. That was that. "Fine, Mother," Shanna said aloud. "I'll do it your way for now. But only because I don't want to call attention to myself. Next time, though..." Shanna didn't finish. She doubted she'd ever be able to move from what her counselor had called her "parent tapes." Even dead, Elizabeth wielded a lot of power.

Blurry-eyed, Shanna leaned into the mirror to apply her makeup, then tossed the eyeliner aside. What difference would it make? She'd be wearing her funeral hat—the one that would cover her face—and judging from the way she felt at the moment, by the end of the service her tears would have washed it all away. Picking up a brush, she worked out the tangles and fluffed the still-damp curls with her fingers, then set in place the wide-brimmed hat that had belonged to her mother. The veil, a delicate mesh, reached just below her chin.

At 10:45 Shanna put on her low black heels and stepped outside, then made her way to the chapel. On the way, she worked on setting aside her fears and concerns about seeing Joshua again. This was Andrew's funeral—a time for mourning. Everything else could wait.

The Morningsong Chapel was a restored turn-of-the-century church and had been part of a township that was now part of the Morningsong Estate. Andrew had restored the church to its former glory. White with a steep, pitched roof and a steeple and a cross, it looked like something out of a Laura Ingalls Wilder novel. He kept it open for employees and family members as a place of prayer and offered it to the community for weddings and funerals and community events. Every Sunday night a minister from one of the nearby towns would come in and conduct vespers.

Shanna used to come often before she gave up her baby. She hadn't had much use for the chapel or for prayer since then.

The bell in the steeple tolled now, calling stragglers inside.

"Shanna. Is that you hiding behind that veil?" Nan stopped her as she approached the concrete steps. She must have been in the depths of grief, yet there she was, playing hostess to arriving guests. The older woman seemed to never change. She was like her home—elegant as a duchess one moment, warm and homespun the next. Nan had that lived-in look, as if several generations had found refuge under her roof. She was a medium-boned woman, with the soft kind of bosom children loved to lay their heads against.

Rather than answering, Shanna embraced her. Nan wasn't wearing black, Shanna noticed, but a bright blue suit that made her look radiant rather than somber. "I'm sorry about Andrew—it must be terrible for you."

"Thank you. Not so terrible at the moment. I suspect I'm still in shock. It'll hit me soon, though. Probably when it's all over. I know in my heart Andrew's in a better place. Just wish he hadn't left me behind." She offered a wan smile and patted Shanna's hand. "You'll come up to the house after the service, won't you?"

"I…I don't know. Our plane got in late last night."

Nan tipped her head, assessing. "I understand. Tomorrow, then. Don't make us wait too long. Joshua and Tom will be wanting to see you."

"I'd like to see them too." The remark was partially true. She did want to see Tom. The younger Morgan brother still remained a good friend. Glancing around, she asked, "Where are they?"

Nan nodded toward an approaching limousine and hearse. "They'll be helping to carry in the casket." She paused for a moment, then added, "My great-grandson is helping too—or at least he thinks he is. Such a darling boy—takes after his father."

"I'm sure he does." Shanna steeled herself against a sea of emotions welling up inside her. It wasn't fair that Joshua should have a child to hold and love, while she held nothing but an empty heart. *That was your choice,* she reminded herself.

"Ryan is anxious to meet you," Nan went on. "He's one of your biggest fans."

"Ryan?"

"Joshua's boy."

"Oh." She was thankful Nan couldn't see her face. The last thing she wanted to do was meet Joshua and Laurie's child. "Well, it's always exciting to meet a fan," she said, struggling to paint herself collected and unmoved.

Shanna's heart took another tumble when Laurie Daniels approached, looking elegant in a demure maroon dress with a white collar. She was taller than Shanna had imagined and more beautiful than her photos.

"Oh, Laurie. I don't believe you two have met," Nan said. "Laurie is Joshua's secretary. More than that, really. I don't know what we would have done without her these last few days. Laurie, I'd like you to meet Shanna O'Brian."

Laurie extended a slender hand. "I've heard a great deal about you, Shanna. It's nice to finally meet you in person." The sincerity in her voice surprised Shanna. She didn't seem at all like a femme fatale. Perhaps Joshua had never told her about their brief marriage.

"Nice to meet you too," Shanna returned the greeting. She wasn't sure what she expected to see in Laurie; arrogance maybe, or some hint of evil. She saw none of that, though—only a gaze filled with caring and compassion. She could understand why Joshua might fall for a woman like her.

"Excuse me for interrupting," Laurie said, shifting her kind gaze back to Nan. "Joshua asked me to escort you in. Are you ready?"

Nan glanced toward the church's open door, then back to the hearse where the casket was being pulled out of the back. Turning back to Laurie she said, "I guess I'm as ready as I'll ever be."

"Would you like to sit with the family, Shanna?" Laurie asked.

"Yes, please do, dear," Nan entreated.

"Thanks, but you go ahead. I'll wait for Max. He should be along any minute."

She watched until the two women disappeared inside, then merged with the other hundred or so people filing into the church. Max caught up with her as she entered the sanctuary. The two of them slid into an empty space near the back just as the music started.

Joshua and Tom, along with four other men and Joshua's son, carried the casket to the front where dozens of flower sprays and wreaths had been placed. Nan was right; the boy did take after his father. Shanna tried not to think about that or about how handsome Joshua looked in his black three-piece suit or how her heart ached with a longing she couldn't even begin to put into words.

The minister led them in singing "Amazing Grace," but to Shanna the sound was anything but sweet. She'd sung the words to that song a thousand times, but unlike the author, she was still blind. Shanna still felt lost and abandoned by the God she'd once loved. Again she dammed up the stream of erratic thoughts and memories and focused on Andrew's eulogy.

The message was short and to the point. Andrew had been a great man and would be missed by his family and friends as well as the world at large. "Andrew Morgan was a man of integrity." The pastor's gaze drifted over the congregation as he brought his message to a close. "He was an honorable man, a philanthropist, who used his wealth to make the world a better place. While he had wealth, it was not money that endeared him to us—it was his compassion and generosity and his striving to live a godly life. We all loved Andrew—not for what he could give us, but for what he was—a husband, father, grandfather, and friend."

The service went on, with Joshua sharing his thoughts about his beloved grandfather. Shanna's heart ached for him. He'd adored his grandfather, and the loss must be unbearable. Shanna sat in numb silence, taking it all in, still unable to comprehend that the music legend was gone.

After the memorial service, they proceeded to the cemetery on the hillside overlooking the lake—also part of the old township. Several generations of Morgans were buried there in a family plot. Now it was Andrew's turn.

The family and some of the guests drove the short distance in a traditional funeral procession to the grave site. Shanna, needing some air, chose instead to walk. "I'll walk with you," Max said, falling into step beside her. Shanna purposely lingered behind the other walkers as they made the winding path to the top of the hill.

"Did you know him well, Max?"

"Fairly. He got me out of trouble a few years back. I'm mighty beholden to him." Max cleared his throat. "He was a good friend."

"What kind of trouble?"

"Well, now, I reckon that's between him and me."

In other words, mind your own business. She thought the words but didn't say them; her gaze following the procession. Except for briefly greeting Nan before the service, she purposely stayed clear of the family. Not that she had to do much distancing. Joshua hadn't attempted to talk to her. But then, he had Laurie beside him. They made a striking couple.

Shanna wondered how Max could have gotten the idea that Joshua was still interested in her. If Joshua and Laurie's closeness now meant anything, they were still very much together. *But this isn't the time to reflect on Joshua's love life,* she reminded herself. *This is a time to bury the dead.*

A three-foot-high stone fence bordered the small cemetery that bore evidence to the tragic history of those who'd lived at Morningsong. Shanna paused by two familiar markers—Harry and Barbara Morgan.

"Who were they?" Max whispered.

"Joshua's parents. You didn't know about them?"

"I knew they were dead, but no one ever talked about them. They died young," Max said, reading the dates on the tombstones.

"Joshua was only five at the time. He brought me up here once, shortly after I came to Morningsong. His father had been an alcoholic—like mine. They were killed in an auto accident. Harry had been drinking."

"Must have been a real disappointment for Andrew and Nan."

"True, but I'm sure Joshua and Tom have more than made up for Harry's failures." She stopped briefly at another marker and knelt down to pull up a weed, then brushed the dirt from the shiny gray marble surface. *Elizabeth Megan O'Brian.*

"My mother is buried here. Have I ever told you about her death?" Shanna knew she hadn't and didn't know why she'd asked.

"No, I don't believe you have."

"I found her in her bedroom—carbon monoxide poisoning."

He frowned. "*You* found her?"

"It was pretty awful."

"That must have been tough. Was it suicide?"

"The authorities suspect it was but said it might have been an accident—or worse." Shanna had no idea why she was explaining it to Max. She hadn't been able to talk about her mother's death to anyone. Now it just seemed to spill out. "Elizabeth may have left her car running in the garage under her bedroom. Or someone might have..."

"Killed her?" Max stared at the grave as though he might find the answer to his question written there.

"Police haven't ruled out foul play. As far as I know, they don't have any suspects. The case is still open, last I heard." Shanna closed her eyes and let the odd mix of feelings wash over her. She missed her mother. On one level Shanna had loved her deeply. On another, she felt a sense of relief. Shanna still nurtured an overwhelming guilt that if she'd been there, she might have been able to save her. They'd taken separate flights. Elizabeth had left earlier in the day since she had business to attend to. Shanna was to do her concert, then come home the next morning. It was one of the few times they'd traveled apart. Though Elizabeth hadn't mentioned what her business was, she'd seemed anxious about it.

Shanna arrived the next morning to find her mother asleep. At least that's what she'd thought at first. The late hour made her check. Shanna shuddered, remembering the lifeless body.

According to the medical examiner, she'd been dead eight hours. *If only I'd been there for you, Mother, maybe I could have...* Shanna stopped in midthought. There was little point in agonizing over it again.

Shanna straightened as she felt a heavy hand on her shoulder. Max's face had turned ashen. He looked weary. "Max, are you OK?"

"I'm fine, darlin'. A little tired is all. Never did take kindly to all-nighters." He raised his head and motioned toward the crowd at the top of the hill. "We'd better get up there with the others."

"Ashes to ashes. Dust to dust." The minister read a passage from the Bible and said a final prayer. Soon the casket would be lowered into the ground. The funeral would be over, and the celebration of Andrew's passage into heaven would begin. Family and friends would eat and talk about old times—something Shanna couldn't face.

After the service, she turned to Max. "I'll see you later."

"Aren't you going to the house?" Max asked. "They're having lunch for everyone."

"No. You go ahead. I think I'll walk down by the lake. I'm not ready to face anyone right now. I'll see you later tonight or tomorrow."

"Suit yourself. The family will be disappointed."

Shanna's lips curled in a half smile. "I doubt they'll even notice. Besides, I already told Nan I wouldn't be there." Shanna glanced toward the row of cars lined up along the road leading to the small cemetery. Her gaze halted at the lead car. Joshua offered his arm to the white-haired woman beside him. After assisting Nan and the little boy into the black limousine, he turned to Laurie, helping her in, as well. He straightened and glanced over the hillside, letting his gaze rest on Shanna.

Shanna hesitated. She thought for a moment he would come to her, and for a moment she hoped he would. But he didn't. He turned away and slid into the backseat. It hurt far more than it should have to see Joshua and Laurie together. Shanna said good-bye to Max and headed in the opposite direction, walking back across the well-kept grounds and down toward the path that led her around the lake and back to her apartment. She could barely see the asphalt path through her tears and the black veil of her mother's wide-brimmed hat.

Chapter Six

Shanna shivered and hugged herself as she nestled deeper into the pale blue velvet cushions of her rocking chair. It had been hours since the funeral. Her mood remained as dark as the night that now surrounded her. She felt as though she'd been shot full of Novocaine and the numbness was wearing off—her heart was beginning to ache again. She tasted the salty tears that slipped along her cheek into the corner of her mouth.

"Not again." Shanna swept a manicured hand across her cheek and stared incredulously at the wetness on her fingers. "What's wrong with you? You have better things to do than sit here and cry all day." Her voice was edged with sarcasm. She seldom cried anymore, but Andrew's death had opened the dam, and now she couldn't seem to stop.

She hadn't shed this many tears since Joshua left. Then she'd cried for days, hoping and praying that he hadn't been unfaithful and hadn't really walked out of her life forever.

"You're wrong," she'd told her mother. *"He'll come back for me."* He never had. Not even when she'd written him about the baby.

Shanna shook the thoughts away, picked up her glittery rhinestone-studded guitar and began strumming, then set it back in its case. Andrew had never liked the instrument. *"Doesn't have the same resonance as your old one,"* he'd said after her first performance with the flashy new guitar.

Shanna agreed with him but didn't dare say so. The jeweled guitar had been a Christmas gift from Elizabeth when Shanna was sixteen. There would be no living with her if Shanna sided with Andrew. The old one had been her first. The Morgans had given it to her shortly after she'd signed on with Morningsong, and Andrew had taught her to play.

"Don't be ridiculous, Andrew," Elizabeth argued. "We want her to look elegant, don't we? Nowadays a star has to be glamorous as well as talented. And this is one of the best guitars money can buy. I want Shanna to have a whole new image. No more child star. She's a woman now, and I want her to look like one."

"She's only sixteen, for Pete's sake. Don't make her any older than she is."

"She's my daughter, Andrew. You make and sell the records; I'll take care of her appearance."

"What do you think, Shanna?" Andrew asked.

Shanna squirmed, knowing which side she had to take and hating it. She picked up the guitar in question. "It…it is beautiful," she stammered.

"Suit yourself." Andrew shrugged and let it go. "Looks like I'm outvoted."

The memory brought a sudden burst of anger—at Andrew for letting Elizabeth have her way, but more at herself for having been such a pathetic wimp.

Shanna rummaged through her closet for the old guitar. Elizabeth had thrown it in the trash, but Shanna had rescued it and hidden it in the back of her closet. Worn and out of tune, the aged wood still felt smooth as satin. She quickly tuned it and began to play. Her fingers skimmed across the strings, bringing the instrument to life as if it were an extension of her body. The guitar responded to her touch like a loving friend. Oh, how she'd missed that sound.

Playing through several of her favorite songs gave Shanna an idea. She rose from the chair, grabbed a jacket from the hall closet, and pulled it on over her ivory cable-knit sweater. As Shanna stepped out into the cool October evening, she hurried down the dimly lit footpath from her apartment to the recording studio. It was time to stop the memories and tears and say good-bye to an old friend. It was time to sing.

The studio, normally buzzing with activity, now reflected the empty feeling inside her. The only light was one someone had apparently forgotten to turn off. It highlighted the stool outside the sound booth, where she often sat to record her songs. She walked toward the light and sat in the center of it.

The great Andrew Morgan was gone. Shanna still couldn't believe she'd never again see his warm smile or feel his welcome-home hugs. "Thanks, Andrew…for everything." She sighed and closed her eyes, sorry that she had neglected those words for so long, wondering if he could hear them now.

Come now, Shanna. She could almost hear his gentle yet authoritative voice rebuking her. *What's all this crying and fussin' about? We've no time for such foolishness. There's work to be done.*

Knowing it would have pleased him, she gazed into the darkness beyond her small circle of light and said, "You're right, Andrew. There are songs to be sung and CDs and videos to be made."

An idea began to germinate for a new album. Tomorrow she would talk to… She swallowed hard to dislodge the lump in her throat. She would never be able to share her ideas with Andrew again. Shanna picked up her guitar and strummed softly. Tomorrow she would have Max and the crew help her choose some of Andrew's favorite hymns and cut a gospel album—a salute to his memory. "Andrew Morgan," she whispered, "this one's for you."

"On a hill far away stood an old rugged cross…"

Shanna sang one gospel song after another, finishing up the medley with "Amazing Grace." There in the light and the silence, she could almost feel God's presence. Maybe He hadn't deserted her after all.

When she finished, she set the old guitar back in its battered case and snapped it shut.

Joshua remained in the shadows of the sound room, hardly daring to breathe lest he disturb the singer seated just beyond the room's open door. The halo of light illuminated her fiery red-gold hair. She looked like an angel sent to assure him that Andrew was safe and happy and probably even recording the angels in his new home.

No wonder fans loved Shanna. She'd slipped some in the ratings lately, but she'd worked her way into legend status and would undoubtedly stay near the top of the recording charts for years to come. He hoped his plan to temporarily pull her out of circulation wouldn't affect her popularity. Though Morningsong would lose money by not having Shanna in the spotlight, he, Max, and Andrew had agreed she needed time off. Joshua wanted, no, needed her to stick around for a while. They had a lot of details to work out on both business and personal levels.

The resonant strains of her alto voice filled the empty room as Shanna sang. As the last refrain echoed in his ears, Shanna returned the guitar to its resting place.

"Don't stop." Joshua jumped at the sound of his own voice. He hadn't meant to say it out loud.

"Oh." Shanna pressed her hand to her chest and squinted to see beyond the light. "Joshua, you scared me half to death. What are you doing here?"

"I didn't mean to frighten you." He paused to turn the light on in the sound booth. "I was here when you came in. I was going to listen to a demo and…"

"I'm sorry. I didn't think anyone was here. Um…I'll leave you to it, then." Shanna slipped her jacket on and started for the door.

"Shanna, that was breathtaking. It's the best I've heard you sing in a long time." Feeling like a schoolboy with his first crush, he left the booth and met her at the door. She seemed even more beautiful to him now than when he'd married her. Cascades of soft curls framed her delicate oval face. Her large brown eyes bore the gentle innocence of a fawn. He let his gaze travel down the bridge of her finely carved nose to her lips, moist and slightly parted. Joshua closed his eyes to control the compelling urge to kiss them.

"I…I'm sorry about Andrew." Shanna's gaze darted up to meet his, then skittered away. "How's Nan? Tell her I'll drop over to see her tomorrow sometime."

"She's doing OK. It was a shock, but then death always is. She made pies yesterday—peach, your favorite. She saved you a piece."

Shanna nodded. "Then I'll have to go for sure."

"Shanna…"

"Joshua…"

They both spoke at once, then apologized. Joshua swallowed hard. He moved toward her as if his body had taken on a life of its own. Placing his hands on either side of her face, he drew her toward him. She grasped his hands to pull them away but closed her eyes instead. He kissed her, gently at first, then again. When she didn't respond, he backed away.

"I…I shouldn't have done that."

"No." Shanna bit into her bottom lip. "You shouldn't have." She picked up her guitar, grasped the doorknob, yanked the door open, and fled.

Joshua stood in the stillness of the darkened room long after she'd gone. His arms still ached with the need to hold her. But it was too soon. He'd rushed her once before, and the results had been devastating—for both of them. Now he was doing it again. "God," he murmured, "give me strength. Help me to do it right this time."

He reached toward the dimly lit instrument panel spread out before him and turned off the recording equipment. He hadn't meant to tape her but was glad he'd already turned the tape machine on to do a sound check for an upcoming project. The mics were in place, the levels were set; he'd simply pressed record when she started singing. The songs had come from the depths of her heart—like an extended love song. He sighed, remembering when she used to sing that way for him, and he prayed that day would come again.

Joshua locked the door to the studio and headed back to the main house. He paused and glanced toward the apartments off to his right. The lights still burned in Shanna's living room. Should he go to her right now, tell her how much he loved her—had loved her from the moment her mother had brought her to Morningsong to audition for his grandfather? Everyone had been delighted with Shanna, adopting the curly-headed cherub as one of the family. He'd only been twelve, she seven, but even then he'd felt a special bond between them.

Bitter memories oozed to the surface of his mind. They'd taken her away from him too many times, and in the end he himself had dealt the final blow—he had severed the fragile thread of love linking them together. If he'd only known the truth. He could have gone to her then and given her his support. Elizabeth had woven a web of lies and deceit around all of them, but no more.

"She can't hurt us anymore, Shanna," he said aloud as if to reassure himself. His feet, seemingly moving on their own accord, began the trek toward the light of her room.

Suddenly the beacon drawing him closer to the woman he loved disappeared. He blinked in disbelief, telling himself it was only a coincidence and that her mother hadn't returned from the grave to separate them again. Joshua shook his head to dispel the crazy notion he'd conjured up. He filled his lungs with the cool, crisp scent of the evening air and released a shuddering sigh. Then he turned, retraced his steps back to the studio, and took another path up the hill toward the house.

Tomorrow would be soon enough to see her. Tomorrow, when he would officially take his place as president of Morningsong. Tomorrow he would set his and Andrew's plan in motion, the ghosts would be laid to rest, and nothing would ever come between them again.

Chapter Seven

Shanna stared at the neon green letters on the clock radio: 6:30. The restless night revealed itself in the tangle of gray satin sheets and the long white lace and nylon nightgown that had twisted around her waist. She tugged at the sheets and finally freed herself from their constricting hold.

Thoughts of Joshua clung to her mind, refusing to obey her commands to leave. All night her brain had used her closed eyelids as a screen, flashing scenes of Joshua on and off like a home movie. There was Joshua in the summer, splashing her and tipping her off her float…Joshua in winter, throwing snowballs and wrestling with her in the snow, kissing away the cold…Joshua in springtime, bringing flowers and brushing their fragrant, feather-soft petals across her nose…Joshua on their honeymoon, loving her.

"Arrgh," she growled in exasperation as she brushed thoughts of him aside like unwanted cobwebs. She would fill her mind with more pressing matters. Things like working out the format for the album she wanted to do in Andrew's honor and scheduling another overseas tour—a long one, as far away from Joshua Morgan as possible. What had she been thinking, letting him kiss her like that? What was even more frustrating was that she'd wanted him to.

She needed to get back on the road, back into the spotlight where fans waited to hear her sing. Besides, she couldn't stay here—not with

Joshua and Laurie so close. His kiss the night before had been a mistake. Joshua had said so himself. A reflex, she supposed. She hadn't expected it, but at least she hadn't allowed herself to respond too deeply. She touched her mouth, wondering for a moment what might have happened if she had.

"Shanna O'Brian, what kind of fool are you, letting the likes of Joshua Morgan get to you? It's obvious he hasn't changed one bit. Imagine hitting on you when he's..." Shanna rubbed the sleep from her eyes. What was Laurie to him, anyway? They'd never married—at least as far as she knew. Yet there was definitely an attachment. If nothing else, they'd had a child together. "It's none of your business," Shanna reminded herself.

After showering, she pulled on a pair of worn jeans and a pale pink sweatshirt. With her wash-and-wear hair still damp, she grabbed the phone to put her plan into action.

"Good morning, Max." The muffled voice at the receiving end of the call told her Max had slept in and was not delighted to be awakened.

"Good grief, girl, don't you ever sleep? What time is it? Oh," he groaned, not waiting for her to answer. "It's only seven. What are you doing up at this hour?"

"I want to go back on the road, Max." She hesitated and held the phone slightly away from her ear, anticipating his reaction. "Tomorrow."

"What? Are you nuts?"

"I want to get back to the tour and leave for the West Coast first thing in the morning. And I want you to schedule a cruise and a concert tour through Europe."

"Shanna Elizabeth O'Brian, if you weren't a grown woman, I'd take you over my knee for even suggesting such a thing." His loud, gravelly voice would have sounded threatening to anyone else, but Shanna laughed at his attempted bark.

"You'd have to catch me first." Her smile faded. "I'm serious, Max. You know what I'm like. I can't hang around doing nothing. Please...call for reservations, and we can fly out of here in time to do the show in Minneapolis Saturday night. I know you canceled that one, but maybe it's not too late."

"Whoa! You know we can't do that. Even if I wanted to, which I don't, we can't leave now."

"Give me one good reason why not?"

"I can give you several but not over the phone and definitely not before I've had my coffee."

"But—"

"Look, put on a pot for me—it's the least you can do after getting me up at this hour."

Shanna sighed. She'd never been able to understand why the bitter black liquid could make a difference in a person's outlook, but if it worked, why not? "You're on. I'll have your poison ready in ten minutes."

Ten minutes later, Max was pounding at her door.

"It's about time," she teased good-naturedly.

Max hauled his lanky but still muscular form over the threshold. In one fluid movement he removed the battered hat and sank into a chair. He reminded her of a gorilla. Coarse black hair and a yet unshaven face topped narrow shoulders. A few tufts of black curls sprang wildly from the V of his shirt.

Shanna poured his coffee, and the two sat in silence. When he'd drained the second cup, she decided he was ready for more than an occasional grunt. "Max," she began. But when he lifted his face to look at her, she stopped. The lines in his face seemed deeper—more pronounced. Why hadn't she noticed it before? Even after his coffee he looked tired, older than his fifty-six years.

"I'm sorry I woke you this morning." She got up and, moving around behind him, placed her hands on his shoulders and began to massage the tight muscles.

"It's OK, darlin'. I should have been up anyway. No self-respecting cowboy would be caught dead sleeping that late."

"Max," she began again, "what I said earlier…couldn't we leave to—?"

"No way."

"But why not?" Shanna's hands stilled.

"It's not my decision. Joshua wouldn't stand for it. Besides, the reading of the will is tomorrow. He's expecting us to show up at the big shindig they got planned for him up at the house tonight."

"Tonight? They're throwing a party?"

Max shook his head. "That's right…you weren't at the house yesterday when they announced it. I was supposed to let you know. It's just a little celebration Laurie and Nan are putting together in honor of Joshua."

Shanna folded her arms and padded to the window. In a voice that sounded childishly desperate even to her own ears, she said, "Max, I don't want to go."

"Look, darlin', I know how you feel." There was no grumbling in his voice now, only gentleness. "But you have to be there."

"Tell them I'm sick or something." She paced to the bar and hooked a leg over a stool.

"It won't work. Joshua wants you there."

"I doubt that. He's got Laurie. Anyway," she continued, "how come they're having a party tonight? We just had Andrew's funeral yesterday. Nan shouldn't have to—"

"Of course she doesn't *have* to. You know doggone well when Nan makes up her mind to do something, she does it. She told me that was what Andrew wanted, and she intends to carry out his wishes."

"Oh." Shanna took the beige phone from the kitchen counter and placed it in front of him. "Please try to get me out of it."

Max frowned and took a long sip of the coffee as if he were going to refuse. "OK," he said at last, "I'll call, but it won't work."

Shanna tried not to listen as Max talked to Joshua. She busied herself in the kitchen, rinsing the few dishes she'd used the day before. The hot, sudsy water felt good. Her hands rarely touched dishwater.

She almost felt domesticated, but not quite. Loving the feel of soap and water on her hands was one thing, but doing household chores like cooking, cleaning, and taking care of kids on a daily basis was quite another—something she would be no good at.

"Shanna," Max called and handed her the phone. "He wants to talk to you."

The old familiar knot worked its way into her stomach again. She paused to dry her hands and throw Max a scathing look before taking the phone from him. "I thought you were going to handle this," she hissed, then resigned herself to the facts. This was her problem, not Max's. She breathed deeply to gather courage before saying hello, yet when the word came out, it was little more than a whisper.

"Shanna…" Only Joshua could say her name that way, like the caress of a breeze on a summer day.

She sank into a nearby chair before her knees buckled. How strange that after so long he could still turn her insides into a quivering mass by simply saying her name. Surely she'd progressed beyond the symptoms of an adolescent crush. Shanna wondered if perhaps he was affected, too, because minutes seemed to pass before he spoke again.

"What's all this about you not feeling well?"

"I…I'm feeling sort of queasy." At least she was telling the truth on that point.

"Still don't like crowds, I take it."

"That's right—unless I'm performing in front of them." She should have known he'd remember that. They both hated to be around large groups of people. Whenever the Morgans threw a bash, she and Joshua would see who could last the longest. It used to be a game with them.

"And you're not really sick."

"Not exactly, but—"

"Good, then I'll see you tonight."

"Joshua…" Shanna decided to use another tactic. "What I really want is to go back on the road again. Max and I could leave right away."

"No!"

"But—"

"Shanna, I don't want to pull rank, but Morningsong still pays your salary."

"Yes…and you're Morningsong now, right?" Shanna didn't bother to hide her annoyance. "I don't like being told what to do."

"That didn't used to bother you." He hesitated, his acrid tone softening as he added, "Look, I don't want to argue with you. But I do want you at the dinner party tonight—it's important to me. And about the tour…I want to make some changes."

"What changes?" Something bearing the name of fear reared up and pounded in her chest. She didn't want anything to change. Not now.

"We'll talk about that tomorrow after we hear the details of Andrew's will."

"Why can't you tell me now?"

"Shanna, give it a rest. I have to help Laurie and Nan get ready for this party Nan insists on having. Take it easy today. And come to the house tonight." He hesitated. "I'll make a deal with you."

"What?" Shanna twisted the phone cord around her fingers.

"Whoever ducks the party first has to buy dinner Saturday night. We'll meet in the garden room…like we used to."

"I don't think that would be a good idea." Even as she spoke she could feel her resolve slipping. "Laurie might not like it."

"What's Laurie got to do with anything? You think…? Forget it. Laurie is staying with Ryan tonight. Shanna, please, don't argue with me. We've got some important industry people coming. It's essential you be there. I'll be by to pick you up at seven-thirty."

"You're going to pick me up? I'm perfectly capable of walking up to the house by myself…or is it that you don't trust me?"

"Let's just say I'm protecting my interests."

"Right. Don't you mean *controlling* your interests?" She let the sarcasm she felt lace her words, then replaced the phone in its cradle.

"I take it you're going to the dinner party." Max adjusted his hat and placed it strategically on his head.

Shanna nodded. "Like you said, he's the boss. I guess that doesn't give me much choice." Her voice broke. Great, she was going to cry again. She grabbed for a tissue from the box by the phone.

Max was at her side in an instant, offering comfort in the circle of his arms. "There, now. What's with the tears?"

"I...I'm sorry." She sniffed and blew her nose. "I don't know what's happening to me. I hate to cry. I know I'm acting like a big baby about this, but I can't seem to stop."

"Like I've been telling you since I came on board, you've been pushin' yourself too hard. First you lose your mother, and now with Andrew dying and the funeral and all...you haven't had a decent night's sleep in months. If you ask me, your body's telling you to slow down." Max guided her to the sofa and lowered her into the deep cushions. "Now, as your manager I'm ordering you to lie down and rest. Read a book or sleep the day away. Then you'll be ready to handle anything that comes along tonight—even attending the dinner party with Joshua."

"Maybe you're right. I've been through a lot worse."

Max brushed a stubborn curl from Shanna's forehead and pressed a kiss there. "Old Max is always right. If you think you'll be OK now, I'll take my leave. I'm needing a bit of a nap myself."

"I'll be fine. You go on."

"You'll sleep?"

She hesitated. "Yes. At least I'll try."

Max raised an eyebrow as if he didn't believe her.

"I promise." She smiled and gave him a playful push. "Now go on."

A few minutes later Shanna stood at the bathroom sink and splashed cool water on her face. *You have got to get hold of yourself, girl,* she cautioned the image in the mirror. Shanna stared, unbelieving, at the dark shadows under her eyes and the red puffy eyelids. "Maybe Max is right," she said aloud. "You look terrible." She went to bed, doubting a nap would repair the damage.

At six that evening Shanna awoke to a pounding headache. She shoved her covers aside and groped her way to the bathroom and gulped down a couple of aspirin.

"I should have stuck to my story about being sick." She glanced at the large old-fashioned tub, with its clawed feet perched on the tiled floor. Deciding a hot bubble bath would relax her and hopefully wash away the headache as well, Shanna descended into the warm water, hoping to alleviate the tension building inside her again at the thought of facing Joshua.

"Come on," she spoke to the swell of bubbles in her hand. "He's just another guy. No reason to get yourself so upset."

She blew the bubbles away. "No, he isn't," she argued with herself. "He's not like any man you've ever known. He's Joshua Morgan.

"This is crazy. He's got me talking to myself." She closed her eyes and leaned back, letting the hot water soothe her frazzled nerves.

"There's no problem," she murmured as the heat soaked away her tension. "All I have to do is go to the party with him…no problem at all. Treat it like a business engagement—another appearance you need to make."

The scented water worked its healing miracle, leaving her limp as a rag doll. Shanna wrinkled her nose at the unmade bed and the pile of clothes that cluttered the floor. This wasn't like her. Even though she never needed to bother with cleaning, she liked keeping her personal items in order. But tonight she didn't care. Something about the sleep, the bath, and the aspirin filled her with a lethargy she couldn't seem to shake.

She walked into the large closet and selected a long teal silk dress with a draped top and low back. The skirt hung nicely over her trim hips—not too loose, not too tight. A slit up the side offered modest glimpses of her long, slender legs. After brushing through her hair and applying makeup, Shanna pivoted slowly to survey the finished product, feeling as though she were watching someone else. The girl in the mirror couldn't be her. She looked more like a princess in a fairy tale.

"Hey, Cinderella," Shanna spoke to her mirror's image. "How'd you like to take my place at this party tonight?"

The image shrugged. Why not?

"You would? Well, then, have a pleasant evening, Cindy. Enjoy Morningsong Palace and your Prince Charming while you can. Just remember that when morning comes, your dreams will have turned to ashes and you'll have to walk away."

For a long moment Shanna stared into the haunting brown eyes, then turned from the image and escaped to the living room. She walked to the large picture window that framed the Morningsong landscape. To the west the sun was setting over smoky hills.

Her breath caught at the sight of Joshua heading up the walk. In his fitted tuxedo, he looked every inch the prince in the fairy tale that had been playing in her mind. If their separation had done anything to change him, it was to make him even more attractive. He'd lost the thinness of youth. His shoulders, broad and more powerful than she remembered, filled the black jacket of his tux to perfection. His muscular thighs strained against his trousers as he sprinted up the steps to her apartment.

Well, Cinderella, your prince has arrived. And he is charming.

Delicate chimes floated into the room. Shanna told her heart to be still, then with all the poise and elegance of country music's number one singer, she moved toward the sound and leaned forward to open the door.

Chapter Eight

"Joshua. Come in." Shanna congratulated herself on her control of the situation, but, then, she hadn't let her eyes focus any higher than his bow tie.

Joshua stepped into the small living room. "Shanna…" His arms remained firmly at his side. *A good thing,* Shanna mused, *or you might be foolish enough to walk straight into them.*

She let her gaze journey upward, past his square jaw to his finely chiseled mouth and nose. Her hands trembled with a desire to touch the smoothness of his freshly shaven face—to run her finger across his lips and the strong, defined cheekbones bronzed now by the California sun.

It would be dangerous to let her eyes meet his. She might be drawn into their ocean depths and drown as she had in her reckless youth. What if his eyes were glazed with the same shades of love she'd seen in them back then? Or worse, what if they were filled with hatred? Either way she'd lose. But when she let her eyes meet his, she saw neither love nor hate. He seemed embarrassed.

"You…you look…great," he stammered, glancing away.

His sudden shyness gave her time to gather her wits. "Thank you," she murmured. "Um…shouldn't we be going?"

A grin broke across Joshua's face. "This is ridiculous. I can't decide whether to shake your hand or hug you or kiss you or…"

"Yes, well…it is a bit awkward seeing each other after so long a time. Considering the circumstances, a handshake would be best." She extended her hand, relaxing in the relative safety of the gesture.

But when his hand touched hers, she thought perhaps they should have settled for a brief hello. There were no lightning bolts, no searing fires—nothing so bold and romantic—only a gentle tremor that vibrated through every fiber of her being.

She didn't have long to think about the impact of his touch. He pulled her toward him and wrapped her in his arms. She started to protest, but as she felt the warmth of his chest and the steady beating of his heart beneath her hand, the objection withered. Shanna let her head rest on his shoulder.

"I was wrong." His Adam's apple shifted up and down as he spoke.

"You were?"

"Yes." His chin rested on her head. "A handshake is not going to be enough."

"Oh?" Shanna's breath caught as he drew back and tilted her chin upward.

"I don't think a hug is the answer, either." His gray eyes glinted with sparks of mischief. "But I think we'd better head on over to the house. And"—his lips brushed the tip of her nose—"maybe we can continue this discussion later."

Shanna cleared her throat, drew herself up to her full five feet seven inches, and backed away from him, ignoring his remark. "I'll get my wrap. Be back in a minute."

She was annoyed. Angry. Had he deliberately baited her, leading her on to see what kind of reaction his advances would get? *Well, you certainly showed him, didn't you? It's a good thing he didn't go any further. You can't afford to let him get to you. You've got to be strong.*

It would serve Joshua right if she told him she had no intention of going with him to the party. She should walk away from Morningsong this instant and never come back, but she wouldn't. Not yet. Tonight was a special time for him, and she wouldn't spoil it by bringing up the past or the future. Tonight, bizarre as it seemed, she'd fall into the role of Cinderella and try to enjoy the ball. Tomorrow she'd be on her way.

"Is it chilly out tonight?" Shanna called from the bedroom. When Joshua didn't respond, she shrugged and pulled out a fur jacket that would suffice in any case.

Shanna entered the living room and found him engrossed in the seascape mural that covered an entire wall. She watched as his gaze shifted to inspect the rest of the room and held her breath for his response. She wondered if he'd see the significance of the room or understand the part he'd played in its creation.

She had designed and decorated the room as a sort of therapy to help her through the tormenting months that followed her short-lived marriage to Joshua. Inspired by a deep love for the sea, the mural depicted a vague, translucent sunset hovering behind a violent storm. Once, it had told her that the sun would shine again. Now it stood as a sharp reminder that the storm would stay forever, like dark and distant memories, obliterating the sun.

A light beige carpet blended with the beach in the picture to continue the illusion of sand.

The furniture she'd selected harmonized with the landscape in soft muted colors of sky blue, gray, cloud white, sunset lavenders, and pinks.

"Nice," he said at last. "It's like you."

"Oh?"

"Yes." His voice softened as he stepped toward her and placed his hands on her shoulders. "Soft, subtle, beautiful." He twisted a curl around his finger and tugged her gently forward. "Natural. Free. A little wild. The way you used to be with me. The way you were last night when you sang for my grandfather. Seeing you convinced me that under the glossy show business facade is the Shanna I fell in love with."

"N-no..." She wanted to think of some quick, humorous retort, something cool and sassy, but his hands slid over the curves of her shoulders, and all she could do was stammer, "You…you make it sound like I'm two different people."

"Aren't you?" The searching intensity of his eyes startled her. He was too perceptive, as though he could look into her soul and learn things she didn't even know herself. Her gaze lingered on his, and the message she read there shook her to the core. If his eyes and actions were any indication, she'd swear that Max was right and that Joshua was still in love with her.

There had always been a strong physical attraction between them. Like it or not, that hadn't gone away. It had nothing to do with love, she told herself. Joshua wanted her. She wanted him. But that didn't make it right. Still, maybe one kiss…

No! You can't let yourself get burned a second time. God, if You're out there at all, help me resist him. Help me walk away intact. I can't afford another broken heart.

"I…I think we'd better go…" She wasn't sure how convincing she sounded, but it didn't seem to matter. Joshua hadn't heard or hadn't wanted to. His thumb stroked the smooth line of her jaw, coming to rest on the racing pulse at the side of her neck. His lips were only inches from hers.

She swallowed hard, her resolve melting. All she had to do was weave her fingers in the thick coarseness of his hair and bring his head down ever so slightly to meet hers. At the moment her thoughts might have been transformed to action, Joshua moved away.

"I'm sorry." He brushed his hand through his hair and offered her a sheepish grin. "Let's go on up to the house. They can't start dinner without the guests of honor."

Outwardly, Shanna rallied quickly and allowed Joshua to drape the jacket over her shoulders. She even managed to say, "Thank you." But it took her a bit longer to quiet the emotional war between her heart and her head. She should have been thankful for Joshua's move away from her. Instead, she felt cold and empty.

Outside she drew in a deep breath of crisp night air to steady herself. They walked up the long, winding path toward the main house.

Joshua eased his arm around her shoulders. Shanna tensed and shrugged away.

Joshua stuffed his hands in his pants pockets. "You'd better prepare yourself for a lecture. Nan's upset that you didn't come up to the house after the funeral yesterday or this morning."

"I couldn't—" Shanna nearly choked on her own words. "I hate being around all those people when I'm…and this morning I was so tired."

"I know. But you could have stopped in to say hello. Show you cared."

Shanna ignored his jab. "How is she?"

"It's been rough for her. You don't stay married to the same man for fifty years without suffering when he's gone."

"No," Shanna said softly. "When someone you love dies or goes away, it's like something dies inside of you. Sometimes the empty space is so big and dark, you wish you could die so you wouldn't have to feel it anymore."

Anguish pierced his gut as he watched her. Joshua reached for her hand. She looked up at him. Her eyes revealed a tormenting pain, then quickly glazed over as if she realized she'd let him see too much. What hurt the most was knowing she blamed him. *It wasn't me. It was Elizabeth. She lied, she deceived all of us.* He wanted to turn around and take her back to her apartment and explain everything, then take her in his arms and kiss away the terrible hurts they'd both endured. But he couldn't. Not yet. His desire for her burned as fiercely now as it had when they'd married. Still, he needed to take it easy—the last thing he wanted was to scare her off. He'd almost done that last night in the studio. Joshua cursed himself for letting his heart overpower his good sense.

He couldn't afford to dwell too heavily on Shanna just now. Morningsong Productions was waiting for him to take over. His own needs, his life, would have to wait. And, like Max said, the timing had to be right. He only prayed the time would come soon and that when it did, she would be willing to take him back.

"Shanna." Joshua stopped and turned her to face him. "We have a lot of things to talk about in the next few days. I know we can't just pick up where we left off six years ago. Too much has happened. But maybe for tonight, at least, we can forget about all the trouble and be friends again, like we used to be, before—well, before things got serious between us. You were my best friend, you know."

"That was a long time ago. I don't—" She stopped when another voice inside interrupted. *Don't argue, Cinderella. His Royal Highness has made a request. Surely you won't deny him your friendship for one night?* Blocking out the tears and the pain should be easy. For her it had become an everyday routine, like brushing her teeth. Ordinarily she was good at it. But ordinarily Joshua wasn't walking beside her.

"Remember when we were kids?" Joshua went on. "Having you at these things always made them easier to take. Like I mentioned earlier, I'd rather not have all the formality, but this is what Andrew wanted. Stepping into his shoes is an honor. At the same time, I'm not sure I'm a big enough man for the job."

"Of course you are," Shanna said, surprised at his sudden insecurity. His vulnerability made him far less frightening. "You've been in the business all your life, Josh. There's no one who could do the job better."

"Thanks for the vote of confidence." Joshua squeezed her hand. "I'd still feel more secure with you at my side. Will you stand by me tonight—for old times' sake?"

Shanna nodded. "I'll try."

They walked a few feet in silence before Joshua spoke again. "Maybe it would be easier if I'd been expecting it, but Granddad's death was so sudden."

"I know how you feel. Since Mother died, I've had so many more responsibilities. Change is always harder when we're forced into it."

Joshua stiffened, visibly angered. "How can you liken Elizabeth's death to my grandfather's? She was *nothing* like him. She abused you and tore people down. Andrew was always trying to build people up, helping them see their potential. You're better off without her. We all are."

Shanna pulled her hand from his and stopped short. Shocked by his outburst, she could only stand there, open-mouthed.

"I..." Joshua turned around. "Shanna, I'm sorry, I shouldn't have said that. It's just that I hate what she did to us."

"What *she* did? She forced me to see the truth about you!"

"Truth? Your mother didn't know the meaning of the word."

"And you do? You always hated her." Something akin to fear rose like bile into her throat. Elizabeth had always looked after Shanna's best interests. She had been uncompromising in making certain Shanna was protected. She may have gone too far at times, but... It suddenly occurred to Shanna that Andrew and Joshua may have grown tired of Elizabeth's demands and wanted her out of the way. They could have killed her and made it look like a suicide. "You...," she stammered, "you wanted her dead. You said that once."

"You think I killed her?" His eyes widened in disbelief.

"Did you?" In her heart she knew the accusation was unfounded. Joshua had been in L.A. when it happened. But Andrew...

"No." Joshua clenched his fists. "I may have thought about it from time to time, but I could never kill anyone—not even your mother." He dragged a hand through his hair. "Look, we can't talk about this right now. Nan is waiting for us. Let's call a truce for tonight. I promise we'll hash everything out tomorrow."

As if saying her name were a magic chant, Nan appeared in the entry to welcome them in. "Shanna." Nan held out her arms in welcome. Shanna accepted the invitation without hesitation, letting herself comfort and be comforted. She desperately needed Nan's warmth—an assurance the world hadn't gone mad. The delicate scent of lavender floated around Nan and reminded Shanna of springtime and home and happier times. Nan was dressed in a full-length emerald velvet gown with an empire waist and a V neck. A blazing diamond broach enriched the simple lines, giving her the regal look of a queen. "My dear child, I have missed you so much."

"I've missed you too." Shanna drew back. "How are you doing?"

"Holding up. Being busy helps.

"Yes, I know." A knowing look passed between them.

"Come have tea with me tomorrow, dear. We can have a nice long chat, and you can catch me up on all that's been happening in your life."

"I'm afraid that wouldn't be much," Shanna said. "Just performing. But tea would be nice."

Nan nodded and turned to Joshua. He bent to kiss her soft, wrinkled cheek. "Are you sure you're up to this, Nan?"

"No, but everyone's here, so we may as well get it over with. You two go on in. I'll join you in a moment."

Joshua fixed his gaze on Shanna's, and for a breathless moment she was distracted by the possibility that they could somehow be a real couple. "Shall we?" Joshua's charm enhanced the spell, and once again Shanna found herself caught up in the fairy-tale world of Morningsong. She took the arm he offered and let him guide her into the ballroom.

Massive crystal chandeliers glittered from the high, ornate ceilings. Candles flickered on linen-draped tables. Their dancing light enhanced, softened, and brought to life the cut-crystal goblets and highly polished silver.

In a far corner, a group of musicians, formally attired, were already entertaining guests with a selection of Baroque music. Shanna smiled at the sight. Not ostentatious, simply elegant—simply Morningsong.

She leaned toward her escort and whispered, "Entertaining royalty tonight, Joshua?" The light, teasing quality of her voice surprised Shanna.

"Only you, princess." The endearing statement struck a chord in her heart.

"And you…Prince Joshua," Shanna said softly, pausing only to catch her breath as his hand touched hers.

He guided her over the dance floor toward the tables, stopping to greet friends and acquaintances along the way. They murmured hellos and stopped for brief greetings. By the time they reached the head table, the others were already seated. She breathed a sigh of relief as Joshua seated her next to Max and took the chair to her right. Nan was seated to the left of Max, then Joshua's younger brother, Tom. An attractive young girl Shanna hadn't met finished out their table, and judging from the warm glances passing between them, she guessed her to be Tom's date. Cascading strands of blue-black hair shimmered like silk in the candles' glow. She wore her hair pulled back from her face, giving her a little-girl look.

"Tom, it's good to see you." Shanna smiled her acknowledgment and was greeted with Tom's flashing blue eyes and sardonic smile. With his classic good looks, Tom could have been a model. He resembled Joshua in build, but his features were finer and his hair a dark brown.

"Ah, if it isn't the lovely Shanna O'Brian. How gracious of you to take the time to join us."

Shanna didn't miss the hint of sarcasm behind the playful greeting. She arched her eyebrow and matched him grin for grin. "Hmm. Missed me that much, huh?"

"Well, you could get off that crazy merry-go-round you ride to stop and say hello once in a while," Tom grumbled.

"We all miss you, Shanna. You're on the road too much these days." Nan sighed and patted Shanna's hand.

"I second that motion," Max drawled. "Trying to slow Shanna down is like draggin' your feet behind a speeding freight train."

"Now you guys quit picking on her," Joshua interrupted. "I have a feeling we'll be seeing much more of Shanna from now on."

Change. Anxiety rose in the pit of her stomach at his remark, but before Shanna could ask him what he meant, he turned away.

Chapter Nine

"Christi." Joshua smiled at the young woman next to Tom. "I hope you're not feeling neglected. I'd like you to meet one of Morningsong's best." Joshua glanced from one woman to the other. "Shanna O'Brian...Christiana Rodriguez."

"Nice to meet you, Christi." Shanna extended her hand in welcome, setting aside the uneasiness from the moment before.

"I am happy to meet you." Christi's shy smile reached her sparkling dark eyes. Shanna guessed her to be about eighteen. She spoke in broken English.

"Christi's one of our new singers." Joshua's voice broke through Shanna's musings. "And an accomplished classical guitarist. We've been working with her at the Los Angeles studio on an album. We're setting up a tour and personal appearances for her. She'll be singing for us later on tonight."

"What do you sing?" Shanna asked.

"Mostly ballads from my country—Mexico."

"She does pop too," Tom said proudly. "We've been thinking of using the L.A. facility mostly for popular music and basing the country western out here. We've got a good lineup of artists ready to go."

Shanna glanced at Joshua, wondering if this was one of the changes he had in mind. "Andrew never mentioned that," she ventured. "I thought he was solely into producing work by country-music artists."

Joshua glanced at Tom. "He was softening. Tom and I have been wanting to expand for several years. Before he died he told me to go ahead with the plan. Christi tipped the scale for us, as she's accomplished in both arenas."

"Joshua, would you lead us in a prayer, please?" Nan reminded him.

"Oh, um…sure." He rose and went to the podium and began the task that had always been Andrew's. He welcomed the guests—around one hundred. Many had attended the funeral; most were employees. "Andrew founded this company on prayer and a deep belief in God. He always said that without God we'd have nothing. Andrew sought God's direction every step of the way. I want to continue that tradition. Please join me now in asking the blessing." After a few moments of silence, he began, "Father, so much has happened in the last few days. We have lost a great man in Andrew. I pray Your hand will guide us as we continue his work." Joshua went on to give thanks for their meal and their many blessings.

Shanna was moved by Joshua's sincerity and humility. He seemed genuine in his seeking of God's help. On the other hand, she wondered if it was all an act. Joshua didn't seem the pious type. Not that it was any of her concern. She certainly had no right to criticize. Shanna had little faith in God or anyone else, while the Morgans never seemed to waver in their faith.

"There are a lot of things to remember," Joshua said, returning to the table.

"It will come," Nan assured him.

Their discussion was halted by waiters who began serving appetizers. Dinner talk remained superficial while they were served, but eventually the talk turned back to business. "Will you be going back to Morningsong West, Josh?" Max asked.

"No. I'm sending Tom out there."

"You're not sending me anywhere!" Tom shot Joshua a sharp glance. "I go where I want, and I haven't decided that yet."

Joshua's jaw tightened.

"Relax, boys, we can talk about that later. So tell me, Christi," Nan said, changing the subject, "how do you like our little valley?"

"Oh, Mrs. Morgan, it is beautiful. I will be spoiled to go back home."

"Where is home for you, Christi?" Shanna stabbed at a slippery, butter-soaked snail.

"San Diego." She ducked her head. "But I don't get home very often. Next week I start a three-month tour to promote my first album." She and Tom exchanged glances. Tom obviously didn't like the idea of her being on the road.

Shanna hoped Christi's relationship with Tom wouldn't go as sour as hers had with Joshua. Her appetite diminishing, Shanna set the escargot aside. Perhaps she should warn Christi of the dangers in pursuing a relationship. Shanna doubted she would listen, though. Young girls in love seldom listen to logic.

As the conversation droned on, Shanna barely tasted the salad; the warm, crusty bread; the sautéed prawns served on a bed of rice pilaf; or the fresh asparagus topped with hollandaise sauce and sprinkles of toasted almonds. She plodded through the meal listening to Max's humorous renditions of his former days as a rodeo junkie.

"The rodeo seems a long way from managing a singer," Christi said. "Why did you quit?"

"Age for one thing." Max chuckled. "Liquor for another."

"You were an alcoholic?" Shanna frowned. "You never told me that."

He shrugged. "Didn't come up. I'm not very proud of the fact. 'Sides, I figured if you knew, you might not have hired me. I was pretty desperate to get the job."

"You're probably right about that. My father was an alcoholic. My mother said it eventually killed him."

"Alcoholism is a terrible thing," Nan said, grief passing across her serene features. "So many wasted lives. You're fortunate to have overcome it, Max."

"Did Andrew know?" Shanna asked.

"Yep. Andrew's the one that got me up and running. I'd been gored by a bull and was in the hospital in San Antonio. Wasn't sure I'd make it. Lot of internal injuries. That's when I realized how bad off I was. Went through withdrawals, the likes of which nearly drove me berserk. When I was discharged, Andrew sent me to a rehab program—paid for the whole thing and promised me a job at Morningsong if I stayed sober."

"We're all very proud of you, Max," Nan said.

"Yeah. Things aren't quite the way I like them, but the good Lord's given me back more than I could ever hope for."

Shanna was proud of Max and told him so. It did grate that he'd never mentioned it to her, but that was as much her fault as his. Shanna didn't often make herself available for intimate chats with the people she worked with.

Guiding the conversation back to more neutral ground, Shanna said, "Since you're thinking of incorporating popular music, I'd like to try a contemporary album."

"Sounds like a good plan," Tom agreed. "You've got a good following in that group. What do you think, Josh?"

Joshua set his coffee cup down. "We might want to think about it in three months or so. I'd like to get myself situated here and see how things go with Christi first. I'd rather not move too fast. There are a number of matters that need settling."

The noncommittal response and the way Joshua had avoided eye contact stirred up Shanna's fears again. Something was going to happen, and it concerned her. Shanna concentrated on her tea and told herself that no matter what it was, she'd survive.

After dinner the board of directors awarded Joshua a plaque with a simple ceremony. Joshua in turn announced his plans to choose a new vice president and that he expected to make his announcement by the end of the week. After a few more bits of news, Joshua introduced Christi, and in the next moment he was beside Shanna again. Applause rose and died, and then Christi took her place on the stage.

"She has great stage presence—reminds me of you when you were that age." Joshua's breath played a sensuous note on her ear and sent vibrations shimmering through her. Shanna forced her attention back to the girl onstage. Christi's voice stroked the air with delicate, clear tones, reflecting the mood around them.

"She's good," Shanna whispered. "A wise choice."

"Glad you think so." The admiration in his eyes told her he was no longer thinking about the singer.

As Christi finished her song, applause burst around them. Shanna reluctantly drew her attention back to Christi, giving her the adulation she deserved. When Christi returned to the table, Joshua stood and hugged her to himself like a proud father. "I'd like to take Christi around and introduce her. I won't be long." He winked, sending her the signal to meet him later in the atrium.

Shanna shivered. She couldn't go through with this charade. It was time for this Cinderella to leave the ball.

"Shanna—"

"Oh!" she gasped and spun around. "Tom, you startled me. I was just—"

"Leaving? Without talking to me?"

Shanna flushed. "Of course not. I…I just needed some air. You know how I feel about these things."

Tom nodded. "I hope I didn't embarrass you earlier. I really have missed you."

"No, you didn't embarrass me. I know I'm gone a lot. Comes with the job. Fans forget you when you aren't out there in the limelight all the time."

He looked at her for a long moment. "Yeah." Then he nodded toward Christi. "What do you think of her?"

"She's good, Tom. She'll make it."

"Mmm. I just wish she'd get her head out of the clouds and think of something besides singing."

"Do I detect a note of jealousy?" Warning signals flashed in Shanna's head again, and her smile faded. "Be careful, Tom." She wanted to say more—to tell him not to become involved with a woman like Christi whose world, like her own, excluded nearly everything that wasn't related to music. But from the pained expression in his eyes, she could tell her warning had come too late.

"Careful? How can I be anything else? Big brother has already seen to that. He's like Granddad, always stepping in to alter people's lives."

"I take it you're not exactly thrilled about moving to Los Angeles."

"Not with Joshua bringing Christi here." He smiled, at least as much as his tightly set jaw would allow. "You didn't know that, did you?"

"You don't think Joshua is interested in Christi?"

"Wouldn't surprise me." Tom shook his head. "Naw, I think he just wants to slow things down between us. Won't do him any good, though. You wait and see. Come next September, Christi and I will be walking down the aisle. And speaking of Christi, I think I'll go rescue her from the masses."

Shanna bit her cheek. Maybe she should have said more, but what chance did a piece of her mind have against determined Morgan will?

She watched Tom's straight, broad shoulders as he sliced through the crowd to reach Christi. She wished she could write the two young people out of the Morningsong script and into one of their own where they might have a chance. Their story brought back memories of another couple—Joshua, determined to marry her, and Shanna, cemented to her music. Before the thoughts could further mar the evening, she scribbled them off the pages in her mind with bold, black strokes.

Too many conversations later, Shanna forgot her earlier resolve to avoid the atrium and slipped through the open stained-glass doors. She breathed in the familiar exotic, musky scent of freshly watered plants and flowers.

The room—a long glassed-in porch drenched in shades of green, splashed with colorful blooms of hibiscus, begonias, and orchids, and complete with a waterfall—reminded Shanna of a lush, tropical paradise. The room was bathed in a glow of muted light cast from the illuminated gardens and paths outside.

Shanna stretched out on a lounge chair near the waterfall. Its welcome babble drowned out the party sounds. She closed her eyes and slipped off her shoes. Weary from too much talk and food, she leaned back. "Just a few minutes," she murmured, "then I'll go home." Water soothed like a lullaby and carried her to another place in time.

It was during her seventeenth birthday party. She could still see his teasing smile when he finally escaped the crowd and met her here.

"OK." Shanna sighed. "What shall I give you this time?"

"Did we bet on anything?"

"I don't remember."

"I know what I'd like." Joshua's voice had grown softer, deeper.

"What?" She looked up at him and felt herself go very still. He'd never looked at her in quite that way before.

"It's a special prize."

"Is it expensive?"

"Priceless."

"But then how could I give it to you?"

"If you loved me you could."

"What is it?" She had loved him for a long time.

"You." He shifted uncomfortably. "I'd like you to kiss me."

Love for him welled up inside her, closing off the flow of words. She lifted her face to his and nodded. A dozen butterflies took off at once as his head lowered to meet hers. She closed her eyes and let the wonder of him fill her senses—the soft caress of his breath on her cheek; the fresh, clean scent of spice and soap; the warm, strong feel of his muscled shoulder beneath her hand. She felt the brush of his lips on hers, the gentle caress of his hands as they framed her face.

In some corner of her mind, Shanna realized her memory had been replaced by the real thing. "You're not a dream anymore, are you?" she whispered against his mouth.

"Would it make a difference?" His finger traced the outline of her eyebrows, her cheeks, her mouth.

"If…if you're real…I shouldn't be here. We shouldn't be doing this."

"Then…" Joshua lowered his mouth to hers, teasing, touching between each word. "I'll…just have…to be…a dream." His mouth closed over hers.

As he lifted his head, she leaned her forehead against his chest, too shaken to speak. His heart hammered in his chest, matching the odd percussion of her own.

He drew in a ragged breath before he spoke. "Shanna…"

She lifted her eyes to meet his. Even in the dim light she could see the fire blazing in them, openly declaring his need. She looked away quickly as though the fire in his gaze might burn her. What he wanted, she couldn't give him. What he offered, she couldn't take. She felt a knotting ache in her chest and knew the dream would have to end.

"I love you," he whispered.

"No!" she snapped, suddenly filled with more than enough strength to refuse him. "Don't talk to me about love, Joshua Morgan."

Joshua took her hand in his, stroking her wrist with his thumb. "Shanna, don't let the past make you bitter."

"If I'm bitter it's because I used to believe in love." Shanna's voice had softened to a whisper. "I believed in princes and fairy tales and dreams. I even believed in a perfect love between a man and a woman—a love made in heaven to last forever. Now I know princes are mere mortals, fairy tales are an illusion, and dreams don't come true. Love is part of the fantasy."

"You're wrong, Shanna. You've gotten a warped picture of what love really is. I'm sorry because I helped you build that image. Things have changed now. Please, give me the chance to show you how wrong you are. Let me prove—"

"No." Shanna rose from the lounge and pulled her hand from his. "What we had is gone, Joshua. I don't want to bring it back—I can't go through all that again. I have all I need now—my career, my music. I won't change my mind, and don't think you can change it for me."

He stood. She flinched as his shoulders rose above her, blocking out the light. "Your career may be enough for now, Shanna, but there just might come a time when you'll want more than a cold guitar and a few old memories."

Joshua stood motionless before her. She forgot to breathe as she watched the anger drain from his eyes to be replaced by a sort of anguish. As she stood to leave, he grasped her shoulders and crushed her against him. Then, with surprising gentleness, he tilted her chin and lowered his mouth to hers. He lingered a moment as if she were the last note he would ever play. She felt his shoulders sag as he released her. When she opened her eyes, he was gone.

She hadn't cried. Her pain reached far beyond the need for tears. Yet a salty wetness lingered on her cheeks. Joshua's? She hadn't meant to hurt him. She hated herself for coming, for being weak and letting him hold her. If she couldn't help the way her body responded to him, she should have stayed away. Shanna straightened. It was over now, and hurtful as it would be, she had to let him know there would be no chance for reconciliation.

"It must be midnight, Cinderella." She glanced at her gown, surprised to see it hadn't turned to rags. "Time to sweep up the ashes and move on."

Chapter Ten

Shanna stretched and wriggled deeper into the satiny cocoon of sheets and comforter. A tiny smile lifted the corners of her mouth. In her dream Joshua trimmed the sails and headed out to sea. A shrill screech from an overhead gull clashed with the gentle swish of the wind, the billowing sail, and the deep turquoise water.

The screeching grew louder, more raucous, changing her pleasure to aggravation and blurring the images of her brilliant dream into shades of stormy gray.

Shanna reached over to quiet the persistent ring and after three tries managed to turn off her alarm. She peered at the offensive clock and set it back on the bedside table. "Your days are numbered. I'm trading you in for a radio alarm." As often as she threatened, she had yet to make the move. Her life was like that in a lot of ways.

Running a hand through her disheveled curls, she yawned and snuggled back under the covers. When quiet filled the room again, traces of a honeymoon and an ancient summer day filtered back into her sleepy brain. She'd been so young and naive then. Such easy prey. As the lethargy wore away, Shanna threw off her blankets in disgust. She had better things to do than ruminate over the past. Letting romantic thoughts fill her head was pure foolishness.

Last night had been a prime example. At times Joshua seemed to have more power over her emotions than she had over herself. She needed to be more careful. She might not have the strength to resist him another time.

Before heading for the shower to wash away the last vestiges of her dream, Shanna quickly made the bed. A maid would be in later and would probably redo it, but some habits were hard to break.

Feeling somewhat refreshed from her shower, Shanna walked into the closet. Though she spent most of her time on the road, Shanna kept a wardrobe in the apartment. This morning she selected a navy blue pantsuit and a white silk blouse from the rack, then pulled out navy shoes. She had too many clothes—too many shoes. Too much of everything. Her mother's choice, not hers. Every time Shanna came back to Morningsong, there would be another outfit in the tightly packed closet. "You're in the public eye, Shanna," Elizabeth would say. "You need a big wardrobe. You don't want to be seen in the same outfit twice."

On the wall just inside the closet was a corkboard covered in black velvet and framed. On it hung more jewelry than she'd wear in a hundred years. Most of it had been her mother's. Shanna lifted off several gold chains in various lengths and styles, then set her choices on the bed. Yawning again, she padded through the thick carpet of the bedroom and living room to the cold tile floor in the kitchen. A few minutes later, she settled into the corner of the sofa with a cup of tea to list the chores she needed to accomplish.

She would stay tonight, but come morning she'd be on the road—with or without Max. Shanna made a note to call Beth. Except for an appearance at the funeral, Shanna hadn't seen or heard from her friend. Not surprising with her recent engagement to Cliff Benson, who managed music productions for Morningsong. Beth had been away from Nashville and her fiancé for weeks. That arrangement wouldn't last long. Already Cliff was bugging her to quit her job so she could be with him. Marriage would definitely put an end to Beth's travels. Or Beth's travels would put an end to their marriage plans.

Shanna chewed on the end of the pen. She wished Beth well. And Cliff. "You don't know what you're getting yourself into. I hope you'll be happy."

Shanna wrote a note to herself to talk to Max about lining up a new makeup artist, then scratched it out. There was no hurry. She could always take care of her own makeup in a pinch. In fact, thinking about it now, Shanna wondered if hiring someone else was really necessary. Why not keep Beth on for as long as she wanted to stay, then phase out the job. No sense paying someone for something Shanna was perfectly capable of doing herself. Elizabeth had insisted on hiring a makeup artist. Now that she was no longer in charge…

It was a small decision in the scheme of things, but Shanna found an odd pleasure in making it. She shrugged and continued her list. There was packing to do, calls to make, ruffled feathers to soothe. Nan and Tom would be disappointed at her hasty departure, but it couldn't be helped.

The next item on her list she wished she could avoid. She'd need to stop by the police station in Nashville sometime today—find out how the investigation into her mother's death was coming. Deep down, Shanna had never believed the suicide story. Elizabeth O'Brian thought too highly of herself for that. Maybe it had been accidental, but Shanna still harbored the gut feeling that Elizabeth had been murdered. Though Shanna had left the investigation to the police, it often nagged at her.

Who had hated Elizabeth enough to kill her? Andrew? That made little sense. If Andrew wanted her dead, he could have done it years ago and probably with less publicity. Though Andrew could be shrewd and demanding, she couldn't picture him as a killer. At heart, he was a kind man. Still, Elizabeth did have the ability to try his patience. Had she pushed him too far?

And what about Joshua? Last night she'd determined he couldn't have done it, but that wasn't necessarily true. He could have flown out here on business and gotten into an argument with her. Shanna realized now he did want her back. Would he have gone so far as to kill

Elizabeth to get to Shanna? It didn't make much sense—but then nothing at Morningsong made sense anymore.

Tom could have done it, but to Shanna's knowledge, he'd never had much contact with Elizabeth. Certainly not Nan. Max? He hadn't arrived at Morningsong until after her mother's death. "If I didn't know better, I would list myself as a suspect. Lord knows I had enough motive with the way she..."

Shanna shook her head. Elizabeth controlled Shanna's life only because Shanna had allowed her to. At least that's what a psychiatrist had told her. She was a victim because she had allowed people to victimize her. Shanna may have entertained thoughts of getting rid of her mother from time to time, but she never would have done it. If Elizabeth was murdered, it had to have been done by someone outside of Morningsong. And that was entirely possible, knowing her mother. She was a shrewd businesswoman and had stepped on more than a few toes on her climb up the social ladder.

Shanna crossed out the names she'd listed and placed the pad and pen on the coffee table. Her gaze settled on the Bible that sat in the center of the table. Shanna hadn't opened it in a long while. She sighed and picked it up and thumbed through it. "I suppose I should thank You for getting me through last night. Though I would have preferred not having to deal with Joshua at all."

She closed her eyes and tipped her head back against the cushions. "Sometimes I think I must be crazy. How can I love someone who is so wrong for me? It isn't fair, You know."

Life isn't fair. Her mother had told her that often enough.

"Tell You what, God. You get me through this and I might start going to church again." Shanna frowned at the shallowness in her comment and set the Bible aside without reading it. She had too many things to think about now. Dumping the scant remains of her cold tea into the sink, she washed the cup and set it on the rack to dry.

Half an hour later, Shanna applied dark brown mascara to her lashes and leaned back to scrutinize herself in the mirror. She'd put her hair in a bun on top of her head. Only a few wily tendrils had escaped.

A layer of foundation nearly covered the freckles that made her look young and vulnerable. A touch of blush lent color to her pale skin. She'd never cared for makeup and didn't wear much offstage. This morning, though, it gave her an air of confidence. While she wouldn't be singing, she would be performing, acting as though she had no feelings at all for the man with the sandy hair and eyes that still seemed to say "I love you."

"Just goes to show how wrong a person can be." Shanna dressed quickly, each layer of clothing covering the vulnerability she felt. She lifted the fine gold chains over her head, separating and arranging the strands across her chest.

Forcing herself to meet her likeness in the floor-length mirror, she raised her chin. "There is nothing to be afraid of. Joshua can't hurt you any more than he already has." Whatever changes he had in mind for Morningsong wouldn't affect her singing career. She was worth far too much to the company to—what? What could he do? Now that she thought about it, her fears seemed unfounded, foolish, and misplaced. The worst he could do was fire her, and she'd be free to sign on elsewhere. She'd been approached by dozens of companies over the years. He certainly couldn't hurt her financially. Though Elizabeth's debts had taken a large cut out of her profits, Shanna still had a sizable nest egg.

The clock on her bedside stand read 8:45. Time to face the music. She made a face and shook away the last of her fears.

A fine gray mist greeted Shanna as she opened the door to the apartment. Grabbing an umbrella from the stand in the entry, she confidently stepped outside.

"Hey, darlin', going my way?" Max stopped on the path to wait for her.

"Sure. Want to share my umbrella?"

"Nope." He touched his hat with the tip of his forefinger, lifting it slightly. "This'll do me fine."

"I take it you've been summoned to the reading?"

"Yep. Can't say as I know why. Doubt Andrew left me anything."

"I'd be surprised if he didn't. Andrew thought a lot of you. And from what you said last night, he was a good friend. Andrew took care of his friends."

"The feeling was mutual. Just wish we didn't have to go through all this rigmarole. A little thank-you note would have suited me fine. I'm the one who owed him—big time."

Shanna nodded. "I'd just as soon skip the whole thing too."

As they neared the house, her anxiety level rose again, though she wasn't sure why. She wished they were meeting in the office complex rather than in the library of the Morgan home. It was too intimate. "Max, as soon as this is over, let's get out of here. We'll hook up with the band in Oregon and—"

Max shook his head. "You can't keep running from him, Shanna. Sooner or later—"

"I'm not running."

"Sooner or later," Max went on as if she hadn't spoken, "you'll have to face the truth."

"Truth about what?"

"Your feelings, for one. You'll have to stop and look inside yourself to see who you really are and what you want."

Shanna's laughter sounded hollow. "You're beginning to sound like my therapist. I know who I am, Max. And I know what I want."

"Do you?" His gaze swept over her face as he reached for the ornate door handle. "I wonder."

Shanna shook out the umbrella, set it in the foyer to dry, then stepped into the marble entry. She shivered as a chill ran through her, not certain whether it came as a result of Max's comment, the weather, or the house.

"Shanna! Max!" Debra Clay, a longtime employee, greeted them at the door. "It's wonderful to see you again." Debra and her husband, Jim, managed the house and grounds and were now renting the house Elizabeth had lived in before she died.

Shanna returned her exuberant hug. "It's good to see you too." Glancing at Debra's stomach, she added, "Looks like something's missing."

"What…oh, the baby." Debra chuckled. "You *have* been gone a long time. Cassie is four months old already. Remind me to show you some pictures later."

"What do you mean pictures? I expect to see the whole family."

"Count on it. Max too. I know Jim would love to see you. Why don't you both come over tonight?"

"Sounds good to me," Max said.

"I'll try to get away." Shanna knew she wouldn't go. The house Debra and Jim lived in held too many unpleasant memories. Shanna hadn't been in it since she'd hurriedly packed up her mother's belongings the day before the funeral, and she didn't plan to go again.

"I suppose we'd better go." Shanna started down the hall. "Hope we're not late."

"Not at all." Debra glanced at her watch. "Just in time."

Shanna and Max slipped quietly into the library, now crowded with a dozen or so folding chairs placed in two rows. Her gaze drifted over walls of shelves and books, coming to rest on Andrew's dark mahogany desk. Shanna had loved this room as a child and had spent hours curled up on the fainting couch, which was now hugging the wall between the two windows, reading *Wuthering Heights, Little Women, Black Beauty,* and other classics. Often she'd write stories of her own. Love stories of how one day she and Joshua would be married and have six children and live in a big house on a hill, surrounded by a white picket fence. A clichéd fantasy, for which she had paid dearly.

She brought her thoughts up short. With a critical eye, Shanna wondered how she could have enjoyed a room like this. Heavy drapes hung at the windows. Even open, as they were now, the room had a dark, brooding feel to it. It reminded her of a room one might find in a medieval castle.

Debra came in behind them and closed the door, then sat beside her husband in the chair nearest the door. There were two empty seats—one next to Joshua in the front row, and the other behind him, next to Laurie Daniels. Shanna thought seriously of standing. She might have, too, if Max hadn't nudged her forward and everyone hadn't turned to watch them.

And if Joshua hadn't come back to escort her. "Shanna, Max, I'd like you to meet Andrew's attorney, Phillip Mitchell."

A heavyset man with wire-rim glasses and salt-and-pepper hair reached for her hand, then Max's. Looking up at Joshua, he said, "If this is everyone, we should get started."

"Of course." Joshua guided Shanna to the chair he'd been sitting in and seated himself next to her. She had never been claustrophobic, yet sitting in the small room beside Joshua, she suddenly felt trapped.

Ignoring him and the emotions churning inside, she turned to Nan, who sat at her left. "I'm sorry if I held things up."

"You didn't." Nan reached over and patted Shanna's knee and whispered, "Do try to relax, dear. Everything is going to be fine."

"I'm sure it will." Shanna squeezed Nan's hand and smiled as though she really meant it.

You're being ridiculous, Shanna scolded herself. *Thousands of women have ex-husbands to deal with.* There was no reason she and Joshua couldn't learn to communicate with each other on a less emotional level. As Max had said, she would need to work with Joshua much like she had with Andrew, at least until her contract was up. Her head saw no reason at all why she and Joshua couldn't relate as business associates. Her heart seemed less sure. Certainly they were still attracted to each other, but she, at least, had learned that physical attraction in and of itself did not make a marriage.

It was about time she came to grips with the reality of the situation. She was no longer a child with foolish dreams of white picket fences. Those dreams had been shattered years ago. Max was right on another score. She did need to face the truth. Joshua had abandoned her. He'd been unfaithful. She glanced behind her at Laurie, feeling sorry for the woman for the first time. For six years Laurie had been with him, and for what? From the looks of things, she was being discarded as well.

Shanna didn't know what Joshua was thinking, but she would have no part of it.

Phillip Mitchell cleared his throat, drawing Shanna's attention back to the reason they were all gathered in the study.

"Andrew brought this to my office several weeks ago." The attorney held up a videotape, opened a cabinet nestled in the shelves behind the desk, and slipped the tape into the VCR. Taking hold of the remote control, he half sat on the corner of the desk. "Said he wanted to talk to you all, person to person, rather than having his will read by someone else. All you need to know before I give the floor to Andrew is that this is considered an official document and is as binding as a standard will. I'll let Andrew take it from here." He pointed the remote at the TV screen, and after a few seconds of static, Andrew appeared in living color.

Shanna held her breath. How odd to see him looking so vibrant and alive, when just two days earlier he'd been laid out in a casket.

"I'm glad you all could make it. As Phil told you, I didn't much like the idea of having him or anyone else read some kind of dry, boring piece of paper. So I said to myself, why not make a video? That way you can tell everyone face-to-face what you really thought of them." He laughed and winked, his blue eyes bright and clear. "First off, I gotta tell you, I don't want you all blubbering and feeling bad about my passing. Don't think of me as being gone, just think of me as being in a better place." He paused to rub his jaw. "It isn't easy doing this—talking about my own death. Guess the hardest thing is saying good-bye—to you, Nan, and Joshua, Tom, and Shanna. Yes"—his eyes seemed to focus directly on her as if he'd known where she'd be sitting—"you, Shanna. Even though you aren't a blood relative, I've always thought of you as one of the family. I've something important for you, so don't you be thinking of leaving."

Shanna gasped. How well he knew her. She glanced at Nan, who seemed intent on her husband. A white, lace-trimmed hankie dangled from the older woman's hand as she reached up to catch her tears.

"I'd like to start this thing with those of you in the second row." He chuckled. "Just so you don't get the wrong idea and start thinking I'm some kind of ghost, I should confess that I asked for you all to be seated a certain way so I could talk right at you—but you've probably figured that out by now."

Andrew individually named the six people seated behind Shanna. Besides Max, Laurie, Debra, and Jim, there were two older men Shanna recognized as board members.

Andrew gave both of the board members a gift of $500,000 and thanked them for their service. They were apparently in the process of retiring and seemed pleased by Andrew's gesture. He also designated that a letter and share of the profits be given to every Morningsong employee. He gave Jim and Debra a bonus of $100,000 each and would allow them to stay in their present home rent-free for as long as they stayed with the family.

"Laurie Daniels." Andrew's gaze seemed to settle on the woman as he said her name. "For reasons I cannot fathom, you have given up what could have been a wonderful career in music to play secretary to Joshua and be a mother to my great-grandson. Nan and I will always be grateful to you for that. I won't go into details on the tape, my dear, as you already know what they are."

Shanna glanced back at Laurie, startled by the look of defiance on her face. Their gazes met and Laurie's features softened. Dry-eyed, she lifted a tissue from her purse and dabbed at the corners of her eyes.

What was going on? What was Laurie Daniels up to? And why did Shanna have the distinct impression the details of Andrew's "talk" with Laurie had something to do with her?

Chapter Eleven

"Max. My good friend. First, thank you for enlightening me. Your insight made our mutual problems so much easier to deal with. I hope you'll soon be able to take care of the matter we discussed on your last visit. In the meantime, knowing how much you love ranching, I've decided to deed my horse ranch up north over to you."

Andrew's gaze lingered on Max. "I know what you're thinking, Max, but I want you to have it. Nan and I talked it over. You're by far the best suited to run it, and this way we can keep it in the family."

Shanna turned in her seat, her mouth open. *Family?* she mouthed. She hadn't known of any family ties between Max and the Morgans. Of course, that didn't mean there were blood ties. Andrew often referred to his employees as family. Still, if Max was a relative, it would explain why Andrew had helped Max overcome his alcoholism. But why had he recommended she hire Max?

Max frowned, met her gaze a bit too briefly, and looked away as though he were harboring some deep, dark secret.

Wondering just how close he and Andrew had been, Shanna turned back to the television screen. She had trusted Max. Had he fed her confidences back to Andrew and Joshua? Had Andrew wanted Max to keep an eye on her?

"It's all yours, Max," Andrew went on without giving Shanna a chance to voice her thoughts. "And we want you to feel free to retire there anytime you get the notion."

"Phil..." Andrew looked over at the lawyer. "I'd like you to stop the tape now. You have your instructions."

Phillip did as he was told, and the screen went blank. "The remainder of the tape is to be viewed by Andrew's wife and grandchildren...and you, Shanna. The rest of you are free to go. Over the next week, I'll be talking to each of you individually to finalize your portion of the estate. We'll start the tape again in ten minutes."

"Well, I'll be..." Max stood. "I never dreamed Andrew would give me the ranch."

Joshua leaned over the back of his chair, offering his hand in congratulations, then pulled him into a hug. "You're worth far more than that to us, Max."

"I still can't believe it. Andrew never even hinted." Max, teary-eyed, slipped his hat on and turned to Shanna.

"Congratulations, Max. I'm happy for you." She knew her voice sounded flat, but it was the best she could do for the moment. "I didn't know you were thinking of retiring."

"Um...we need to talk, Shanna." Max cleared his throat. "I should have said something before now."

"Of course," she managed to say. "Later. I'll call you."

He nodded. His gaze swung over to Nan, who embraced him and walked him into the hall.

Feeling disappointed and betrayed, Shanna sat back down, trying for all the world to act as though nothing out of the ordinary had happened. She was losing Max. *He's only an employee,* she told herself. *He can be replaced. Should be replaced.* Still, he had come to mean so much to her. Apparently the feeling wasn't mutual. The ache in her heart was one more reason not to get too attached to anyone. Eventually they leave you.

Behind her, Joshua was talking to Laurie. She tried to tune them out, but they were standing too close not to hear.

"Are you sure this is what you want, Josh?" Laurie said. "Andrew may be your grandfather, but you don't have to let him dictate—"

"I'm sure," Joshua interrupted. "It's for the best."

She sighed. "I think you're making a mistake. We're good together. You can't deny that..."

Their voices faded. Stunned, Shanna tried to make the pieces of this bizarre puzzle fit. Laurie and Max were both leaving. Andrew seemed to be moving people about as though they were pawns in a game of chess. Soon he would be announcing his next move for her.

Laurie's comment lingered in her head. *"You don't have to let him dictate..."* Shanna held on to it as though it were a lifeline while she listened to the murmur of voices outside the door, waiting for Andrew's plan for her to unfold. She would listen, of course, but then she would do as she pleased.

"We never were together," Joshua reminded the slender brunette at his side. He hurried her into the hallway lest she say too much in Shanna's presence.

"In my mind we were. I've always loved you and Ryan." Her tender gaze brought him up short. "And you have to admit I'd make a good mother."

"I'm sure you will. You'll make a good wife too—to the right man." Joshua closed his eyes. Maybe he was being a fool. Laurie had always been there for him. Shanna had run at the first sign of trouble. "Look, I really do appreciate all you've done for Ryan and me, but..."

She slid her hands to his shoulders and stretched up to kiss him. "If it doesn't work out, I'll be waiting," she murmured.

He took a step back, pulling her hands from his shoulders. To say he was unaffected by Laurie's advances would have been a lie. *You really are some kind of fool, Joshua Morgan,* he told himself as she walked away. *You could have it all—a woman who loves you, a stable home, a mother for Ryan, but here you are throwing it away on a woman whose only love is the stage. Shanna doesn't want you.* But for some strange, inexplicable reason, Joshua didn't want anyone else.

His gaze lingered on Laurie's beautiful figure until she'd stepped into the entry and out of sight. He turned to find Shanna standing in the hall. How long had she been there? How much had she seen and heard?

"We'd better go back inside." He took her elbow and began to steer her back into the library.

"When I'm ready." She pulled out of his grasp and walked down the hall, turning into the guest bathroom. He started to follow, then thinking better of it, went back into the library alone.

Shanna's hands shook when she washed and dried them. She'd known Joshua and Laurie were an item. Seeing them kiss shouldn't have shocked her. But the pain ripped through her insides like a fire and still burned. Shanna dabbed the damp towel against her hot forehead and cheeks.

"They can't hurt you unless you let them," Shanna told her mirrored image. "No matter what happens, you'll come out on top." Elizabeth had drummed that into her. And it was true. She was one of the nation's most popular singers. She'd won too many music awards to count. Her songs consistently made the top ten on radio stations across the country. She had it made. The only thing that could hurt her was if someone were to take away her music. That would never happen.

Shanna straightened and set her jaw. She'd go back to the library, watch the rest of Andrew's video, then be on her way. She pulled in several deep breaths and released them slowly, the way she always did when she got a case of stage jitters.

"Here she is."

Nan tossed Shanna a warm smile as she came back into the room and took her assigned seat. She'd always seen Nan as an ally, but now she wasn't so sure. How much did Nan know about all this? Was she as manipulative as Andrew? It seemed to run in the family. Shanna had never really thought of Andrew as controlling. Maybe because compared to Elizabeth, he was a lamb. Or maybe he was just more subtle.

Now, however, the evidence was clear. He had the power to put people where he wanted, when he wanted.

"Are we ready, then?" Phillip asked.

Joshua nodded. "Go ahead."

Andrew's image appeared on the screen again. "Welcome back. I know this may seem rather unusual, but there are matters meant for your ears only. Shanna..." His gaze moved to her. "You are no doubt wondering what this is all about. I'll come to that in a moment. First I'd like to tell you how the corporation is to be divided."

"He'd better hurry." Tom sprang out of his chair. "I've had about all of this spooky stuff I can take." He paced back and forth across the floor.

Andrew chuckled. "Patience, Thomas, I'm coming to you next."

"How does he do that?" Tom glared at the screen and leaned against the window sill.

"He knows you well, darling." Nan smiled. "Your behavior is very predictable."

"Yeah, well, that's about to change."

"Thomas," Andrew went on, "as my youngest grandson, you will receive one-quarter of Morningsong Records—"

"All right."

"—to be held in trust until your twenty-sixth birthday."

"What? What am I supposed to do in the meantime?"

"Tom, would you just shut up? He's getting to all that." Joshua glared at his younger brother.

"Until that time you will head the Los Angeles operation. Should you decide, however, before that time to seek other employment or return to college, Joshua will buy your portion of the company for the amount stipulated in the contract I've already drawn up. You will receive an adequate monthly allowance out of that fund. What I'm offering you, son, is freedom. Use it wisely. Joshua and I have worked out all the details, so the two of you can deal with all that later. My prayer for you, son, is happiness. You're not going to find that by rushing into marriage or being wealthy. You'll find it by getting your life in order, discovering who you are and what you want to do—and in making your peace with God."

Tom groaned and dragged his hands through his hair. Grief drew his handsome features into a deep frown. His shoulders sagged.

"Whatever you decide to do, Thomas, know that I love you."

Shanna wondered if she'd judged Andrew unfairly. His love for Tom wasn't that of a controlling father figure. He'd cut Tom loose to make his own choices.

"Shanna..."

At the mention of her name, Shanna jumped and focused her attention back to the video.

"It's finally your turn."

Her heart pounded so loudly in her ears, she could hardly hear him.

"You will also receive one quarter of Morningsong Productions."

"What?" she gasped. "You can't...I don't..." She clasped Joshua's sleeve.

"I know this comes as a surprise, my dear, but you have played an important role in making Morningsong what it is today. You've been like a granddaughter to me." Andrew glanced down at his hands. "Owning a portion of Morningsong can never make up for the pain I've caused you over the years." His blue gaze swept up and seemed to meet hers. "I'm more sorry for that than you'll ever know. I've written documents—confessions, if you will—and have asked Joshua to go over them with you. I wish I could have told you all this in person, but the time was never right. Perhaps I'm a coward at heart." He sighed. "At any rate, you are a full partner in the business. I pray you will, at long last, find the joy your mother and I took from you all those years ago."

The rest of Andrew's video went quickly. He'd left everything else to Joshua with lifelong provisions for Nan. Even after the lawyer left, Shanna sat in a daze, trying to make some sense of what Andrew had said and done. She didn't want to own part of Morningsong. How could Andrew possibly think he was doing her a favor? He had offered Tom freedom. Yet he had imprisoned her as surely as if he'd placed her in shackles. Andrew had legally bound her to the one man from whom she wanted to escape.

"Shanna." Nan touched her arm. Her gentle voice did nothing to allay Shanna's panicked thoughts. "It's all right, darling. We all agree with Andrew's decision. As he said, you're one of our own. Being Joshua's wife, you're entitled—"

"His wife!" Shanna drew back. "You make it sound like we're still married."

Nan looked at Joshua. "You haven't told her?"

"No." Joshua dragged his hands down his face. "I was planning to do that when I gave her the letters."

"Oh dear. I'm sorry. Perhaps Tom and I better leave you two alone, then." She patted Shanna's knee as she rose. "We'll talk later. There's a lot to catch up on."

"Apparently." Shanna gripped the sides of the chair. "What is this all about, Joshua? What are you and Andrew trying to pull? Why would Nan refer to me as your wife?"

"Because you are."

Shanna shook her head. "No. The annulment…my mother and Andrew…"

"Andrew only let your mother think he'd filed the papers. He never did." Joshua pried her hands from the chair and held them in his own. "We're still married, Shanna."

She pulled her hands away. "No, that's impossible. I don't believe you."

"Why would I lie?"

"I don't know. I don't understand any of this. No!" She pushed Joshua's hands away. "Don't touch me." Getting to her feet, Shanna moved to the window, out of his reach.

"I know it's a shock. It was for me too. I didn't know until a few days ago. He gave me the letters and…" Joshua came up behind her, cupping her shoulders. "He told me a lot of things about you—and Elizabeth. I never meant for you to find out this way. I'd planned to tell you everything this afternoon."

Keeping her shoulders rigid and unyielding, Shanna continued to stare out the window at the manicured lawn and islands of flowers. She should tell him to keep his hands off but felt strangely comforted by his presence behind her. "Maybe you'd better tell me now." Her voice came out as strong and stingingly sharp as she wanted it to.

He stepped away from her then. She folded her arms and turned around, resting her hip on the window sill. "I'm waiting."

Hands clenched in his pocket, Joshua took a seat behind the desk. Her attitude infuriated him. She wasn't supposed to react like this. Certainly he'd expected her to be surprised, but not angry. In his oft-played-out version, she would look up at him with those tender doe-brown eyes, and all the trouble between them would melt like ice chips in the sun.

He remembered his own reaction had been one of shock and denial. Then, as his grandfather's words took root and he realized he and Shanna had both been the victims of her mother's lies, Joshua thanked God for his good fortune. The woman he had loved all these years, and always would, was still his wife.

Her obvious contempt tore him apart. Joshua yanked open the top drawer, extracted a thick manila envelope, and slapped it on the desktop. "First, like it or not, you and I are still married."

"Then I want a divorce."

He glared at her. Maybe he was crazy for even trying, but he couldn't let that happen—not yet. Not a second time. "We'll talk about that later. First we need to discuss your new position with the company. For the next year you'll be working as vice president."

"You're joking. I'm not—"

"Hear me out." He held up his hand to silence her. "Your contract with us isn't up for a year. During that time, you'll continue to sing on occasion. You'll produce one album. You'll go to the Country Music Awards ceremony and do the Christmas special CBS booked you for. The rest of the time you'll be here at Morningsong learning the business."

Shanna stared at him. “I can’t believe what I’m hearing. I have no intention of learning the business. I’m a performer. I don’t want part ownership, and I definitely don’t want to be vice president.”

“Look, Shanna, I know this is pretty hard to absorb, but don’t say no just yet. Give yourself a few days to think about it. There really aren’t that many options—Andrew acted in what he thought was our best interests.”

“And that’s supposed to make it right?” Shanna pushed away from the window and sank into the straight-back leather chair near the right corner of the desk. She’d have preferred standing, but her legs felt like she’d been put together with clay. “All right. What else does Andrew *recommend* I do?”

“I’ll get back to that in a minute. First I want to apologize for the letter I sent you after our son was born.”

“What letter?”

Joshua closed his eyes. “You didn’t get it? Now, why doesn’t that surprise me? I did write you a letter. Apparently Elizabeth thought it best to keep it from you.”

“Maybe she was right.”

“You can’t be serious.”

“*If* there was a letter, and if she did keep it from me, it was to protect me.”

“It was to keep us apart. She knew if you read it, you’d know the truth about her.”

“Oh, really?” Shanna clasped her hands together to keep them from trembling. “And just what did you say?”

“Some angry things actually. I couldn’t believe you’d give up our baby. You should have told me. Maybe it’s just as well you didn’t see it.”

“What did you expect me to do, Joshua? You were in L.A. and I was alone and…”

“I know. Andrew told me how Elizabeth forced you to give him up for adoption. I should have known you wouldn’t have made that kind of decision yourself.”

"She did what she thought was best for me," Shanna said coolly, not wanting to linger on the most painful memory of all. "I eventually came to realize she was right. With my schedule and at my age, I could never have taken care of a child—or a husband."

"Maybe I was too hasty in apologizing. You're not the same person I married." Anger emanated from his icy blue gaze.

"Oh, you are so right. I've changed, and for the better, as far as I'm concerned. I'm no longer the weak and impressionable teenager you took advantage of. I've grown up, and I have no interest in you or marriage or children or Morningsong. I'll finish out the terms of my contract, but don't expect me to stay here. Or play Andrew's and your games. I have no intention of taking on an executive position. You don't fool me for one minute."

She propelled herself out of the chair. "Now, if you're finished, I'm going back to the apartment to pack. I'll be leaving this afternoon to resume the tour." Shanna lifted her chin, proud of the way she'd handled him.

"The tour has been canceled."

"What?"

"You heard me. We're rescheduling all your tours and sending Christi to fill in wherever possible. Naturally, she won't be able to do as many—she's only a woman, while you, Shanna, are like some kind of machine. You need some time away from the music. You're losing your touch. You used to be sweet and sincere. The last thing we need out there is a singer whose heart has turned to stone."

"That's not true," she sputtered. "My fans still love me."

"Some of them do, but do you love them?" He stood up and came around the desk, then leaned forward, placing his hands on the arms of her chair, trapping her in. "You don't have any options left. You'll either have to play by our rules or you don't play at all."

Shanna leaned back and closed her eyes to block out his powerful presence. He was trying to intimidate her. She couldn't let him do that. Opening her eyes again, she steeled herself against his angry gaze. "Move away from me. Now."

To her surprise, he did.

"You can't control me anymore. I do have another option. There are plenty of other record companies that would love to sign me on."

"True, but they won't touch you. You belong to Morningsong." He glanced at the papers on his desk as if they disgusted him. "Now that I think of it, maybe that's our loss."

Shanna hated it that Joshua still had the power to hurt her so deeply. She opened her mouth to retort, but nothing came out.

"Shanna, I'm sorry. I didn't mean..."

She just stared at him and, not wanting him to see her cry, bit her lip to keep her tears at bay. Moments later, Shanna stood and walked to the door. All she could think of was to get as far away from Joshua and Morningsong as possible.

Chapter Twelve

"Shanna, wait!" Joshua stepped between her and the open door. "Please. Talk to me. I shouldn't have gotten angry. I still love you. Truth is, I always have."

She stared at him, feeling as if she were somehow outside herself watching a stage where she and Joshua were the actors. Finally she spoke in a tone so cold and harsh it frightened even her. "You don't know what love is." She ducked under his arm.

"Wait. We need to talk about this."

"I have nothing to say to you. Not now. Not ever."

"Mr. Morgan." Debra's voice crackled over the intercom. "There's a Mr. Angelo from Vermont Video Productions here to see you."

"Tell him to wait, I..."

Shanna hurried down the hall and out of sight.

"Never mind," he told Debra. "Send him in."

Outside a heavy mist drizzled from a gunmetal gray sky. Shanna thought briefly about going back inside to get her umbrella but wouldn't. She'd made her decision, and there would be no turning back.

"Shanna?" Nan called after her. "I believe this is yours."

Shanna stopped and slowly turned around and reached for the umbrella. "Thank you. You didn't have to bring it. I could have gotten it later."

"I take it your talk with Joshua didn't go well."

"No—no, it didn't." Shanna opened her umbrella and held it over their heads.

"I suppose I'm a romantic old fool, but I was so hoping—"

"Nan, please. There's no point. What Joshua and I had was over a long time ago."

"I see. What do you plan to do now?"

"I'm not sure. Since Joshua is living here now, I'll be looking for another place. With so much friction between us, it would be better for me to move off the estate."

"I'm sorry to hear that, but I suppose I can understand. Any idea where?"

"No, not yet."

"Well, promise me you'll stay in touch. I wish there were some way to convince you to stay."

Shanna wrapped her arms around the older woman. "I can't, Nan. It isn't you." She reluctantly pulled away. Tears filled her eyes. She really would miss Nan and Morningsong and Andrew.

Deep worry lines etched Nan's forehead. "Well, whatever you decide to do, I'll be praying that you find contentment. Lord knows you deserve it."

Inside her apartment, Shanna stared at the ocean scene in the mural. She wasn't certain how long she'd been standing there. Joshua's words crashed against her mind over and over like an angry sea.

"You're still my wife."

"The tour is canceled."

"You have no options left."

"You need some time away from the music."

"You're losing your touch."

"You used to be sweet and sincere. The last thing we need out there is a singer whose heart has turned to stone."

"Stop it!" Shanna covered her ears and closed her eyes to drown out the incessant sound of his voice. Turning away from the mural, she shivered in the cold silence.

You can't let him get to you, Shanna told herself. *You're strong now. You've worked too hard to let him tear you down.*

Dropping into the rocker, she reached for the phone and dialed Max's number. At the sound of his gruff hello, Shanna felt a sudden rush of tears. Her voice cracked as it climbed around the lump in her throat. "Max, I need to talk to you."

"What's wrong, darlin'?"

"Everything. Andrew left me a share of Morningsong. Joshua insists I'm still married to him and...I can't..." Her voice broke. "Max, he's canceled my tours. He wants me to stop performing and learn the business. He says I don't have any other options." Anger buoyed her again, giving her renewed strength as she finished telling Max what had transpired. "They can't do that to me, can they, Max? I mean, I have my rights."

Max hesitated. "As I recall, the contract allows Morningsong to call the shots. 'Course, there's nothing says you have to accept the position or the share in the company, but you might want to wait before you decide something like that. It sounds like a great opportunity for you. You could be cutting yourself out of millions. Face it, Shanna, the looks and the voice ain't gonna last forever."

"What are you saying? Max, you're not suggesting I go along with this...this—"

"Just calm down a minute. Being vice president of Morningsong would definitely have its advantages. Maybe you should give it a shot."

Air rushed out of her lungs like a punctured balloon. "I can't believe you'd go along with him. You know how much singing means to me. You've got to talk to him, Max, and tell him the best thing for me is to keep doing what I have been doing." Panic crept into her voice again. She struggled to remain calm.

"Um...I can't rightly do that. You see, I happen to agree with

Joshua. You've been pushing yourself too hard. I figure the best thing for you is to take some time off—get to know Joshua again. You're his wife." Max cleared his throat. "Your place is at his side. Who knows, in time you might come to love him too."

"You knew about this?" Shanna's throat had closed up. "I trusted you, Max. How could you betray me like this?"

"Oh, sugar, I ain't betrayin' ya. I'm doing you a favor. I know it's hard to see that just now, but down the road, you'll be thanking me. You wait and see. In the meantime, I'll be around if you need to talk. Come next week, though, I'll be heading for the ranch. Still can't believe it's mine. Maybe you could come stay awhile. Lots of peace and quiet. It'll help you sort things through."

"I'm sure it's very nice." She hesitated, then added, "I guess that's it, then."

"Oh, now, darlin', don't sound so down in the mouth. This is all gonna work out for the best. God is doing a great thing in your life. You wait and see."

Somehow Shanna managed to sound almost normal as she told Max good-bye. "I wish you well, and if ranching is what you really want to do, then—"

"Whoa, now. I'm not leaving yet. I'll see you later—tonight. You're still coming to Debra's, aren't you?"

"Sure, Max, tonight." She dropped the phone into its cradle. Despite the fact that he was dead wrong, she believed he really was trying to act in her best interests. *My best interests.* For once, Shanna wished the people around her would let her decide what was best. After all, who knew her better?

The one thing she did not need in her life was a husband—especially one named Joshua Morgan. The man was insane. Coming on to her one moment, hating her the next. And then there was Laurie. Had Andrew forced her out of Joshua's life and tried to force Shanna back in?

Maybe Joshua had promised Andrew that he would at least try to work things out. Joshua obviously had feelings for Laurie. Remembering the way he and Laurie had kissed, Shanna felt more convinced than ever that staying with Morningsong and trying to reconcile would be a mistake. The only thing she'd gain in the end would be more heartache.

Joshua would insist she give up her music—he'd already moved in that direction. So she had no other option, huh? "We'll see about that."

The large clock on the wall behind her chimed twelve times. On the last chime, she pushed herself out of the chair and padded to the bedroom knowing what she had to do. It was noon, not midnight, but for Shanna Elizabeth O'Brian, the fairy tale had ended. Like Cinderella, the party was over. Unlike Cinderella, there was no glass slipper to leave behind. No prince on a big white horse. No happily ever after.

The time had come to leave the castle and move on.

Shanna pulled two bags and her guitar out of the closet. She wouldn't need much—toiletries, underwear, a few pairs of jeans, slacks, shorts, some T-shirts, sweatshirts, and a comfortable, loose-fitting dress—the wash-and-wear kind you could scrunch into a little ball and stick in your suitcase. She could always buy clothes later if she needed them. In a second suitcase she placed personal items—books, her journal, some jewelry, things that had come to mean a lot to her. There wasn't all that much—a favorite mug, some tapes, a few small antique pieces that had belonged to her grandmother.

Deciding to leave was the easy part. Knowing where to go proved much more challenging. While she packed, Shanna thought of a hundred different towns and just as many people. Unfortunately, none of the people were close enough friends to run to in time of trouble. Shanna briefly considered staying put and turning to God but ruled the option out.

As far as she was concerned, God had pretty much abandoned her when she'd needed Him the most. What puzzled her was that the thought even entered her mind. Not that she didn't believe in Him. She'd been baptized as a child and had attended church until Joshua left her.

Shanna folded several layers of tissue paper around the antique music box that had been her mother's and before that her grandmother's. The movement set off a few notes of "Jesus Loves Me." As if by habit, her hands pushed the paper aside, wound the mechanism, and opened the lid. Single notes still pure and sweet rang in Shanna's ears, filling her mind with a distant memory of a child's laughter. A tiny angel popped up and twirled around on a small velvet stage. She listened to the music and watched the little girl dancing and singing in the small bedroom that had once been her own. She snapped the lid down, shutting off the memory and the music.

In that instant she knew where she needed to go.

"I'd be safe there," she mused. No one would think to look for her at the old house. No one other than her parents knew about the cabin. And they were both dead. Of course, there was Nancy Blake, the neighbor who'd been taking care of it all these years, but Mrs. Blake certainly had no ties to Morningsong. Shanna vaguely remembered the scent of chocolate-chip cookies and sitting in a warm, cozy kitchen.

She felt a strong sense of reassurance as she weighed the idea more thoroughly. Her parents' cabin—hers now—sat on a bluff overlooking the Washington coast. A cozy place, as she recalled, with two bedrooms, a loft, and a fireplace. She'd sent Elizabeth's personal belongings there, thinking someday she'd get around to dealing with the property and her mother's effects at the same time. It had been too painful to think about before. And she'd had no time. Now, however, she had all the time in the world.

Something else that had been floating around in the periphery of her mind came into focus as well. Shanna had wondered for a long time if the answer to her mother's death might somehow be locked away in those boxes. The police had gone through everything, but what if they had missed something? What if there was some crucial piece of evidence that only she or someone who knew Elizabeth very well would be able to spot? Perhaps something written in a journal or tucked away in some secret place.

Shanna sighed. Wishful thinking. If Mother had left a clue, surely the police would have found it. No, there would be nothing like that, only boxes full of memories. Still, she had to face them sooner or later.

She changed into a pair of faded jeans and a T-shirt over which she wore a long-sleeved denim shirt, then donned a blonde wig and sunglasses. Escaping the estate was far easier than Shanna had imagined. Stopping at the gate, she told the guard she was going into town to shop.

"Do you think anyone will recognize me?" she asked.

He chuckled. "Not for a minute, Ms. O'Brian," he drawled. "Where will you be if anyone comes lookin' for you?"

"Dollywood, I think. Maybe I'll see if Dolly's free for lunch. That would be fun."

"Oh my, yes. It surely would." His eyes glazed over. "She's some woman. You tell her I said hi, you hear?"

Shanna laughed and waved. "I'll do that."

A strange fear gripped her as she drove through the gates and away from Morningsong. Shanna blamed it on the fact that she'd never gone out alone before. There had always been someone—her mother, Joshua, Max, companions, bodyguards, limo drivers—to transport her and keep her safe. Now she had no one. *Wanted no one,* she reminded herself. Shanna shoved her unfounded fears aside. *This is no time to get cold feet.*

Taking several long, deep breaths to calm herself, Shanna headed for the sheriff's office. Halfway there she changed her mind. If Sheriff Kerns had found anything new, he'd have called her. Going to them now seemed pointless. Besides, the last thing she wanted at the moment was to call attention to herself.

"On the road again..." Shanna sang the familiar Willie Nelson tune as she drove the stretch of highway from Nashville to Memphis. The wind whipped through her hair, making her feel wild and daring. The fresh, heady scent of freedom nearly obliterated the guilt she felt at leaving Morningsong behind. *Running away isn't going to solve anything,* her inner voice chided. *You should have talked to Joshua. You should have told Max.*

"There's no reason to feel guilty," Shanna answered back. "Running may be a coward's way out, but the alternative..." She shook her head. There was no alternative. Joshua had canceled her tours. He'd planned her every move for the next year. What kind of life was that? Joshua was as manipulative and controlling as Elizabeth had been. She had no intention of succumbing to that kind of abuse again.

"You did the right thing." She caught her gaze in the rearview mirror. "Anyway, it isn't as if you're running away. You did leave a note."

And she had—to Max. *"I'm going home. Wishing you the best, Shanna."* They'd never be able to figure out where *home* was. When she felt stronger and more in control, she'd call Max and Nan...maybe. For now, though, she needed to plan her next move. Max had been right about one thing. She did need time away—not from her singing, but from Morningsong and from everyone who thought they could manage her life better than she.

The driver of a black van followed Shanna's teal blue Lexus off the freeway at the airport exit in Memphis. Picking up his cell phone, he punched in his contact's number. "Yeah, boss. It's me, Jimbo. You were right. She's flown the coop. Got no idea where she's headed, but wherever it is, looks like she'll be flying. Oh, and boss, she's traveling alone." The last phrase brought a grin to his rugged features.

"Stay with her. Whatever you do, don't let her out of your sight." The boss's voice cut in and out with static. "I want to know every move she makes. Sooner or later she's going to go to wherever she shipped her mother's belongings, and we're going to be there. Hopefully we can find the tape before she does."

"And if we don't?"

"What do you think?"

The line went dead. Jim pushed the disconnect button. He didn't much like the idea of killing someone as pretty and famous as Shanna O'Brian. Now, Liz had been a different story. She had deserved to die. Imagine trying to set them up like that. He'd searched that house from top to bottom trying to find the damaging evidence Elizabeth claimed to have gotten on them. They should have know better than to trust her in the first place. He'd had a gut feeling she was up to no good from the beginning. First she wanted in on the take. But that wasn't enough, so she resorted to blackmail.

Much as he hated the idea of killing Shanna, he'd do it. If she ever found the evidence Lizzie claimed to have, it would put him and his partners in prison for the next twenty years.

Oh, he'd kill her all right. First, though, he'd have himself a real good time.

Chapter Thirteen

Joshua sat in the library long after his visitor had gone. He'd blown it big time with Shanna. The worst thing he could have done was get angry and try to force the issue. Yet that's exactly what he'd done.

"OK," he told himself, thrumming his fingers on the desk. "You've got to think this through." Where had he gone wrong?

You rushed her, for one thing; a voice in his head seemed to say. *And you insisted on having things your way.* It wasn't the first time, he realized. Maybe that's where he'd made his mistake. Not just today, but several years ago.

With his head resting on his folded arms, he thought back to a day when a much younger and less mature Joshua Morgan had asked for Shanna O'Brian's hand in marriage. Andrew had been giving one of his parties. Joshua, then only twenty-two, couldn't wait to see his Shanna again.

She was there somewhere. He straightened to his full six feet two inches and scanned the two hundred guests packed into the massive Morningsong ballroom. He spotted her easily—the girl surrounded by a crowd of admiring males. Her fire-gold curls never failed to set a flame in his heart.

Shanna stood beneath one of the many crystal chandeliers Andrew had purchased from the famed Dorchester Castle in England. Except for the fashionable lines of her coral pink evening gown, she might have been a princess, imported from the same castle in another place in time. But that night his princess entertained a different kind of royalty, the kings and queens of the recording industry—singers, songwriters, agents, and producers.

Shanna's rebel curls captured the shimmering lights in a halolike aura. A handful of rays escaped to illuminate her face in a radiant glow. The light danced in her cocoa brown eyes when she saw him.

Joshua paused for a moment to catch his breath. It almost hurt to have her so near and not be able to touch her. With a longing more urgent than anything he'd ever known, Joshua began the short trek to her side.

"Hey, Josh. I hear congratulations are in order." Tom stopped him.

"What? How did you…" Joshua turned toward his younger brother, feeling a moment's panic. *How could he know?* Joshua was certain he hadn't revealed to anyone the secret trail his thoughts had taken over the past two months.

"Gramps just told me he was sending you to Los Angeles to open a branch office."

"Oh, that." Joshua's sigh of relief didn't go unnoticed.

"What did you think I meant, big brother?" A mischievous grin spread across the Tom's face. "It wouldn't have anything to do with our star singer, would it?"

"Of course not."

"Does that mean I get to move in on Shanna when you leave?" Had any man but Tom made the remark, Joshua would have found good use for the doubled-up fists concealed in his pockets. Even coming from his seventeen-year-old brother, the teasing reply released a spark of anger. Joshua took a moment to loosen his jaw and force his raw emotions under cover. Shanna had been on tour for two months, and he'd gone half crazy from missing her.

Joshua forced a grin. "Touch her and you die. We may be brothers, but when it comes to Shanna, I don't share." The lightness he'd aimed for eluded him, and he cursed himself for being so transparent.

"Hey." The smile died on Tom's lips. "I was just kidding. You're not going to do something weird, are you? I've never seen you so uptight before."

"No—nothing weird. I'm OK." Control edged its way back into Joshua's voice. "I just need to get out of here. Have you talked to Shanna tonight?"

"She was busy turning down offers from our competitors about half an hour ago. She looked as anxious to get away as you do."

"Then I guess I'd better go rescue her." Joshua's voice trailed off as he searched the sea of familiar faces once again.

"Um…if I can do anything to help…like maybe throw Shanna's old lady off the trail, let me know."

Joshua grinned down at the young man who barely reached his shoulder. "Thanks." Joshua wrapped his arm around Tom and gave him an affectionate hug. "Appreciate the offer, but I can handle Elizabeth." His bravado waned as he thought about Elizabeth O'Brian. She was the only thing that stood between him and Shanna. Elizabeth knew how he felt about Shanna, but for some reason he couldn't fathom, she hated him. Maybe she hated all men, because to his knowledge Elizabeth had never allowed any guy near Shanna.

Pausing to snatch a drink from one of the servers, Joshua made his way to Shanna's side. "Do you plan to do more television specials after this one?" A tenor voice from the group of people surrounding her asked.

"No…well, I'm not sure. I haven't been asked yet," Shanna replied, not sure who'd asked the question and obviously not caring.

"When is your new album being released?" came another voice.

"This fall sometime. You'll have to talk to Morningsong about an actual date."

"How long do you intend to record with Morningsong? I heard Tennessee Music Productions just offered you a better contract."

"I love Morningsong and everyone here. If he still wants me, I'll be signing on with Andrew again."

Joshua knew she'd be weary of answering questions about her new album, her tours, and her upcoming television special. If her thoughts were anything like his, he felt certain she wanted to slip away from the crowd and be with him.

She loved him—had told him so before her last tour. What Joshua couldn't understand was why Elizabeth kept trying to keep them apart. She kept Shanna so busy, the poor girl hardly had time to eat, let alone be with him. They were meant to be together, and the few cherished moments they'd been able to sneak over the past year weren't enough.

"It's for your own good, Shanna dear," Joshua had overheard Elizabeth say when she booked Shanna's latest cross-country tour. *"I wouldn't do this if I didn't love you."* Joshua cringed at the memory, convinced motherly love had nothing to do with it. Elizabeth had gotten rich off her daughter's career. Marriage and kids would change things. Shanna would have to slow down, perform less often. Elizabeth wouldn't like that.

A shiver ran through him as he watched Shanna. He loved her so much yet felt fear stirring inside of him. Was he doing the right thing?

"Excuse me," Shanna said to the guests surrounding her. She raised her eyes to meet Joshua's and took a step toward him.

The gesture left him short of breath. It had been two months since they had last seen each other. Did she still love him?

Joshua felt his mouth go cotton dry as she approached. Did he dare ask the question that had been haunting him day and night? What if she refused? He took a sip of the chilled punch before handing the goblet to her.

Her finely carved eyebrow arched delicately. A smile lifted the corners of her mouth, dimpling her flushed cheeks. "Thank you." Their fingers brushed as she took the glass from him. The touch had been brief but potent. Shanna raised the glass to her lips, her warm brown gaze clinging to his as she drank.

Joshua yearned to close the distance between them. Hang the crowds and watchful eyes. He needed to lose his hands in the shining thickness of her curls, to taste her sweet mouth.

"Shanna, darling, come along." The crisp-voiced woman with a shock of thick black hair sliced between them, forcing Joshua back. "There's someone over here you simply must meet." Elizabeth tucked a slender arm around Shanna's waist, pulling her away. Elizabeth tossed a look of triumph over her shoulder. "Excuse us, Joshua dear."

After a few steps, Shanna stopped. A flash of anger sparked in her eyes. "Just a minute, Mother. Joshua and I weren't finished talking." She retraced her steps and handed him the near-empty glass. "This won't take long, I promise. Meet me in the garden—fifteen minutes," Shanna whispered. She spun around and hurried back to her mother.

The jaw that had clamped tight in near rage at the woman who'd separated them relaxed into a smile. He'd never seen Shanna openly defy Elizabeth before. She might agree to his plan, after all. Shanna would be eighteen in a couple of weeks. She'd be of age and able to make decisions on her own. High time to put the overprotective Elizabeth in her place.

He lifted the glass to his lips and let the remaining liquid slide to the back of his parched throat, then stubbornly followed Shanna and her mother to the other side of the room.

Shanna allowed her mother to guide her through the maze of friends and business associates who had gathered to celebrate her latest success. One week from tonight she would host her first television special.

Andrew Morgan cast Shanna a look of genuine admiration. "Ah-h-h, Shanna. Your mother finally found you." He held out his age-roughened hand and drew her forward. "I've a dozen or so very important people I'd like you to meet. Gentlemen, ladies, you've met Elizabeth...and this is Morningsong's pride and joy, Shanna O'Brian."

"A pleasure to finally meet you." The tall, thin man with a French accent lifted her hand to his lips. "I caught your show in Boston the other night—you are a very talented lady. I must try to persuade Andrew to set up a tour in Europe soon."

"Why, thank you." Shanna lowered her head and drew her hand back. As much as she loved performing, Joshua doubted she'd ever outgrow the embarrassment of praise. "To be honest, the credit for my success should go to Andrew and Elizabeth. They do all the work. I just sing and do a little pickin' and strummin'." Shanna emphasized her subtle Southern accent for the Frenchman's benefit.

"Nonsense." Elizabeth spoke for the first time since the introductions. "Shanna is a talented and dedicated young lady. Her music career is, of course, our first priority. We began singing lessons before she could walk. By the time she turned four we had her performing. And she loved it, didn't you, darling?"

"I did, most of the time. I love singing and honestly don't know what I'd do without it."

Joshua felt a tightness in his chest. He could think of a lot of things she could do that didn't include music. He left the party through the open sliding-glass doors that separated the gardens from the ballroom. Making his way through the atrium, with its tropical plants and waterfall, he followed the steppingstone path through the terraced gardens. Rainbows of colored lights illuminated the Morningsong grounds, turning it into a fantasyland. His steps slowed as the beauty of it seeped into his senses. He drew in a deep breath to fill his lungs with the cool night air. The crisp scent of freshly mowed lawn mingled with the sweet, heady fragrance of roses and lingered in his nostrils.

A familiar rush of water beckoned from the far side of the garden. The waterfall originated in the atrium from a natural spring and descended through an opening in the tiled floor. Silver strands of water veiled the rock wall, then spread their woven brilliance into a jeweled pond below. From the pool, water trickled into a narrow stream, ribboning into the moonlit night, heading toward the lake.

The familiar scent of Shanna's gardenia perfume heightened his senses. The soft caress of her breath whispering his name stirred the tiny hairs at the back of his neck.

"Come on. Let's get out of this fishbowl." He grabbed her hand and pulled her along the dimly lit footpath. "I've been waiting all night to get you alone, and I know just the spot."

"Joshua..." She hung back, unable to keep up with his pace. "Slow down."

He stopped and turned to face her. "I'm sorry. It's just that I..." How could he tell her he needed her so much even his bones ached? He tucked his impatience away with all the other feelings meant to be controlled.

"I want to be alone with you too." She laughed. "But...my shoes...I dropped them by the waterfall."

He looked down at the stockinged toes that wiggled and peeped out from under the long evening gown. A wide grin spread across his face. "We'll get them later." He swept her up into his arms and strode purposely down the path into their secret world beyond the lights.

"Mmm," Shanna whispered as she wrapped her arms around his neck and planted feathery kisses under his ear. "I think I'm going to like your transportation system. Where are we going?"

"To the lake. But I'll never make it if you don't stop that."

"To swim?" She giggled.

"If you want."

"But I don't have a swimsuit."

"We could always go skinny-dipping..."

"Joshua!"

Even as she protested, he could see her cheeks warm at the forbidden, but not at all unpleasant, thought.

The path before them dropped away to a wide expanse of lawn that sloped gently to a sandy beach before disappearing into the moon-glazed waters.

Joshua set her down, and they walked hand in hand to the lake's edge.

"I can't believe we're finally alone." Shanna turned to face him. "I missed you so much."

"I missed you too." He held her tight and with his free hand lifted her chin until her gaze met his. "I've been waiting so long"—he lowered his head the remaining distance to kiss her eyes closed. As if the freckles that bridged her nose were sprinklings of brown sugar, he paused to press his lips to each, savoring the sweetness—"to do this." His mouth descended on hers. "Shanna..." A low groan escaped his lips.

Her breathing sounded as ragged as his own when he pulled away. He shook his head and took a deep breath to calm the turbulence still churning inside. Dropping to the sand near the water's edge, he pulled her down beside him.

Shanna was trembling.

"Cold?" Before she had a chance to answer he'd shrugged out of his jacket and draped it over her shoulders.

"A little."

"I've frightened you, haven't I? I'm sorry..."

"Hush." Shanna lifted a finger to his lips to silence them. "Don't spoil it. I liked the way you kissed me. I'm not afraid. Not of you." She looked away, unsure of herself. "I just never felt this way before." She scooped up a handful of sand and let it sift through her fingers.

"How did you feel?"

"Like I was so full of...of...I don't know—something!" She brushed the sand from her hands and turned to face him. She turned away again to draw circles in the sand.

Love for her rose inside of him like a swollen stream. Joshua took her face between his hands and brought her around to look at him. "You're crying." He leaned toward her and caught the salty tears in his lips, then covered her mouth with his as if to share the treasure he'd tasted. "Please don't cry. I didn't mean to upset you."

"You didn't."

The sobs grew more persistent. He lifted her onto his lap and cradled her in his arms. Shanna sniffed and blew her nose on the handkerchief she'd pulled out of his jacket pocket. The tears subsided. "I'm the one who should apologize. You must think I'm really stupid, crying like that."

"I don't think you're stupid. I think you're"—he paused to kiss the still-moist cheeks—"beautiful and sweet...and I love you."

"Oh, Josh, I love you too." Shanna wound her arms around his neck.

He pulled her hands together at his chest. "Let's get married."

Joshua watched as the joy drained from her face. "No." Horrified, she pulled her hands from his grasp and jumped to her feet. Shanna walked along the water's edge, drawing back as the cool water licked her toes. "We can't."

"But you just said you loved me." He stood and brushed the sand from his slacks before coming to walk beside her.

"Oh, I do…but—"

"Then why?"

"I would think that would be obvious. My age…I'm not eighteen yet. And my career…"

"Wait a minute." Joshua grabbed her by the shoulders and pulled her around to face him. "What's your career got to do with marrying me?"

"I can't give it up. I love singing. It's my life. I could never—"

"Give it up? You think I'd ask you to give up singing to marry me? What on earth gave you that idea?"

"Mother…"

"Your mother." Joshua nearly spat the words out. "I might have known." Fear registered in her eyes at his anger, and she backed away from him. "I love you." His voice softened as he pulled her close again. "I'd never ask you to give up your music. You should know that."

Shanna rested her forehead against his chest and draped her arms loosely around his waist. "I'm on the road so much. It wouldn't be right."

"Have you forgotten? I'm in the music business too. I could travel with you. We couldn't be together all the time, but we'll work it out. I promise."

"I don't know…," he heard her say over the pounding of his heart. "I saw what happened between my parents. Joshua…" Her voice grew urgent. "They ended up hating each other, all because my mother gave up her career to marry Dad and…to have me."

"I understand what you're saying, but none of that applies to us. You're not Elizabeth. She's a selfish, overbearing—"

"Don't." Shanna raised her hand to stop him. "Mother isn't perfect, but she cares as much about my career as I do. She loves me and wants what's best for me."

He sighed. *Why did she have to argue?* There was no alternative. He wanted to marry her. He needed her now. He raked his hand through the sandy locks that had fallen onto his forehead. "We love each other. What happened to your parents can't possibly happen to us. I can't imagine anything coming between us. I want you with me, Shanna—forever."

"Mother would be furious and hurt. In her own way she really loves me."

"Maybe, but she's controlling you. Someday you're going to have to make your own decisions and go your own way."

"Couldn't we just let things be like they are? Why do we have to get married? We could try to spend more time together."

"That's just it. Time is running out. Andrew is talking about sending me to Los Angeles to set up an office there. Unless we get married, it will be months between the times we can be together."

"Oh no! Joshua, that's impossible…you can't just go away. I'd never see you."

"I have no choice. Someday I'll be taking over Morningsong for Andrew. Morningsong West will allow us closer access to our clients out there. Andrew wants me there, and I'd like to go—but not without you."

"I don't see how it could work. A husband and wife should live together and have babies. I'd still be on the road over 50 percent of the time. Joshua, don't you see? It can't work."

"It can if you love me. Shanna, please. I promise we'll work it out. Just trust me."

Shanna pressed her hands against his chest and leaned back to study his face in the moonlight. "I do trust you. You've always been there for me, but…I…I don't know what to say." Shanna's fingers came to rest on his lips.

Joshua forgot to breathe. The delicate touch of her hand against his mouth sent shock waves through him. Love for her drove him beyond reason. He had to convince her. He covered her hand with his and pressed a kiss against her fingertips. "Just say yes," he whispered.

Shanna raised her head until she met his gaze. "Yes," she whispered.

Joshua let out the breath he'd been holding. "You won't regret this." He grabbed her by the waist and swung her around, nearly landing them in the lake.

After a lingering kiss, he lifted his head. "I wish we could get married right this minute, but I think we'd better get you back to the party. I wouldn't want Elizabeth coming after me with a shotgun."

"Mother…" Shanna drew in a ragged breath. "How are we going to break the news? She'll never—"

"Relax. I've got it all figured out. Next Sunday, after the television special, we'll sneak away. I've got plane reservations for Miami. Once we're married we'll cable home. Then we'll fly to Florida and go sailing. We'll be gone for a week. By the time we get home, they'll have cooled off. They might be upset for a while, but we'll be married and there won't be a thing your mother or Andrew can do about it."

"Sunday? Sailing? How long have you had this planned?"

"About a month. After Elizabeth scheduled your last concert tour, I swore I'd never let her separate us again."

"She won't."

"No." Joshua spoke with all the determination he could muster—perhaps to quiet the opposing voices that taunted him. "No one will."

But they had. Joshua stood now on the sandy shore where he had proposed to Shanna all those years ago. Somehow he'd made his way from the library to the lake and wasn't even aware he'd done it. The ink had barely dried on their license before they'd been forced apart.

The shrewd and deceitful Elizabeth had managed to turn their joy into heartache in less than five minutes of their coming home. He'd been so sure of himself. But he had underestimated his enemy.

Like a cunning spider she spun her web of lies, entrapping them all. She'd threatened to file suit against Joshua for the abduction and rape of a minor. Said she'd go public if he and Andrew didn't go along with the annulment. All these years Andrew had been paying for her silence.

But Elizabeth was dead now. He hurled a pebble into the smooth, sun-glazed waters, fragmenting the silver into a million shimmering fragments. The only thing keeping them apart now was a dark and clouded past—and Shanna's stubborn pride. They were meant for each other; why couldn't she see that? Though he wanted to go to her that very moment and make her listen to reason, he wouldn't. He'd give her time to think about what he'd said, then talk to her again. He wasn't trying to control her. How could she even think something like that? He just wanted what was best for her—for both of them—and for Ryan.

"God." Joshua bowed his head and closed his eyes. "I can't do this alone. Please help me convince her that she belongs with Ryan and me." Joshua took a deep breath. "Ryan," he breathed. "Maybe that's the answer." Tomorrow morning he'd take his son to meet his mother. Then she would have to listen.

About halfway between the lake and the house it hit him. Like a rock between the eyes, the truth of what he had done nearly brought him to his knees. No wonder Shanna hated him so much. "Dear God. What have I done?"

His mind replayed the memory of his proposal over and over, leaving no doubt in his mind. Shanna hadn't wanted to marry him back then. If he'd been thinking with his head instead of his hormones, he might have realized that. He'd coerced her into marrying him. She'd said no, but he couldn't take that for an answer. In some ways, he'd acted no differently than Elizabeth. He'd been bound and determined to have his way. And this morning he'd done it again.

Tried to force her to see things his way. He was *still* trying to manipulate her.

What would have happened, he wondered, if he'd accepted her "no" and not tried to talk her out of it? She must have known from the beginning it wouldn't work. Even then she'd determined that her music was more important than him. Why had it surprised him to hear it again?

"You're a fool, Joshua Morgan," he muttered. "A complete and utter fool."

He'd still go see Shanna in the morning, but not to talk her into staying at Morningsong with him. And he might even bring Ryan. Whatever she decided to do, she had a right to know about her son. He would lay all the cards on the table and back off. He would not, God help him, make the same mistake again.

Chapter Fourteen

"Would you like a beverage?" The flight attendant paused at Shanna's seat and grinned down at her.

"A Perrier with lime." Shanna lowered the tray and set the book she'd been reading open on her jean-clad thighs.

"Sure enough." The young man popped open the can, poured the bubbly clear liquid over ice, and set it along with a bag of peanuts on the tray, then shifted his attention to the man in the window seat.

"I'll have the same." The man stretched his long legs and muttered, "I hate window seats."

Shanna glanced over at him. He was a large man, over six feet, and obviously would have fared better in first class. A ragged scar over one eyebrow marred what was otherwise a pleasant face. His eyes were a quiet mix of brown and green. She almost offered to give up her aisle seat for him, but the thought of having his bulk between her and the aisle increased the uneasiness that had been building up in her since she'd entered the terminal in Memphis.

Several times she'd caught him studying her as though he were trying to place her. She'd taken her sunglasses off but still wore the blonde wig. If he were an ardent fan of country music, he might recognize her anyway. "Perhaps someone will trade with you," she said.

He shrugged and accepted his drink from the flight attendant. "I was hoping you might."

She shook her head. "Afraid not."

After a few moments he said, "I see you're a Hillerman fan. So am I. Um…I'm Donovan Hill, by the way."

Shanna flashed him a polite smile.

"Ever been to Portland before?" he asked.

"Several times."

"I never have." His lips parted in a wry smile. "What does one do for fun in Portland?"

"I wouldn't know."

"You go there on business, then?"

"Business. Yes." She'd performed there two or three times. Shanna picked up her book and began reading again. Something about the man unnerved her. Though he seemed pleasant enough, she sensed an underlying tension and wariness about him.

"Not much of a talker, are you?"

She looked at him again. "No, I'm not."

"I'm not, either, usually. But it's a long flight and…I thought the time might pass more quickly if we talked."

"They show a movie. That'll help."

Donovan Hill finally took the hint and left her alone. While she tried to focus on Hillerman's *Chee and Leaphorn,* her thoughts kept drifting back to Morningsong. Had she done the right thing by leaving? She wondered if anyone had missed her yet. Probably not. They wouldn't start worrying until late that night when she didn't show up at Debra's. Max would go looking for her. He'd worry, but hopefully not too much.

She wondered how Joshua would react. He'd be angry that she defied him. Then he'd probably be relieved. Her leaving would free him up to pursue Laurie again—if that was what he wanted.

His handsome features etched themselves in her mind. They were still married? She didn't believe that. It was too crazy, too far-fetched. Yet why would he lie? None of it made much sense. Joshua was a fool to think they could pick up where they'd left off. He'd said he wanted them to try again. But why would he say that when he obviously still cared for Laurie? Yet there had been moments when their eyes met, when he'd touched or kissed her, that she could easily believe that Joshua really did love her.

She closed her eyes and tipped her head back against the seat and allowed herself the luxury of dreaming about the way things might have been if Elizabeth and Andrew hadn't interfered. Oh, how she had loved him then.

No, blaming Elizabeth and Andrew wasn't fair. She shouldn't have let Joshua talk her into the marriage in the first place. She'd been right all along. Marriage and babies weren't for her. They weren't now, and they never would be. She'd never be happy without her music and her fans. Though she'd found a few moments of happiness with Joshua, it had been short-lived. Sure, she'd loved him—maybe she still did. But Shanna didn't dare entertain the notion of trying again.

You did the right thing by leaving. You're not right for Joshua—or for any man. Max had once likened her to a moonbeam. *"Don't see much of you in the daylight, but come sundown, you rise and shine. Spreading that light of yours on all those people who come to hear you sing. Come morning you're gone—off to another town, leaving them with nothing but a memory."*

What kind of memories had she left at Morningsong? Certainly not pleasant ones—not the kind a moonbeam brings. Shanna reined in her thoughts and looked out at the brilliant orange sky. In a ritual as old as time, the sky gave up its color and its light. Shanna felt her own color fade away as reality darkened her world. Night eased in with all its fears. She wouldn't shine on anyone tonight. There would be no performance, no audience, no songs, and no applause. The thought left her feeling empty and about as useful as a stringless guitar.

It hardly seemed possible. This morning she had it all; now she had nothing. *That isn't true. You still have your voice and your guitar. You have enough money to live comfortably for at least a couple of years. Best of all,* she reminded herself, *you're free.* Her lips curled in a satisfied smile. "Free as a moonbeam."

"What did you say?"

"Oh." She jumped. "Nothing. I was thinking out loud."

He chuckled. "So what's with this free-as-a-moonbeam business?"

"Nothing, really. A friend of mine called me a moonbeam once. Private joke. Sorry if I disturbed you."

"Don't be. You can disturb me anytime."

She turned back to her book, pretending to read. Eventually Hillerman drew her out of her problems into his imaginary world of intrigue.

When she disembarked the plane in Portland and made her way to the baggage-claim area, she again had the feeling she was being watched or followed. Had Joshua hired someone? She wouldn't put it past him. It was something Andrew might do, and Joshua seemed intent on walking in his grandfather's footsteps. She glanced around but saw no one suspicious.

Maybe she was getting paranoid. It came sometimes with stardom: the fear of being recognized and followed. Or stalked. Unfortunately, all three were very real possibilities. *But not here,* Shanna told herself firmly. She'd used an alias to book her flight. Some time ago Elizabeth had given her a pseudonym complete with an ID card and driver's license for traveling so she didn't have to use her real name. No one else knew about that. At least she didn't think they did.

Her seatmate from the plane caught up with her at the escalator and rode down with her. "Feels good to be out of those cramped quarters, doesn't it?"

"That it does." She shifted her bag from one shoulder to the next. Great, all she needed was for this guy to hit on her again. She was about to tell him to take a hike when he announced he had to hurry to make a phone call and sprinted on ahead. *He was just being friendly,* Shanna told herself. She was getting too uptight and paranoid. Standing in the baggage-claim area, she saw Donovan again, but only briefly. Once the luggage began circulating, she forgot about him, concentrating instead on reclaiming her bags and her guitar.

Gathering her belongings, she placed them in a luggage cart, then made her way through the crowds to the car rental area. While waiting for her flight at the Memphis airport, she'd called ahead and ordered a rental car for the week she planned to be here.

"Well." Donovan came up behind her in the line. "We meet again."

She sighed. "It appears that way."

"You wouldn't be following me by any chance, would you?" His grin disarmed her.

Shanna laughed at his comic gesture. "I don't think so."

"Good. But I'll bet you think I'm following you, right?"

"No, I..."

He winked at her. "All right, I won't deny it. The minute I saw that dazzling smile of yours, I said to myself, now, there's a girl I'd like to follow." He laughed again. "To be honest, I saw you standing over here, and since I need to get a car, too, I thought, why not give it another try? All she can do is say no. So...ah...would you maybe consider having dinner with me this evening?"

Shanna's first impulse was to say no. But he seemed harmless enough. Besides, the idea of having dinner alone held no appeal whatever.

"Silence is good," he said when she didn't answer. "It means you're thinking about it, right? I hope you'll say yes. I really hate eating alone."

"All right. I suppose dinner wouldn't hurt. I'm staying at the Sheraton just down the street. I've stayed there before. They have a nice restaurant." She glanced at her watch. "I could meet you there, say around eight?"

"Eight is good. My parents had eight kids. I was the eighth one. Is that a sign or what?"

Shanna raised an eyebrow. "If you say so."

He pointed to the desk. "I think you're next."

When Shanna finished her paperwork, she saw no sign of Donovan. He'd apparently jogged through the red tape of the car rental business while she, never having rented a car on her own, had had to crawl. She had to use her real name and driver's license and pay a mint for the insurance, but the clerk didn't seem to recognize her.

And now all she needed to do, apparently, was take a shuttle to the lot, pick up her Honda, and be on her way.

Part of her regretted accepting Donovan's invitation to dinner. Part of her looked forward to seeing him again. Though he seemed nice enough, she knew nothing about him except his name. If that *was* his name. Of course, he knew even less about her. On the other hand, what could happen in a hotel dining room? She'd be safe enough there. She'd have dinner, a pleasant conversation, then go to her room—alone. The next morning she'd drive to the coast and never see the man again.

~

A few minutes before eight, Shanna stepped out of her hotel room on the second floor, pulled the door closed and checked it, then walked to the elevator a few doors down. A man stood waiting in front of the elevators. He reminded her of an over-the-hill athlete—a football player, maybe, whose muscles had turned to fat and drifted to his middle.

"Evening," he murmured, nodding at her, then shifted his gaze to the display numbers above the door.

The elevator dinged and the doors opened. The man stepped inside and held the door open for her. The thought of stepping into the confined space with him unnerved her.

"Oops, silly me," she said, backing away and hurrying toward her room. "I'd forget my head if it wasn't attached." The moment the elevator doors closed, Shanna came back. Maybe she was being overly cautious, but something about the man frightened her. Of course, her dinner date frightened her too.

"Maybe you're just afraid of men in general," she mumbled to the image on the mirrored elevator wall as it closed and dropped to the first floor.

Finding her immediately, Donovan's appreciative gaze drifted over her. "You look even better tonight than you did on the plane."

"Thanks." He looked good, too, though she didn't say so. He seemed more relaxed and less threatening.

"Shall we?" Donovan held out his elbow, and she looped her arm through it, then he guided her toward the maître d' and gave the man his name.

"Certainly, Mr. Hill. Right this way."

Becoming more at ease, Shanna found herself slipping easily into the role of Donovan's date. He'd provide a nice diversion, and she needed that. The alternative would have been staying in her room alone.

"So tell me about yourself," he said once they'd been seated. "You could start with your name."

She hesitated a moment, wishing she could be honest yet knowing she couldn't trust him—not just yet. Still, lying to him didn't feel right, either. "I'd rather not say," she admitted finally.

He eyed her curiously, then nodded. "OK. I guess I can understand that. A woman traveling alone—wise to be cautious."

Shanna nodded.

He grinned. "How about if I call you Moonbeam?"

"What?"

"You said something on the plane about being as free as a moonbeam."

Shanna shrugged. "Why not?"

"Do you travel a lot?" He picked up the menu and glanced at it.

"All the time. How about you?"

"A fair amount. Don't much like it, though."

"What do you do?"

"I guess now it's my turn to be mysterious."

"Let me guess, you're a spy and are sworn to secrecy."

"Close." His gaze moved back to capture hers. "I do work for the government, but I'm not a spy."

She groaned. "Don't tell me you're IRS."

"OK, I won't."

The waiter showed up to take their orders, and Donovan seemed relieved at the disruption. They both ordered the house special—prime rib—then sat for several moments in awkward silence.

He glanced at her hands. “No ring—does that mean no husband?”

“No. I mean…” She sighed. “I don’t know.”

He arched an eyebrow, giving her a skeptical look. “You don’t know?”

“Sounds strange, doesn’t it?”

“For most people, but maybe not for a moonbeam.” His warm gaze seemed empathetic. “Want to tell me about it?”

“No, I…” She hesitated.

“I’m sorry, I didn’t mean to pry.”

“It’s all right. I’d like to talk about it, actually. Maybe explaining it to someone outside the family will help me make some sense of it.

“I married very young. Too young. Joshua and I ran away when I was a couple of weeks short of turning eighteen. He was twenty-two. When we returned home from our honeymoon a week later, my mother…” Shanna closed her eyes. It still hurt to talk about it.

“Let me guess,” Donovan said. “Your mother had the marriage annulled because you were underage.”

“Yes. She was furious. She threatened to bring Joshua up on kidnapping and rape charges.”

He winced. “Nasty business. What happened?”

“Joshua left town the next day—didn’t even bother to put up a fight or say good-bye. He turned up in L.A. with another woman.”

“Sounds like a prince.”

“I thought he was, until then. At any rate, Joshua informed me this morning that the papers had never been filed and that we are still legally married.”

“Is that good or bad?”

“It’s a shock. He says he wants to reconcile, but it’s all wrong. And I’m not sure I believe him.” Shanna twisted the napkin in her lap. “I never should have married him in the first place. He’s a stay-at-home kind of guy with roots a mile deep. I'm on the road nine months out of the year. We're like oil and water."

He nodded. "I know the feeling. I almost married once. My high-school sweetheart back in Iowa. Few days before the wedding we had a big fight. Julie expected me to take over her father's farm. I had other plans. Like your Joshua, her roots ran deep. Mine didn't. I wanted college and travel."

They spent the rest of the meal commenting on their food, places they'd been, and places they'd like to go. When they finished, Donovan paid the bill and walked her to the elevator. At her door he kissed her lightly. Shanna didn't turn away. His kiss was sweet. Comfortable. Not at all like Joshua's kisses. Joshua set off a dozen fireworks in her heart at once.

For a moment she thought he was going to ask to come in, but he didn't. "Listen," he said, "I'm only a couple of doors down—240. If you need anything...get lonely and want to talk or—"

"I'll let you know. Thanks for the dinner. And for the company."

Shanna waited until he left, then closed the door. Leaning against it, she sighed, glad she'd had the company and feeling disappointed the evening was over. When she stepped farther into the room, her senses kicked in. She first noted the difference in lighting. She'd turned off all but one light. Three were on now besides the light oozing from beneath the closed bathroom door. The contents of her suitcase had been strewn across the floor, and her nostrils burned with the scent of a man's cologne.

Chapter Fifteen

Her hands shaking, Shanna grasped the door handle. She tore down the hall and pounded on the door of room 240. A cry for help squeaked past the terror-sized lump in her throat.

The door swung open. "What the— What's wrong?"

"My room…" Shanna couldn't finish as her gaze fastened on Donovan's holster and gun. She backed away. It hadn't occurred to her that she might have been set up. While Donovan had entertained her at dinner, his partner had gone through her things.

She wanted to run, but her feet were as heavy as lead. Donovan stepped partway into the hall. "What happened? What about your room?"

She didn't answer and finally managed to take a step back.

"Shanna," he demanded, "give me your room card."

When she didn't, he pried the card out of her tightly clenched fist. "Stay here." He grabbed her by the shoulders and pushed her into his room, then ran down the hall to 236. She started to follow.

Drawing his gun, he inserted the plastic card and pressed down the handle. Opening the door, he raised the gun and cautiously stepped inside.

He was a cop, she realized then. Relief sent the adrenaline through her body gravitating to her knees, making it impossible to stand. She backed into his room and leaned against the open door. Donovan came back a few minutes later. "There's no one in your room. Come on." He led her over to one of the chairs. "You'd better sit before you fall down." His concerned gaze drifted over her. "You OK?"

She nodded and folded her arms around herself to stop the shivering.

"Good. Now, what's this all about?"

"You..." She looked down at the holstered gun again.

His hand brushed over it, then pulled a wallet off the nightstand and flipped it open to reveal a badge. "FBI."

She released a long sigh. "For a minute there I thought you might have been working with whoever was in my room."

He shook his head and seemed surprised she'd entertain such an odd thought. "Did you see anyone?"

"No. But there were lights on, and I could smell cologne. I didn't go all the way in, but I could tell someone had been there. My things were scattered everywhere."

Donovan picked up the phone. "I'll call security."

Two hours later hotel security and the police had come and gone. Shanna's jewelry had been taken, and they called the robbery an unfortunate incident. Police doubted they'd ever find the perpetrator. The hotel manager apologized for the inconvenience and changed the code for her room, then issued her another card.

After giving his initial statement to the police, Donovan watched the proceedings with a sour look. Now he turned to her. "Are you certain the jewelry is all that's missing?"

"I think so." She shrugged. "Fortunately, it's not a huge loss. Most of it can be replaced."

He rubbed the back of his neck. "I don't like you staying here by yourself."

Shanna didn't relish the thought, either. "I'll be fine," she said, opening the door for him. "I doubt they'll try again."

"Probably not," he admitted. His gaze lingered on hers. "What am I going to do with you?" he murmured.

Shanna stepped back. "Why would you say something like that? It's not as if you—" She stopped, remembering the moments just after she discovered the break-in. "Who are you?"

He frowned. "We've been through this before. I'm an FBI agent."

"That's not what I mean. You didn't just happen to meet me on that plane. You followed me from Memphis."

He shook his head. "Where would you get an idea like that?"

"Because you know my name. You called me Shanna."

He rubbed his eyes. "I was hoping you hadn't noticed."

"Why? Did Joshua send you?"

"No."

"You know him, though. You weren't guessing about the annulment. You already knew that. What's this all about?"

"It's a long and complicated story." Glancing at his watch, he added, "I doubt either one of us is up to dealing with it tonight."

"I'm used to late nights. Does this have something to do with my mother's death?"

He drew in a deep breath, stepped back into her room, and dropped onto her king-sized bed.

"Why were you following me?"

Folding his hands behind his head, he leaned back against the pillows and crossed his legs at the ankle. He closed his eyes as if shutting her out. His chest rose and fell in the pattern of a deep sleep. She was about ready to pummel him when he sat up. "You're a suspect and your life could be in danger. I took over the investigation of your mother's death two weeks ago when we found a black-market CD with your name on it. Been following you ever since. We know you figure into this some way, we're just not certain how."

Her mouth hung open and Shanna couldn't seem to close it. She sank into the chair near the small, round table. "Black market? You mean someone has been copying my label?"

"And selling at discount prices. We have reason to believe your mother was involved in a black-market ring, and that's what got her killed."

"That's absurd. My mother wouldn't…" Shanna rubbed her forehead.

"Wouldn't she?" Donovan swung his feet off the bed. "We have witnesses linking her to a racketeering group operating out of Las Vegas."

"It's just not possible." Though Shanna felt duty bound to defend Elizabeth, she also entertained the notion that Donovan might be right. Her gaze drifted over to meet his. "You said I was a suspect."

He nodded. "One of many."

"I didn't kill my mother."

"I know that now." Donovan stood and paced to the window and back. "Shanna, I'm going to level with you. I don't believe for a minute your room was ransacked by some hotel jewel thief. And I don't think I'm the only one who followed you out here."

"I don't understand."

"I'm not sure I do, either. But I do believe you're in danger."

"Why?"

"Maybe you have information or evidence that could be used against them—or they think you do."

"That's ridiculous." Shanna's heart pummeled the wall of her chest. She thought about the boxes of things she'd packed up and sent to the cabin.

"Is it possible she left something for you that might indicate what she was up to? Something the authorities overlooked?"

Shanna shook her head. "I don't see how. They searched the house, and when I packed her things, there was nothing."

"That you know of," he added.

For a moment she considered telling him of her plans to go through her mother's boxes, but she couldn't bear the thought of having anyone else there looking over her shoulder. No, she'd go through Elizabeth's belongings herself, and if she found anything at all suspicious she'd call the authorities. "You'd better go," she said.

"Yeah. We'll talk more about this tomorrow. Right now I want you to get some sleep. And don't worry. I'll be standing guard right outside your door."

"You don't need to do that."

"Yes, I do."

"Why?" She swallowed hard. Fear crept in like a pervasive cancer. Not because of the burglar, but because she couldn't stand the thought of being locked in.

"I don't want to take any chances. If the guy comes back..."

"All right." Shanna gave in. There was no use arguing. And having him outside her door would guarantee her safety. "I'll see you in the morning."

"Right."

Shanna closed the door and secured the deadbolt and the chain. She stood in the same spot for several minutes shivering and rubbing the goose bumps from her arms. An eternity had passed since she'd arrived in Portland, yet the glowing red numbers on the digital radio alarm told her it was only midnight. Moving to the window, Shanna pulled the drapes and wriggled out of her dress.

She should have slipped into her nightgown but didn't. Instead, Shanna pulled on a pair of jeans, a T-shirt, and a denim jacket. She turned out the lights, then opened the drapes and the patio door. Stepping out into the brisk autumn air, Shanna moved to the railing and leaned over. She was on the west side of the hotel, while the main entrance faced south. The parking lot was narrow and lined with tall trees. Beyond the trees was an industrial area. About twenty feet below, her rental car waited beneath the narrow balcony. There was no one in sight. She could easily escape without being seen. All she had to do was figure out a way to climb down.

"You can do this," she murmured to herself. "You have to." Donovan would be furious when he learned he'd lost her, but that couldn't be helped.

Packing the one bag she'd brought into her hotel room took less than five minutes. Stripping the bed, she tied the two sheets together, then secured one end of her makeshift rope to the top rail of the balcony. Though she'd seen it done in movies, she wasn't certain it would work in real life. Fortunately, she only weighed 125 pounds. The sheets looked sturdy enough. She hooked her bag over her shoulder and climbed over the rail. Hand over hand, legs wrapped around the twisted sheets, she began her descent. Now all she had to do was hope no one would come around the corner of the building.

~

"A clean getaway." Shanna couldn't help but smile as she drove up the ramp to the I-205 freeway and headed north. She'd take the Washington route to the coast, following the Columbia River. Frequent checks in the rearview mirror assured her that no one was following. She felt a twinge of guilt at leaving, but that couldn't be helped. She didn't trust the FBI agent—if that's what he was. And she didn't want anyone looking through Elizabeth's belongings until she'd had a chance to do so herself. More than that was the fear that a man had broken into her room.

Shanna shuddered at the thought that someone other than Donovan might have followed her to Portland. In ditching the FBI agent, she'd be rid of him as well. She checked the rearview mirror again. She'd been going only fifty-five since getting on the freeway, and though several cars had passed her, none lingered behind. "You lost them," she said aloud to reassure herself. "They'd never expect you to leave the hotel in the middle of the night." She had the advantage now. Not that she planned to stay hidden forever. Just long enough to find out what was going on—and whether or not Elizabeth had been involved in the black-market scheme.

She'd studied the map at the Memphis airport and had memorized the route. North to I-5, then exit the freeway at Longview and head west onto the Long Beach Peninsula. Once there, she would check into a motel for whatever was left of the night, then tomorrow she'd drive to the cabin.

For the first time in as long as she could remember, Shanna was actually looking forward to being alone and not having to perform.

Jim Broadman wrapped the jewelry he'd taken from Shanna's room in a white hanky and stashed it in his garment bag. Most of it was worthless, but maybe it would bring him a few bucks. Looked like three or four of them had real stones in the settings.

The real prize, though, was not the trinkets but the paper he'd found folded between the pages of her appointment book. He'd copied the address down word for word and left the paper where she'd put it. She'd never suspect that he'd seen it.

He snorted. *Smart thinking to make it look like a robbery, Jimbo,* he congratulated himself. There'd be no prints, no evidence that he'd been after anything other than the jewelry.

Settling down on the firm hotel mattress, he examined the address again. He knew without a doubt it was where she'd be heading. Lizzie had once told him about a place she had at the coast.

His grin disappeared as he remembered the look on Shanna's face when he'd held the door open on that elevator. Thinking she was too good to share the ride down with him. It still rankled. He'd been tempted to run after her then. Teach her a thing or two about manners. But he had to bide his time. He'd give her a couple days' head start, then go after her.

He'd always heard that Portland was a nice town. He'd do some sightseeing. First, though, he'd have to take care of the fed who'd been tailing Shanna.

He stretched out on the bed and turned out the lights. Seeing the two of them hunched over dinner, making eyes at each other, laughing and talking. Killing him would be a pleasure.

Chapter Sixteen

Joshua stared into the inky black night. The door opened and light from the hall spilled into the room, turning the window into a mirror reflecting his pajama-clad image.

"Joshua?" Nan moved up beside him, slipping her arm through his. "I thought I might find you in here."

"What are you doing up so late?"

"Couldn't sleep. How about you?"

Joshua looked down at his grandmother. "She's gone, Nan. Just like that. I went over to see if I could talk some sense into her and found this." He pulled a crumpled paper out of his robe pocket and handed it to her.

Nan took it from him. "Oh dear. I should have suspected she'd do something like this. When did she leave?"

He drew in a ragged breath. "This afternoon. The guard said she was going shopping. She never came back."

Nan reached up and gently rubbed his shoulder. "Have you any idea where she's gone?"

"No. The note said she was going home," he murmured. "Morningsong is her home. She hasn't lived anywhere else since she was a little girl. I thought about that old run-down place they had in Nashville when we first signed her on, but the houses in that neighborhood all came down fifteen years ago when they built the shopping center."

"Perhaps she owns a place somewhere else. Have you spoken to Max?"

Joshua nodded. "He said as far as he knew, Shanna had no use for anything as permanent as a home. She never even talked about staying on anywhere."

Nan frowned. "Oh, Joshua, you don't think she means home—as in heaven?"

Suicide? He couldn't say the word. "The thought did cross my mind." He dragged his hands down his face. "I'd never forgive myself if I pushed her to that, Nan. With her being as upset as she was, I shouldn't have let her go back to her apartment alone."

"You mustn't blame yourself." Nan drew him away from the window. "I spoke with her after you did. She was upset. She told me she'd have to move away from Morningsong, but I had no idea she planned to go so soon. Have you called the sheriff?"

"Not yet. Max said it was too soon to put out a missing person's report. She's an adult. Besides, she left a note. There's no evidence of foul play. If we haven't heard from her by morning, Max will do some checking. He thinks she might have gone somewhere to cool off or something."

"Yes, I'm sure he's right. We all need to do that from time to time. Still, saying she was going home...that worries me."

"Yeah. She might have just said that to throw us off her trail." He shook his head. "This is my fault. I shouldn't have pushed her. What am I going to do? I love her, Nan. I didn't give her Andrew's letter or tell her about Ryan, and now she's gone."

Nan paused at one of the bookshelves, withdrew a black leather-bound Bible, and handed it to him. "I know the advice I'm about to give you may seem paltry in light of what you're facing, but worrying and fretting over what Shanna does or doesn't do won't help you or Ryan one bit. You need to pray, darling. Pray that God will give you wisdom and strength in the days ahead. Pray that He will protect Shanna and help her to make the right decision as well. And pray that you will be able to accept the decisions she does make—even if she decides not to come back."

"In other words, put it in God's hands." Joshua added the sarcastic remark, then apologized. "I don't mean to sound like an ungrateful degenerate, but God hasn't been doing much where Shanna and I are concerned."

Nan sighed. "Perhaps He's doing more than we realize. I don't know what God ultimately has in store for you and Shanna, but I do know that He can take all this turmoil and all the evil perpetrated by Elizabeth and work it for good. Just trust Him, Joshua."

Joshua cast her a sidelong look. "Easy enough for you to say. You've always got it together."

She bristled. "Sit down." Pulling a chair around so the two faced each other, she sank into one of them and waited until Joshua took the other.

"First of all," she said, "trust is never easy. It should be, but it isn't."

Joshua tilted his head back. "Why do I get the feeling I'm about to get a lecture?"

"Not a lecture. A story. I've never told you this before. Never told anyone except Andrew. I'm ashamed of how weak and unforgiving I was back then."

"You don't have an unforgiving bone in your body."

"Oh, but you're wrong. I spent a number of years being bitter and angry."

"Somehow I have a hard time imagining that. You've always been so easygoing."

"Only on the outside. When your grandfather and I were younger, life was good to us. I thought we must have been doing all the right things because God had blessed us so. We had wealth, status, a growing company, and a wonderful son. Then everything seemed to go wrong. Harry was a junior in college. The sheriff called asking us to come pick him up. He'd been drinking. I was devastated, but we pretended it didn't matter, that his partying was just a phase—like many young men go through. Then a few months later came his first drunk-driving arrest. He ran into a ditch and hit a telephone pole."

Joshua frowned. "There were two accidents?"

"Three. Each time we made excuses. We disciplined him, of course, even made him go to AA meetings. He'd stop drinking for a while, then a few months down the road he'd be at it again. When he met and married your mother, he seemed to grow out of it. I'd see him with an occasional drink, but it wasn't until after…" Nan bit into her lower lip and closed her eyes. Tears slipped beneath her eyelids, and she wiped them away.

Joshua leaned forward and took her age-spotted hand in his. "You don't have to talk about it, Nan."

"Yes, I do. You need to hear it." Her watery gaze lifted to his. "For a long time I blamed myself for Harry and Barbara's deaths. If I'd seen the signs, if we'd intervened, maybe we could have prevented the accident that took their lives and left you and Tom homeless. I was angry with myself and with Andrew. Though I wouldn't admit it for the longest time, I was most furious with God and blamed Him for all that had happened."

Joshua could relate all too well. He'd blamed himself for his parents' death, as well. He knew better now. At least he'd been told often enough that he couldn't have made a difference.

"It took me a long time to realize that Andrew and I didn't cause the accident," Nan went on, "and neither did God. Ultimately, the only person to blame was your father. Not that he chose to run a red light or drive too fast—at that point he was beyond reason—but that he chose to drink too much. The point is, darling, once I stopped blaming myself and others, things changed for me. I began to see how God had turned the terrible tragedy of Harry and Barbara's deaths into something good. We had lost a son and daughter-in-law, but we gained two sons. You boys have brought Andrew and me more joy than either of us ever thought possible."

"And more trouble."

Nan laughed. "Ah, but you kept me young and on my toes." Her smile faded. "Joshua, not a moment goes by when I don't wish that Harry and Barbara were still alive. The pain of losing them will never completely go away. But the bitterness I harbored against God and myself and Andrew is gone. When I let that go I found I had more energy, more love and hope and happiness…" Nan smiled. "Listen to me going on like that. I sound like a saint."

"You are." He leaned forward and kissed her cheek.

"I've loved having you and Tom here. And along the way I found true joy. I know there will be joy for you, as well, Joshua. Perhaps not with Shanna—for it's impossible to change other people's hearts. Shanna has to make that choice for herself. But you will find joy. The key is to look in the right places."

"I wish I had your faith."

"Not my faith, darling, yours—it's enough." She stood, signaling the end of their discussion.

Joshua lingered several minutes after Nan left, leafing through the Bible she'd handed him. It had been a long time since he'd studied the Good Book. Sure, he'd gone to church on a regular basis and repeated the psalms and verses printed in the bulletin. But the time so often seemed wasted, his participation rote. He touched the gold-edged pages and felt the stirring of conviction.

Andrew had made a practice of spending time each morning in devotions and prayer. *"Helps me gain perspective on the day. Life without God at the helm,"* he used to say, *"is no life at all."*

Joshua decided it was high time he carried on the tradition. Not that he expected it to open in just the right place and give him the answer to all his troubles. That sort of sudden revelation was rare.

"It isn't the Bible itself that changes lives," he remembered Andrew saying. *"It's developing a personal relationship with the God who inspired it."*

Joshua sighed and closed the cover. "God," he whispered, "regardless of what happens, I want to be the kind of man You want me to be. The kind I need to be to raise Ryan. I know I don't deserve it, but please give me another chance to talk with Shanna. Keep her safe and…"

Joshua felt a presence in the room. He looked toward the open door, then smiled at the small figure running toward him. Scooping Ryan up in his arms, he settled him on his lap. "Hey, big guy, what's going on? You're supposed to be asleep."

Ryan wrapped his skinny arms around Joshua's chest, snuggling against him. "I had a bad dream, and I couldn't find you in your bed. Nana was up. She said you wouldn't be mad if I came in here."

"I'm not." Joshua held him close. "A bad dream, huh. Want to talk about it?"

He sat up, his face animated. "These bad guys chased me, and I almost drowned. I ran and ran and then I founded a stick and I knocked 'em out and took 'em to the sheriff and he put 'em in jail…but then they got out again. And then I had to kick 'em and hit 'em again."

Joshua raised an eyebrow at what was quickly turning into another of Ryan's tall tales. "Guess you showed them, huh?"

"Yeah." He grinned, then looking up at his dad's face said, "How come you're in here by yourself? Were you sad like last time? I don't like you to be sad."

Joshua looked into his son's wide blue eyes. "I don't like it, either. And sometimes sad things happen. But you know what? Seeing you makes me feel much better."

Ryan yawned and leaned back against him. "I love you, Daddy."

"I love you too, Son." Joshua kissed the top of his head, then held him until he fell asleep. Ryan's deep and steady breathing comforted Joshua and seemed to drain away the frustration he'd been feeling all day. Love for the boy almost filled the empty hole in his life where Shanna should have been. Though he might never have Shanna, he did have a part of her.

Something stirred inside him as he held Ryan. A tiny shred of hope that came as a picture flitting through his mind. Shanna was sitting in the rocking chair in front of the fireplace in the older portion of the house. She was holding an infant to her breast. Joshua and Ryan were playing a game on the worn braided rug.

Ryan stirred and the image fled. Joshua carried Ryan to bed and a few minutes later crawled into his own.

Sunlight poured into the room Shanna had rented early that morning in Long Beach, Washington. Since the window faced west, it had to be after noon.

Another image of Joshua haunted her sleepy mind. She pushed it away along with the bedcovers. She didn't want to think about him. No matter how hard she tried to keep those thoughts away, they crept in when she wasn't looking. Sometimes it seemed Joshua's roots were buried as deeply into her heart as they were into Morningsong.

The moments just before she fell asleep or woke up were the worst. Unwanted thoughts could take over then—when her mind lay naked, stripped of control by exhaustion and sleep.

She stretched and wandered to the window. The view was spectacular. She hadn't seen the ocean in a long time. Now the blue sky, ocean, waves, and sand called her to come and play, but Shanna ignored the yearning. She'd have plenty of time for beachcombing later. What she needed right now was a shower, then breakfast. Then she would contact Nancy, the woman Elizabeth had hired to maintain the cabin.

An hour later, Shanna checked out of the motel. She called Nancy Blake's number, but no one answered. After eating a scrumptious clam chowder at the hotel's restaurant and enjoying the view, Shanna tried the number one more time. Still no answer.

Not wanting to wait around any longer, she drove north to Ocean Park. It was a quaint little one-stoplight town with its own post office, library, and two grocery stores. Shanna stopped at the country store that claimed to have everything to pick up groceries, then asked for directions to the cabin. Luckily one of the clerks was a friend of Nancy's and knew the landmarks well.

A few minutes later, Shanna turned onto a narrow, treelined drive, then crossed over a rustic wooden bridge. On either side a marshy green meadow bordered a creek. Then trees again for a hundred or so yards. The drive wound up a hill, then stopped at the top, giving her an unhindered view of the shoreline.

Her heart fluttered like the wings of a frightened bird as she emerged from the trees and pulled up in front of the cabin. It was smaller than she remembered. She loved the natural look of the gray weathered wood and the bright blue trim that had recently been painted. The flower gardens, though somewhat overgrown with weeds, looked well cared for. Pieces of driftwood scattered around the yard gave it a beachy flavor. Seeing the place again made Shanna wish she had come back sooner.

"This is it," she whispered. "Home." A lump lodged in her throat. Tears stung her eyes, blurring her vision. Brushing them away, Shanna turned off the motor and stepped out of the car. While she wanted desperately to throw open the door and explore every nook and cranny of the place, something held her back.

Along with excitement, Shanna once again felt tentacles of fear wrap themselves around her chest, making it hard to breathe. What she felt had little to do with being in an isolated cabin at the end of the world, or with vandals and thieves. The mounting terror came from the thought of entering a house haunted by painful memories. It came, too, from not knowing what lay ahead and anxiety about what she might find in Elizabeth's possessions.

"You've come this far," she said, giving herself courage. "Might as well go in."

Following the instructions her mother had left, Shanna reached for the ledge above the kitchen window and felt for the key. Yes. Grasping it, she took a deep breath and inserted it into the lock.

Chapter Seventeen

"Call for you on line two, Mr. Morgan," Debra's crisp voice stated over the intercom. With Laurie gone, Debra was acting as Josh's secretary until he could hire someone else.

Joshua stopped pacing and leaned over his desk. "I told you to hold my calls," he grumbled. It had been two days since Shanna's disappearance, and despite all his efforts to remain calm and entrust Shanna to God's care, Joshua was a basket case. Pure and simple.

"I think you'll want to take this one, Joshua. It's Max."

"You're right. I'm sorry." Joshua sank into the leather executive chair behind his grandfather's desk. Grabbing the phone, he immediately asked, "Did you find her?"

"Not yet, but I may have a lead."

"Thank God. Where is she?"

"Hold on, Josh. I didn't say I'd found her. I had a friend of mine check the flights out of Memphis the day Shanna left. One of the attendants remembered that a woman with freckles and a blonde wig and sunglasses using the name Jennifer Page flew out of Memphis Tuesday night—the same day she left here."

"Jennifer Page?"

"One of her fake IDs. Elizabeth had gotten them for her for traveling. She took flight 706 to Dallas, then went on to Portland, Oregon."

"Portland?" Joshua couldn't have heard him right. "Why on earth would she go there?"

"Beats me. I called the hotels that were listed, but they claim no one named Jennifer Page or Shanna O'Brian checked in. 'Course, she might have used another name. One clerk I talked to, though, said he remembered a gal who could have been Shanna, but she was hanging out with some FBI agent. He remembered her because her room was burglarized while she was having dinner with the guy. She left via the balcony sometime during the night without the agent. Seems he was none too happy about it."

Joshua rubbed his forehead. "It might have been Shanna. We need to know for sure."

"I faxed him a photo. He should be responding any minute now. I'd be surprised if we come up with a positive ID."

"Did Shanna ever mention Portland?"

"Not as I recall. We played there a couple of times—hold on a sec. I have a fax coming in now." Several seconds passed before Max came back on. "Looks like we have a positive ID, Josh. The desk clerk says no question. And the gal he saw was a blonde."

"Doesn't make sense. You said she was with an FBI agent. Can you find out who he is and why she was with him?"

"Will do. I'll get back to you. If it's OK with you, I'd like to head out to Portland myself—see if I can track her down."

"Thanks, Max. I appreciate it." Joshua hung up, then tipped his head back. What in the world had possessed her to go to Portland? But the more pressing question was, where had she gone from there, and why had she run from the feds? Putting his feet up on the desk, he stretched out and closed his eyes. He'd have to leave that part of the mystery to Max. Once they got the agent's name, they could contact him. In the meantime, Joshua needed to figure out where in the Portland area she might have gone. He'd already asked Debra to go through her personal files, but only one previous address had been listed. He had no way of knowing where she'd lived before she and Elizabeth had moved to Nashville.

He lowered his feet and snapped his chair forward. Of course. After chastising himself for his ineptness, he buzzed Debra and asked her to look on the personal history forms that should have been filled out when they first signed Shanna on.

"I'm sorry, Josh. There isn't one. While I was looking for an address, I checked the original forms Elizabeth filled out for Shanna. Her place of birth was left blank. I thought that was rather strange and did a computer search, but our records show no birthplace."

"It has to be somewhere."

"That's what I thought. I've got a call in to the Social Security office. I'm trying to think of all the things you need a birth certificate for. Passports, Department of Motor Vehicles might have it—I'll try them."

Joshua thanked her and hung up. At least now he knew where to look. Shanna would have written her birthplace on their marriage certificate. That was in the files he'd gotten from Andrew.

Remembering back to their wedding day, he cringed at how he'd bribed the justice of the peace in Watson Country to overlook the fact that Shanna was underage. Joshua had taken him aside and lied to him about Shanna being in a family way. No wonder so many things had gone wrong. Their marriage was based on lies. His lies. Had he not been so impatient, they might have had a proper wedding a year or two later, with Shanna dressed in white satin and lace. They might still be together today.

Or maybe that was wishful thinking on his part. How often had Shanna insisted she didn't want marriage and a family? She'd cited her career as an excuse, but what if she really didn't want to make room in her life for him and Ryan?

"No," he mumbled, shaking off the possibility. Shanna wasn't like that. He'd tell her about Ryan, and she'd change her mind. Wouldn't she? Somehow Joshua wasn't so sure.

"Hey, Josh?" Tom opened the door and poked his head in. "Can I talk to you?"

"Sure. What do you need?"

Tom ambled in and sank into the chair. "Well, I've been doing some thinking, and I've decided to take over the L.A. office like Granddad wanted. I'll leave in a few days—unless you need me here."

"What happened? Did you and Christi break up?"

"No. This has nothing to do with Christi. I just decided that if I'm going to do it, I might as well go now. Never did like sitting around doing nothing."

Joshua had mixed feelings about turning Tom loose on Morningsong West. Andrew had sent Joshua there at about the same age, but Tom lacked maturity. On the other hand, the responsibility would be good for him.

"What's the matter?" Tom asked. "Thought you'd be happy to see me go. It's what you wanted, isn't it?"

Joshua looked at him a long moment. His little brother was no longer a kid. He was a grown man now. After their parents died, Joshua had felt a deep sense of responsibility for Tom. He'd been overprotective, and lately Tom had taken to baiting him and picking fights. He resented Joshua's help, looking at it as interference. Fine. Joshua didn't want to fight with him anymore.

"What I want doesn't matter," Joshua said at last. "It's your decision. As far as Christi is concerned, you have to do what you think is right. I know I've been pretty adamant about you waiting to marry her. I guess that's because of what happened between Shanna and me. I don't want to see you get hurt."

Tom grinned. "So you're saying…it's OK for me to marry her?"

"If that's what you both want. I still think you'd be better off waiting a couple of years. A lot can happen."

Tom shrugged. "Nan said the same thing. I guess I can wait another year."

Relieved, Joshua came around the desk and leaned against it. "I'm glad to hear that. What does Christi think about your going to L.A.?"

"She's OK with it for now. Once she finishes her work here, she'll head out to L.A. to see her family. We'll spend some time together before she starts her tour."

"Sounds like you've got things pretty well worked out."

"Yeah. Things are looking good." He sobered. "Have you heard from Shanna?"

"No." He straightened and walked over to the window.

"Max told me he'd tracked her as far as Portland. You planning to go after her?"

"I don't know. Not if she doesn't want me to. At this point I just want to make sure she's OK."

Tom nodded. "Well, if you need any help let me know."

"Thanks. I think you'll be helping most by running Morningsong West. It'll take a load off my mind."

Tom joined his brother at the window, which faced the apartments. "Why would she run, Josh? You were the only guy she was ever interested in. I always figured you two would end up together."

"People change. Situations change."

"I guess." Tom turned and headed for the door. "So you going to be OK with my taking off tomorrow?"

"Sure. We'll need to go over some things before you leave. After dinner be OK?"

Tom agreed and left, saying he was going to pack.

He'd been gone only a few minutes when Debra appeared in the doorway. "I'm sorry to bother you again, Josh, but Sheriff Kerns is here to see you."

Before she could finish, Nate Kerns squeezed around her and strutted into the room. "You can skip the formalities, Deb." Nate tossed her a grin. "Josh and I go way back." Nate and Joshua had gone to school together. Nate was now the sheriff of Watson County. The two had been friends, but time and distance had taken a toll on their friendship. Nate still had the build of a quarterback—broad shoulders, narrow hips—all accentuated by the khaki sheriff's uniform and the way he held his arms out to keep them clear of the gun and miscellaneous equipment that hung on his belt. "Hey, Josh. How's it going?"

"Not too good." Joshua shook Nate's extended hand and offered him a chair. "What brings you out here?"

"Got a call from Max this morning. He told me Shanna had taken off. Want to tell me what's going on?"

"Not much to tell at this point. Max traced her to Oregon."

"So he said."

"I'm trying to find out if she has roots there."

Nate nodded in sympathy. "I might be able to help you with that. I'll run a check on her through Motor Vehicles. You should have called me right away. The sooner we start looking the better."

"I didn't think you guys would be interested since she left a note. Too soon to file a missing person's report."

"Ordinarily that might be the case, but Shanna's a celebrity. Max said this is out of character for her."

Joshua sighed. "I'm not so sure about that. She was pretty upset yesterday. My guess is she just decided to run away."

Nate leaned back, resting an ankle on his knee. "What or who do you think she's running from?"

"Me. Morningsong. I don't know."

"I'm not sure how to tell you this, Josh, but there's another reason she might be on the run."

Joshua frowned, thinking about the FBI agent in Portland. "Don't tell me she's a fugitive. The worst thing Shanna's ever done is gotten a parking ticket."

"I'm not saying she's done anything wrong." He pinched the crease on his pants. "I'm saying she might know something."

"About what?"

"The record piracy."

"What?"

Nate pursed his lips. "I take it Andrew didn't tell you."

Joshua covered his eyes. "Nate, I hate to seem dense here, but I have no idea what you're talking about. Are you saying someone is involved with pirating our records and Shanna knows about it?"

"Can't believe Andrew didn't mention it to you." Nate rubbed his hand against the arm of the chair.

"There were a lot of things I didn't know. Working out in L.A., I didn't get in on everything that went on out here. He was in the process of filling me in on the various aspects of the business when he died. Didn't mention anything to me about pirating, though. *That* I would have remembered. There may be something on it in his files, but I haven't had a chance to go through everything yet."

Nate nodded. "Sure was sorry to hear about Andrew's passing. He was a good man."

"So tell me more about this pirating business. When did you hear about it?"

"Andrew came to my office a few months back. Seems that just prior to her death, Elizabeth had been complaining about Shanna's drop in royalties. He'd told her sales were down, which they were. Elizabeth pointed out that, according to the charts, Shanna was as popular as ever. Two of her songs were in the top ten at the same time. Apparently Elizabeth mentioned the possibility that someone might be pirating. Andrew told her he'd look into it."

"Did he?" Joshua scribbled notes on a pink Post-it.

"Not right away. At first he thought she was trying to pull something. It wasn't until after she died that he started wondering if she might have been right."

Joshua stared at him. "Let me get this straight. Andrew thought there might be a connection between the pirating and Elizabeth's death?"

"He was worried she might have started looking into it on her own and maybe stumbled on to something and gotten herself killed in the process."

"Whew. That's pretty wild. Did he have any proof?"

"Not to my knowledge."

Joshua was tired and irritated. Everything around him seemed to be off kilter. Why hadn't Andrew mentioned anything to him?

After a heavy sigh, he said, “The press reported Elizabeth’s death as a suicide.” Joshua tapped a pen against his hand. “I didn’t even know you were still investigating it.”

“We haven’t officially closed it. I’m not actively working on it anymore. The FBI has pretty much taken over. I haven’t heard anything in weeks, so when Max told me about Shanna, I got worried. Might not be a connection, but if there is, Shanna could be in danger.”

“I’m afraid I don’t follow. What does Shanna’s disappearance have to do with this?”

“Maybe nothing. Or maybe she knows more than she’s letting on.”

The entire conversation sounded like something out of a made-for-TV movie, the plot too convoluted and frightening to be real. “Then we’d better find her, and fast.”

“My thoughts exactly. I’ve called the FBI office in Portland. They’re supposed to be getting a message to Agent Hill.”

“The agent who was with Shanna?”

“I suspect so.” He rose. “Look, Josh, I’m sorry about all this. I’ll let you know as soon as I hear anything. In the meantime, check your files—see if you can come up with anything on the piracy thing.”

Chapter Eighteen

"Oh…" Shanna's breath caught as she stepped into the front room. "It's… I knew it would be great, but this…" She dropped her bag and crossed the hardwood floor to a wall of windows that framed the sea. It reminded her so much of the mural on the wall in her apartment back at Morningsong. Shanna wondered if the mural had come out of her memory of this place.

The late afternoon sun melted over her, and she stood mesmerized, shading her eyes from the glare as the sun turned the water to shimmering silver ripples. A streak of something white shot by, glanced off her leg, and kept going. Shanna yelped and jumped aside. Whatever it was skidded to a stop just short of the window seat, leapt up, and after flashing Shanna a regal look, began washing her paw.

"What are you doing here?" Shanna gasped. "You scared me half to death."

"Excuse me…"

Shanna whirled toward the voice. A tall, slender woman with salt-and-pepper hair pulled into a loose bun leaned in and smiled. "I didn't mean to frighten you. Saw the car and…"

"I'm Shanna—Elizabeth O'Brian's daughter." Shanna held a hand to her chest as if the motion might calm her wildly beating heart.

"Oh, of course." She stepped forward and offered her hand, her long skirt—a colorful gauze material—swaying gracefully as she moved. "I'm Nancy Blake."

"Hi. I tried to call you earlier to let you know I was coming."

She groaned. "I've been in Astoria all day visiting my grandkids. Just got back." For Shanna's benefit she added, "Astoria is on the other side of the Columbia River, in Oregon."

"Oh, right, I remember seeing the bridge."

Nancy scanned the kitchen. "Do you need anything? I'd invite you over for dinner, but I'm off to a birthday party. Of course, you could come along. I'm sure the girls wouldn't mind."

"Thanks, but I stopped at the store before I came."

"How long will you be staying?"

Shanna shrugged. "I wish I knew. Um…thanks for taking care of it. And the packages I sent—they did get here, didn't they?" Shanna looked around but saw no sign of them.

"Sure did. I stuck them up in the attic—hope you don't mind. It's just that I don't like a lot of clutter, since I try to make the place look lived in. Henry says if a house looks vacant it attracts vandals—not that we have problems like that around here. We have very little crime."

"That's good to hear," Shanna said. "I take it Henry is your husband."

"Yep. He's a peach. I'll bring him over to meet you sometime. I'd do it right now, but he's out of town."

"What does he do?"

Nancy grinned. "Depends on the season. Summers he fishes. Winters he writes novels."

"A writer! Should I know him?"

"Only if you read mysteries. One of his novels, *A Friendship to Die For,* is being considered for a television movie."

"Sounds intriguing. I'm sorry I haven't read it."

"Not to worry. I'll bring you a copy. By the way, my husband and I have a couple of your albums. Maybe you could sign them sometime while you're here."

"I'd be happy to." Shanna smiled at the ease with which Nancy had asked. "Um...about my being a singer. I'd appreciate it if you wouldn't tell anyone else. I managed to slip past the news hounds." She sighed. "As much as I like having fans, and even an occasional interview, I—well, I'm not up to that just now."

"Sure, no problem. Though people around here are used to seeing celebrities."

"Really?"

"Sure. Besides Henry, we've got a number of well-known writers, artists, and musicians who live here, and several others who come up here to work. They like the atmosphere."

Shanna nodded toward the water. "I can see why. It's so—I don't know—peaceful here. And beautiful."

"It can be. We've had some gorgeous fall weather. Come winter, though, we get the rain. Depresses a lot of people." She chuckled. "We love it. Gale winds. Let's just say the reason Harry gets so much writing done is that it's usually too wet to do anything else."

"I don't suppose I'll have to worry much about that. I'll be gone before winter."

"So will half the peninsula. Lot of retired folks head south. Well, I'd better be off. Have to meet the gals at five-thirty. Sure you don't want to come? Our birthday girl is a singer too. Connie plays piano at the Sand Dollar Lounge on Friday and Saturday nights. She's not quite your caliber, but she's very good. We're eating at 42nd Street Café—they serve fantastic food." Nancy tipped her head back and groaned in ecstasy. "Their sturgeon is to die for."

"I appreciate the offer, but I'm exhausted. I'll just unload the car and eat a light supper. Then probably crawl into bed."

"OK, catch you later, then."

"Nancy?" Shanna stopped her at the steps to the porch. "Could we maybe get together tomorrow sometime? I have tons of questions about the place."

"Sure. How does ten sound?"

"Great. See you then."

Shanna dealt first with the kitchen, putting away her prepared foods, setting a teakettle on to boil, and making a list of supplies she'd need. She hadn't really expected to find anything but was surprised that someone had stocked it fairly recently with essentials like flour, sugar, and various spices. That seemed odd, considering her mother hadn't been there in years—at least not that she knew of. She'd have to remember to ask Nancy about it. Maybe Elizabeth had given her permission to rent it out. Or maybe the supplies were Nancy's way of making certain it looked lived in.

The kitchen was small but functional. It overlooked the living room and had the same spectacular view. A counter with two tall wicker-and-chrome chairs served as a divider between the kitchen and living room. Shanna poured herself some hot water and tore open a box of fruity herbal tea. She dunked the tea bag and sat down on one of the stools. Inhaling the delicate scent of berries, Shanna looked out over her new domain.

The cabin had a homey feel. On one level Shanna sensed a comforting familiarity. On a deeper level she sensed an odd, almost frightening, sensation—as though something terrible had happened there. If she didn't know better, she'd have suspected the place was haunted. Certainly not by Elizabeth. Elizabeth had always spoken of the place with such disdain, Shanna wondered why she'd kept it. Shanna shrugged away the unpleasant notion, grounding herself in the delicate taste of raspberry tea and the feel of the warm mug in her hands.

"I'm glad you kept it, Mother," she mused. "Whatever the reason."

She spent the next few minutes staring out at the water, enjoying the sound of waves crashing and sea gulls squawking overhead. Not ten feet away, Shanna noticed a lone gull perched statue-still on a piece of driftwood that resembled a piling. After a few minutes of marveling at the bird's ability to be so still, Shanna ventured outside, laughing aloud as she approached. "No wonder you didn't fly away. You're a fake."

For show. *Like you, Shanna.* She sobered, puzzling over the disturbing thought that seemed to come out of nowhere. The bird was a showpiece, a copy. Something for the public to look at and enjoy. It sat alone, unmoving—unable to feel or eat or fly. An object with no life of its own. Shanna hugged herself and frowned. Joshua's words ripped into her again. *Cold. Unfeeling.*

Shanna tore her gaze from the concrete gull and shook her head to rid her mind of the disturbing thoughts. *"Get a grip, girl,"* she imagined Max saying as she went back inside and closed the door behind her.

Glancing at the bags that still littered the living room floor, Shanna picked up her luggage. Time to stop daydreaming and get to work.

The cabin had two bedrooms. One had been hers, with a ruffled pink bedspread. Shanna was surprised to find children's clothes still hanging in the closet. She closed it quickly without giving herself a chance to dwell on what it all meant. The second bedroom had belonged to her parents. It had a double bed with a brass frame. No clothing here—no real memories. She plunked her suitcase on the bed and began stashing her clothes in the small closet and antique chest of drawers. Going to her music box, she opened the lid, letting the sweet song of "Jesus Loves Me" fill the room as the tiny angel turned.

When she finished unpacking, she took her suitcases up to the loft to get them out of the way. The loft or attic, accessible via a ladder, made a third possible bedroom. It served as a storage area now. The boxes Shanna had shipped were stacked neatly against the wall. There was a large cedar chest, as well, and several other boxes. A heavy layer of dust covered the floor, except for the area leading from the three-foot-square loft opening to the boxes against the right wall. She was once again reminded of her promise to go through Elizabeth's effects—but not now. She was in no mood to open the door or the boxes to the memories she knew would be buried there.

Shanna hurried downstairs and back into the kitchen, where she quickly washed the cup she'd used and set it in a rack to dry. With everything put away and the cabin tidied, Shanna showered and slipped on a pale pink sweat suit, then wandered through the house looking for a way to turn on the heat.

Finding the thermostat, she turned it to sixty-eight degrees.

Without the solar heating the sun had provided, the room was growing cold. The north wall to the right of the window had a cozy floor-to-ceiling stone fireplace. Three logs, complete with kindling, waited in the grate. While lighting the fire, Shanna made a mental note to check into getting more firewood. She'd need to stock up for the winter.

The moment the thought entered her head, Shanna shook it away. What was she thinking? She'd be here a week—two at the most. She frowned. *If you don't stay here, then where? You can't go back to Morningsong.* "Well," she mused, "as Max would say, we'll just have to cross that bridge when we come to it."

Shanna fixed a salad and sat down in the window seat to eat. The bright afternoon sun had turned to deep orange. Scattered clouds hovered on the horizon, highlighted by the brilliant sky. Not a silver lining exactly, but cheery nonetheless.

"M-e-eow." Her feline visitor from earlier in the day jumped up beside her and sniffed at her food.

"Hello again. I forgot to ask Nancy about you." The cat dropped to the floor and wrapped her purring self around Shanna's leg. "You must be getting hungry. Want to go home?"

Shanna wondered how the cat had gotten in and where she'd been hiding all day. Setting her plate on the counter, she opened the door. The white fur ball stood in the entry, peered outside, then scurried back in. Shanna laughed. "All right. You win for now. But in the morning, it's back to Nancy's or wherever it is you belong."

Once she'd acquainted herself with the cabin's light switches and other things necessary for the night, Shanna picked up her old guitar, settled into the rocker, and began to play. The cat, as if on cue, curled up in the narrow space between the chair's arm and Shanna's thigh, resting its head on her lap. Soon its purrs added a percussion to the chords Shanna strummed.

The strings responded to her touch as they always did, coming to life in medleys she'd known since childhood. How often, she wondered, had she sat in this very room singing and listening to songs like "You

Are My Sunshine," "I Dream of Jeannie," "Goodnight Irene," and "Beautiful Brown Eyes." She caught and held a passing memory of herself as a little girl, laughing and singing while her daddy sang songs his daddy had taught him. The memory fled, leaving Shanna feeling warm and strangely comforted.

She began humming the notes to an unfamiliar song. Then came the words. "Home is a place you can go to." Shanna faltered. It had been a long time since a song had come to her like this. Yet the words hung in her mind like a gift from God, ready to be opened.

Home is a place you can go to…when no one seems to care. Like the Father it is waiting, ever present, ever there. Home is a place you can go to…when the tears don't seem to end. Like a long-lost friend it holds you and helps your soul to mend.

Shanna set her guitar aside and reached for her journal. There she jotted down the words. *Is it true?* she wondered. *Can coming home really help me?* Shanna closed her eyes and let the pen drop to the floor. The fire's warm glow and the kitten's gentle purr almost convinced her it could.

She stared into the fire, tears blurring the flames, absently petting the cat, which had inched onto her lap.

"Oh, Shanna, what a mess you've made of things. Marrying Joshua was the biggest mistake of them all. I was stupid to think it could ever work."

One question kept coming back like the ocean waves just beyond her window. Why couldn't she get over him? After all he had done to hurt her. After all they'd been through… But she still loved him. Like Romeo and Juliet, theirs was a relationship destined to end in tragedy.

"Maybe that's the answer. Maybe I should kill myself. That way Joshua would be free to marry Laurie, and I wouldn't need to worry about him or anything else anymore. There's not much of a future for me without my music." She sighed.

But was that really the answer? This wasn't the first time Shanna had entertained thoughts of suicide. She hadn't succumbed to the temptation then and doubted she would now. She'd been eighteen years old and pregnant. Losing the baby had almost driven her over the edge. Shanna fought against the memory at first, then let it come.

When Shanna first discovered she was pregnant, Elizabeth was furious. Shanna felt a strange mingling of fear and joy. In her tender young heart, she clung to the belief that Joshua still loved her. Now that she was having his baby, he'd come back. She would forgive him his indiscretions with Laurie Daniels. She was certain once he knew about the baby, he'd come to her and take his place as her husband and the father of their child. But her letters and phone calls went unanswered. Shanna was left to face the pregnancy alone.

At first Elizabeth insisted she have an abortion. "It's the only feasible way."

Shanna couldn't do that. The baby was a viable human life. She couldn't add to the tragedy by snuffing out the life of an innocent child. The baby was a part of her and Joshua, and even though she had made the mistake of allowing herself to become pregnant, she knew she'd never forgive herself if she took her mother's advice. Thankfully, Andrew backed up her decision. The situation was bad enough as it was.

"Let her have the child," Andrew told Elizabeth the day the three of them sat in the library discussing what should be done.

"Impossible. Think what this kind of scandal would do to her career."

"These days it hardly matters, but you're right; we can't take that chance. I'll pay for the expenses," Andrew offered. "We'll make certain no one ever finds out about it."

Her mother backed down almost immediately. For Elizabeth, money was the answer to nearly everything. "It will mean going away for a while. Perhaps Europe."

"Fine. Go anywhere you like. I'll take care of the medical care and legal aspects regarding the adoption as well. I know people I can trust to keep this quiet."

Elizabeth agreed.

Shanna cowered in her chair, grateful the baby's life would be spared but terrified of what lay ahead. She was glad Andrew and her mother were taking care of the details.

For the few prenatal visits to a nurse practitioner in Nashville and the eventual delivery, she became Jennifer Page. During the last trimester, when she could no longer hide her pregnancy, Shanna and Elizabeth supposedly went to Europe but, in fact, rented a condo in Palm Springs. There, in the sterile, air-conditioned atmosphere, Shanna sat day after day, playing her guitar, singing, and composing songs—most of which were too personal and depressing to share with the world.

Nearly every day Elizabeth would remind her of how fortunate she was to have people like her and Andrew taking care of her and keeping the scandal out of the papers. Every day Elizabeth would assure her that she had Shanna's best interests at heart. "I know you better than you know yourself, darling," she'd say. "You are definitely not the motherly type."

The plan was for Shanna to have the baby at home with a midwife who knew her only as Jennifer Page. Shanna wore no makeup and hardly looked like the Shanna O'Brian who graced the stage and television screen. She looked thin and gaunt, gaining little if any extra weight during the pregnancy.

Two weeks after the delivery, she and Elizabeth would return to Morningsong and her career. As far as the rest of the world knew, Shanna was vacationing in Europe, getting some rest after a grueling work schedule.

Shanna hated being pregnant. More than that, she hated the deception and the secrecy. Every day she prayed for Joshua to come back—to answer her letters or call. He never did. Knowing she'd eventually have to give up the baby, she fought desperately against the attachment she felt for the life growing inside her.

After she gave birth, the midwife placed the baby on her belly. In those few seconds, Shanna fell deeply in love with the tiny, red infant.

It lay kicking and screaming, and Shanna wanted nothing more than to hold and comfort him, to let him suckle at her sore and leaking breasts. Shanna reached for him, but Elizabeth grabbed her hands and held them firm. "Lay back and rest, darling. The nurse will take care of him."

The midwife clamped the cord and handed the baby off to a waiting nurse who wrapped him up and carried him out of the bedroom.

"No, don't take him, please. I want to see him. Please." Shanna's cries went unheeded. She tried to sit up, but exhaustion forced her head back to the pillow.

"Hush," Elizabeth cooed, brushing the hair from Shanna's perspiring forehead.

"Just let me hold him for a minute, please."

"It's better you don't. We don't want you becoming too attached." Turning to the midwife, she said, "Can't you give her something to settle down?"

"I don't need that. I need my baby."

"Get her something now!" Elizabeth demanded between gritted teeth.

The midwife nodded and minutes later came back with a syringe.

"No, don't." Shanna had no energy to fight and managed only a whimper when the needle sank into her hip.

"I can't do this, Mother, please. I want my baby."

"No!" Elizabeth snapped. "It's too late for that. Have you forgotten who the father is? You've signed the papers. It's for the best, darling. Andrew will see that he gets a good home. You are in no position to care for a child."

Shanna fought against the drug, struggling to stay awake. Her body refused to cooperate, and all she could do was weep until she faded into nothingness. When she woke up, everyone but Elizabeth was gone.

Over the next few days she existed in a drugged stupor. Medication numbed the pain, and whenever Shanna asked about the baby,

Elizabeth gave her a sedative. Where and how she got the medication, Shanna didn't know. She finally stopped asking. Maybe it was at that point she stopped living.

Shanna wrapped her arms around herself and rocked. Though she'd convinced herself she'd done the right thing, the baby haunted her dreams with as much regularity as Joshua did. Every time she saw a child, she wondered about her little boy. Did the baby look like her or Joshua? What had the adoptive parents named him? Where did they live? Several times she'd thought about trying to find the child. Elizabeth had always discouraged her. *"What would be the point?"* she'd say. *"His adoptive parents are good people. Trying to get him back now would break their hearts, and it wouldn't be good for the boy."* She was right, of course. Elizabeth was always right. A search would only cause more heartache in the end.

Shanna comforted herself with the thought that someday the child might want to know who his birth parents were. It happened often these days. She imagined herself looking into her child's face and catching a glimpse of herself or Joshua. Maybe someday…

Tossing words heavenward, she said, "Please don't make me wait that long. If there's any way…" Her empty arms ached with the need to hold her baby. An anguished sob escaped her lips. "Oh, God, why does it have to hurt so much?"

She rocked harder, willing the pain to go away. One thing she knew for certain. If healing were ever going to come, she would need to see her little boy again. Maybe just knowing the child was healthy and well cared for would help. She only hoped Elizabeth and Andrew had gone through the proper channels for adoption and that Elizabeth hadn't sold the child on the black market or somehow gotten rid of it. No, she couldn't let herself think that. Her mother may have been ruthless at times, but she wouldn't…she couldn't have been that inhuman. Besides, Andrew had promised to make certain the child was adopted by a responsible family.

Shanna set the cat aside and hoisted herself out of the rocker. "I'm going to do it," she said aloud. "Somehow, some way, I'm going to find my baby."

She turned out the lights and headed for bed, ignoring her own haunting questions. *What if you do find your child, Shanna O'Brian? What are you going to do then?*

Chapter Nineteen

Jim Broadman wanted to stay at the Sheraton but figured it might be better to lay low after spotting the FBI agent there. He doubted the agent would recognize him from the plane, but better to be safe. He'd chucked his plan to kill the fed. There were too many guards around. Didn't see much sense in it now, anyway. Jim left the hotel at ten o'clock Wednesday morning and took the bus downtown, where he checked in to the Starlight Motel. Once he'd settled in, he walked around the neighborhood, past the adult bookstore, the topless bar, and a couple of art galleries, then went into a tavern, where he ordered a beer and found a pay phone.

"Did you find her?" The voice on the other end of the line sounded uptight, and Jim wondered if maybe things weren't going so good.

"Yeah, I found her. So did the FBI."

"What?"

"Hey, it ain't no big deal. An agent got on the plane with her in Memphis and checked into the same hotel. I couldn't get near her."

"How do you know he's FBI? What did he do, flash around a badge?"

"Yeah, as a matter of fact he did. After she bought a ticket in Memphis, he showed the ticket agent his badge. He got on her flight and stuck close to her like dirt to a turnip. But don't worry. I got what I wanted. Well, not the evidence, but I think I know where she's stashed it. I plan on heading out that way tomorrow."

"What about the fed? If he's tagging around after her, we'll never get close enough to find out what she's got."

"She ditched him, but I know right where she's headed." Jim related the details of his jewelry heist and the address he'd lifted from the room.

"All right. Just sit tight. I'm coming out there. Where are you?"

Jim gave him the name and address of the motel. "It ain't necessary for you to come all that way. I can handle this myself."

"Didn't say you couldn't. We have to talk, and I don't want to do it over the phone. Now, stay put until I give you the go-ahead. If the FBI agent spots you, you can bet he'll drag you in for questioning. We wouldn't want that, would we?"

"He's not going to find me."

"See that he doesn't."

Jim hung up, feeling frustrated and in need of another beer. What was the matter with the guy—didn't he trust him anymore?

Just after midnight, Jim paced the floor, drawing a deep drag of his cigarette. He'd been cooped up in this cheap motel for twelve hours too long. Except for meals and a couple of hours at the bar down the street, he'd stayed put. He didn't much like being put on hold. He'd already decided to wait a couple of days before following the O'Brian broad to the coast. That part he didn't mind. It was hanging around for further orders that bugged him. He probably shouldn't complain. He was getting good money for the work he'd been hired to do.

What he couldn't understand was why the boss had to see him in person. He normally kept a distance—didn't want to take the chance of people seeing them together. Of course, no one would know him out here.

Someone tapped on the connecting door to his room. He hesitated a moment, wondering if he'd heard right. The knock came again, harder this time. "Jim," a familiar voice said. "It's me, open up."

Jim grinned. Finally. Turning the knob, he pulled the door open and backed into his room. "So you finally made it," Jim said. "What took you so long?"

The boss barely acknowledged him. A deep frown creased his forehead. "Where is Shanna's address?"

Jim shrugged aside the boss's lousy attitude and went to the dresser. He tore off the top sheet of the note pad and tossed the pad back on the dresser, next to the phone. "It's right here. I told you there was nothing to worry about. You didn't have to..." Jim turned around, his gaze dropping to the gun his boss was holding—pointing—at him. "Hey, what are you doing—?"

The gun went off, a silencer muffling the blast, making it sound less deadly than it was. Shocked, Jim staggered back, clutching his chest. He looked down at the hole in his shirt and the blood slowly leaking out if it. Another shot. The bullet sliced the side of his neck. He grabbed for his throat; his hand came away wet and bloody. His last breath exploded in rage. He dove for his assailant, landing just short of the target. Blood splattered on the dirty beige carpet and on the boss's expensive leather boots.

~

Donovan Hill had reached another dead end. Literally. He'd spent the better part of two days looking for Shanna O'Brian. Finally last night he had gotten a lead on where she might have gone. A call to the sheriff in Watson County, Tennessee, confirmed that Donovan wasn't the only one looking for Shanna. Sheriff Nate Kerns thought she might be headed for the coast to a place where she'd lived the first six years of her life. Her mother had still owned the house when she died, and Shanna inherited it.

Donovan had been writing down the address when he spotted a familiar face on the local news program. That face was what had brought him to the morgue.

Shelly Graham, the medical examiner, unzipped the body bag, exposing the corpse's head, neck, and chest. "Well, here he is."

Donovan grimaced. "Poor guy never had a chance."

"Not much. Took a bullet in the heart—another severed his carotid artery. Do you know him?"

"Not his name, but I've seen him three times in the last few days." He suspected the guy had been following Shanna and was probably the one responsible for breaking into her room. For some reason Shanna O'Brian had gone into hiding. Maybe she knew the guy had been stalking her. Or maybe she had something to hide. Donovan was still miffed about her giving him the slip, but he could understand her motive if she was frightened and running from this goon. He looked forward to telling her she wouldn't need to worry about him anymore. Of course, she might already know that. It was entirely possible she'd killed the man herself.

Though Donovan had a hard time seeing Shanna as a killer, he wouldn't rule it out—not now. Taking off the way she had gave him cause to believe she might not be as innocent as she looked.

"Where?"

"What?" Donovan pulled his gaze from the body to the medical examiner.

"Where did you see him?"

"Oh, sorry. I remember seeing him at the airport in Memphis. He was on the same flight I took. I saw him again in the lobby of the Sheraton Hotel Tuesday night. The news anchor said his body was found in a different motel—Star something."

"The Starlight Motel—downtown."

"Have you ID'd him yet?"

"That was the easy part. Prints are on file. His name is Jim Broadman. A few arrests for petty theft back in Nashville. Not too impressive."

"Theft, huh? Didn't by any chance find some jewelry on him, did you?"

"As a matter of fact, we did. In his suitcase. We think it might belong to a woman whose jewelry was taken at the Sheraton a couple of nights ago. Woman registered under the name Tracy Monroe." The attractive blonde scrutinized Donovan before continuing. "You had dinner with her the night of the burglary." Her tone held a hint of accusation, as though she knew something she wasn't telling him.

"Yes. We were seatmates on the plane and…" He shrugged. "Since neither of us felt like eating alone…"

"So the Memphis connection here…should we be looking at that? If Broadman was following her and stole her jewelry, could she have killed him?"

Donovan's gaze met her unfaltering blue one. "It's possible but not likely. She left the hotel a good twenty-four hours before this thug turned up dead." At that point he should have revealed Shanna's real identity but couldn't see exposing the singer to a ruthless pack of press hounds—especially if she turned out to be innocent. He wouldn't name her as a suspect unless or until he had proof.

"She could have come back."

"I don't think so."

"What about you, Mr. Hill? Where do you fit into all this?" Shelly asked.

He showed her his badge. "FBI. Came out on a business trip."

"I see. And which one were you following? The woman? Or"—she zipped up the bag containing Jim Broadman's body and shoved the rack back into the cooler—"him?"

He flashed her a grin and folded his arms. "What's with the interrogation, Doc?"

"I'm thorough. And I don't like officers—regardless of what

department they work for—withholding what could be crucial information. We have the woman's comparison prints on file from the burglary. We have no prints on file for her. That's not unusual in itself."

Dr. Graham walked out of the morgue and into an office two doors down the hall. Donovan followed. He knew exactly where the conversation was going. There would be prints on file for Shanna. The sheriff handling Elizabeth O'Brian's murder case would have taken comparison prints. Sooner or later they'd find a match. Judging from the M.E.'s smug demeanor, they already had.

Picking up a file folder from her cluttered desk, Shelly thumbed through it, then fixed her steady gaze on him again. "Do you have any idea who you had dinner with Tuesday night, Mr. Hill?"

"Why do I get the feeling you're about to tell me?"

"Let's not play games, OK? There's a definite connection here between your case and this one. I can understand your hesitation. You don't want our findings leaked to the press prematurely. Neither do I. If we work together on this, we'll both benefit and save valuable time and taxpayers' money. And we may save Shanna O'Brian a lot of embarrassing and certainly damaging publicity. I happen to be a big fan of hers. I'd hate to see her get hurt—especially if she's as innocent as you seem to believe."

The decision wasn't a hard one. He liked the idea of exchanging information with Shelly Graham. "I'm all yours," he said finally. "But only if you'll let me buy you coffee."

She arched an eyebrow and tossed him a crooked grin. "Not a chance. I buy or it's no deal."

He held up his hands in mock surrender. "Hey, no arguments from me."

Over coffee Donovan explained the case involving Elizabeth O'Brian's suspicious death and the piracy of several Morningsong artists. "Piracy is pretty common these days. Usually someone with connections who has access to original tapes feeds them to someone on the outside. The records are produced in Mexico, South America,

China—wherever they can get cheap labor—then shipped back into the States and sold on the black market."

"So you think Elizabeth O'Brian was the insider?"

Shelly sipped her Starbucks latte, cradling the mug in her small hands. Hands, Donovan thought, that were much too pretty and delicate to be doing the kind of work she did.

He moved his gaze to her face. That was nice too. She had a cute nose that curved up at the tip, and angel blue eyes. She wore a suit—the kind fashion magazines touted as a power suit. Maybe it worked; she certainly seemed to hold a good deal of power over him. He cleared his throat. "I know Elizabeth was involved somehow, and the more I learn about the woman, the more convinced I am her death was made to look like a suicide. I think whoever she fed the original tapes to ordered a hit on her."

"Why?"

"Who knows? Maybe she was getting greedy. Maybe she threatened to go to the cops."

"Do you think Shanna was in on it?"

"I doubt it. She seemed surprised when I told her about the piracy."

"And you believe her? Even though she gave you the slip?"

"Yeah. I am planning to track her down, though. There's just one thing that's got me worried."

"What's that?"

"Jim was working for somebody. I don't think he followed her all the way from Memphis just to take her jewelry—it wasn't worth all that much."

"Which means he was after something else."

"Right. Shanna claimed nothing else was missing. So what's this guy looking for? What does Shanna have that he wanted? And did he find it?"

"The bigger question here is, who killed him and why? We're certain the victim knew his assailant. There's no sign of forced entry. No weapon at the scene. From the blood spatters, we got a partial shoe print on the carpet and tracked it to the adjoining room. Found blood evidence in the bathroom—probably cleaned up there."

"Any prints?"

"One. After he was shot, Broadman apparently lunged at his killer. The killer grabbed the table. Though the surface was wiped clean of prints, we got a nice, clear thumbprint from the underside of the table."

"A professional hit?"

"Could be. Looks like it was premeditated. The guy checked in to the room next-door under the name of John Nelson. Paid cash. Clerk wasn't much help. He was average looking, wearing a cowboy hat, boots, and jeans."

"That's it?"

"'Fraid so. Apparently the clerk was more interested in his television set than his guests."

"Anything else?"

She frowned. "We found a partial address the victim had written on a pad by the phone. The pad was from the Sheraton hotel, which is how we made the connection to the jewelry and Shanna. The original note was gone, but we were able to get most of it from the indentation on the next page."

"Do you have it?"

"Not with me. But I remember most of it. Ocean Park—on the Washington Coast. It was 235 something Sand Dollar Lane."

Donovan covered his eyes and dragged a hand down his face. "That's the address the Watson County Sheriff gave me. Broadman must have found it in Shanna's room. I can't believe I didn't realize that until now. Broadman must have copied it from her appointment book and planned to go there later."

"The note was not on his person or in the room."

Donovan shook his head. "Then whoever killed Broadman must have it."

"Do you think that's where Shanna has gone?"

"I'm betting on it."

Their gazes locked in understanding. "I wouldn't worry too much about your singer, Mr. Hill," Shelly said. "The homicide investigator on the case has either gone up there himself or he's asked an officer there to check on the address. If she's there, they'll keep an eye on her."

"We'd better hope that's the case."

Chapter Twenty

"Nancy!" Shanna greeted her neighbor a few minutes before ten. "Thanks for coming."

"I hope you have that coffee ready. I'm sure needing it." She groaned and collapsed on the step.

"What have you been doing?" Shanna asked. "You look like you've done battle with a dirt devil and lost."

"Working in my garden, weeding, and getting stuff ready for winter." Nancy pulled off her headband, revealing a clean patch of skin beneath it. She wore a green plaid flannel shirt that no self-respecting thrift shop would take. Her faded jeans had mud caked on the knees. "Hope you don't mind—couldn't see taking a shower and changing when I have to go right back to it."

"Oh no, I didn't mean—you look…comfortable in…dirt."

"Maybe we could start a new trend—the grungy look."

"I think that's already been done." Shanna looped her arm around the post at the top of the porch steps. "Would you like to wash up?"

"Already did—my hands, at least." Nancy grimaced as she examined her fingernails. "Going to have to bleach these babies."

Since Nancy didn't want to track dirt into the house, Shanna brought coffee and muffins she'd picked up on her trip into town that morning out on the porch.

"Ahh. Poppy seed—my favorite." Nancy closed her eyes as she munched a piece. Chasing the muffin with coffee she asked, "Where's your car?"

"It was a rental. I turned it back in this morning." Afraid Donovan, or someone else, might be able to trace her, Shanna had taken the forty-five-minute drive over to Astoria, across the Columbia River in Oregon, early that morning. "I took a taxi back and had them drop me off at the Sand Dunes Restaurant. While I was having breakfast and trying to figure out how to get back home, I found an ad for a pickup, called the guy, he met me at the restaurant, and I bought it."

"Fast worker." Nancy peered at the empty driveway. "Don't tell me, they have this new invisible paint. Part of your disguise?"

Shanna laughed. "Actually, it's a periwinkle blue. It's used and the owner is going to fix a couple of things and bring it to me this afternoon."

Nancy eyed her curiously over her coffee. "You know, you're different than I thought you'd be."

"What do you mean?" Shanna flushed under her scrutiny.

"You're much more—approachable. Whenever I've seen you on television, you seem so controlled. In person you're—you know—like real people."

Shanna stared at a knothole in the porch. Some of the wood was rotting. It would need to be replaced soon. "It's always been difficult for me to relax and be myself on stage or television. Half the time I'm not even sure who I am." She sat up straighter. "Don't get me wrong. I love performing. Usually I'm more comfortable onstage than I am anywhere else. I guess I almost always feel like I have to perform or be on guard. Sitting here with you, I feel different. There's something about you..."

"Maybe it's the dirt."

Shanna laughed. "Maybe."

Nancy patted Shanna's knee. "You don't have to put on a show for folks around here."

"I'm beginning to see that. Jake—the guy I'm buying the truck from—didn't seem at all impressed. In fact, I don't think he recognized my name."

Nancy chuckled. "The only thing that would impress old Jake would be a fifty-pound Chinook or a six-pack of beer."

"Chinook? Isn't that the name of a town I went through to get to Astoria?"

She nodded. "It's also a type of salmon."

"Nancy," Shanna began, "I wonder..."

"Well, spit it out, sweetie. Do you need a favor, a ride somewhere?"

"I was just going to ask if anyone has been living in the cabin. It's so well stocked and...well, it looks lived in."

"I was afraid you might notice that. Elizabeth would have had a tizzy fit if she'd found out. You might not be too thrilled, either."

"I thought as much. You've been renting it out. It's OK, really. I mean, it looks wonderful and it's much too nice to have sitting vacant all the time."

"Actually, no, Shanna. We've never rented it out. Elizabeth didn't want that." She took a long sip of coffee. "There's a man, a friend, who comes down every so often. He loves the place and, well, when he asked if it would be OK if he stayed a few days, I couldn't refuse him."

"It's OK, Nancy, really. I'm just glad someone's gotten some use out of it."

Nancy nodded. "I think he really needed it. The beach is so therapeutic." She gave Shanna an expectant look, as though she wanted to say more but didn't.

"Therapeutic," Shanna echoed. "I think that's true. I already feel better, and I've been here less than twenty-four hours."

"I'm glad." Nancy set the cup on the wicker coffee table and stood. "I'd best get back to work. If you ever feel like weeding, come on over. Oh, and if you have any questions, I'll be around all day."

"I did want to ask you a couple of things."

"Shoot." Nancy turned and sank onto the top step, leaning her back against the railing.

"There's a little white kitten that's been hanging around. Any idea who he belongs to?"

"Ah, that's Snowball. She's a stinker, that one. Runt of the litter but wild as they come. She's yours if you want her—or I should say, if she wants you. Cats tend to select their owners."

"I'd like that. How long have you lived here?" Shanna sat on the steps opposite her.

"Oh my. Let's see—twenty-five years at least."

"So you were here when I was little."

"Yes." An odd look crossed her features. "Didn't your mama ever tell you about that?"

Shanna shook her head. "Mother didn't like to talk about the time we lived here. I think it upset her too much to remember how my father was. Too many bad memories, I suppose."

"That's unfortunate. There were a lot of good memories in this house too. One of the best was the night you were born." Nancy's eyes lit up as her gaze met Shanna's.

"You were here?"

"Honey, I was not only here, I delivered you."

"You—you're kidding."

"I'm not." Nancy's gaze drifted over her. "I'll never forget it. We were right in the middle of the most awful squall. Winds gusting eighty to ninety miles an hour. We'd been without power all day. Your mother went into labor around dinnertime. Problem was, we couldn't get out to get her to the hospital. A tree had fallen across the driveway just east of where ours forks off. Neither of us could get out."

"Weren't there other neighbors?"

"At that time the nearest neighbor was about a mile away. Elizabeth couldn't walk that far. Henry and Mike tried to clear away the tree, but they didn't make it in time. Finally decided they'd better hike out and see if they could find the doctor. Storm or no, you weren't waiting around another minute."

"So I was born here? In the cabin?"

"You bet. I'd delivered a baby before and had a couple of kids of my own, but we were all pretty scared. I guess what frightened me most was whether or not you'd need medical attention. Elizabeth didn't take well to pregnancy and she'd been sickly."

"Well, I'm here, so it must have worked out OK."

"Wonderful." Nancy tipped her head, her gaze teary. "I'll never forget catching you in my hands and holding you. By the time the men came back with Dr. Stephens, you were already an hour old and suckling like you were born to it. And your daddy. Oh, honey, he was so proud of you. Henry and I were too. I probably took care of you as much or more than your mother did those first few years until Elizabeth…until you moved away."

"That must be why I feel so comfortable with you," Shanna said. "I used to call you Aunt Nanny, didn't I?"

"Yes. I'm surprised you remember."

"It's the house. I get these little pictures sometimes." Shanna hugged her knees, wanting to know more. "Did my father live here very long after he and my mother split up?"

"No. He stayed for a couple of years. We still keep in touch, but—"

"What did you say?" Shanna interrupted, certain she hadn't heard right.

"We keep in touch—"

Shanna found it hard to breathe. "As in present tense? Are you telling me my father is still alive?"

"Yes, of course. Didn't you know?"

"My mother told me he was dead." Shanna rubbed her neck, unable to grasp the notion that her father might still be alive. "I don't understand. There must be some mistake. Are you sure?"

"Very sure."

"I can't believe Elizabeth would lie to me about him." Shanna sprang to her feet and paced across the porch. "It's not possible. It can't be."

"Oh, sweetie, I'm so sorry. No wonder Mike…" She sighed. "Maybe she had her reasons. Mike was an alcoholic at the time…"

Shanna bit her lip. "Right. Mother always had her reasons. Probably got tired of my asking about him." Shanna ran her hands through her hair. She could hardly catch her breath. Her father was still alive.

Nancy folded her hands and pressed them against her mouth, tipping her head down, as if in prayer.

"Do you have a number—an address where I can reach him?" Shanna regretted the words as soon as she spoke them. Her father was an alcoholic. He'd been a terrible father, never calling, never remembering her birthdays or Christmas. She didn't want to see him—yet she did. But she couldn't.

"I'm sure he'd love to see you. I'll see if I can track him down. I'd have to call him, see if it's OK."

"No!" She startled herself with her sharp retort. "Don't bother. It's been too long. He probably doesn't want to see me. After all, he hasn't tried to contact me all these years. It's not as though I'm invisible."

"Oh, but he did try, Shanna. Maybe Elizabeth—"

"Wouldn't let him near me? You're probably right. She was always very protective of me. But she's been dead for six months. Six months, Nancy. And he had to have known—it was all over the papers. He could have contacted me if he'd wanted to." She sighed. "It's better to leave it alone."

"Shanna, sweetie, I know how hurtful this must be for you. I don't know what your mother told you, and I don't know why Mike hasn't been in touch, but don't judge him too harshly. At least not until you've heard his side of the story."

Shanna tipped her head back. "I suppose you're right, but I don't think I could handle seeing him right now. I need to think this through. Please don't contact him. Not yet. I don't expect you to understand, but I need to get used to the idea of him being alive. Maybe later on I can think about talking to him."

"I understand. More than you know." Nancy rose again, dusted off her jeans, and started back down the stairs. "My door's always open, honey. Anytime you want to talk."

"Thanks." This time Shanna let her go.

She sat on the steps for several minutes letting the cool ocean breeze fan her warm face and feather her hair. So many thoughts clamored for attention; Shanna wanted to shut and bolt the door on all of them. Why had Elizabeth lied about her father's death? How could she have been so cruel? *She was protecting you.* Shanna answered her own question. But at what cost? Shanna closed her eyes, resting her head on her folded arms. "Oh, Mother, what have you done?"

~

In the first few years at Morningsong, Shanna entertained dreams of her parents being reunited. She desperately missed her father. Though Elizabeth had repeatedly called him a loser—a good-for-nothing—Shanna could never quite believe that. Rather, she clung to the memory of Mike O'Brian singing her to sleep, carrying her on his shoulders, and drinking her pretend tea.

"Could we invite Daddy to my party?" Shanna asked on her twelfth birthday.

Elizabeth, who'd just made arrangements with a caterer, glared at her. "Don't be ridiculous."

"But—"

"No!" Elizabeth took a deep breath and grasped Shanna's shoulders. "When are you going to get it through your thick skull that your father doesn't want you?"

"That's not true—he loves me."

"You don't need the likes of him. You have me. I've given you everything you could possibly need. Isn't that enough?"

"I...I just want to see him."

Elizabeth moved away from her daughter and lowered herself into a straight-back chair. Her voice gentle now, she said, "Shanna, I know this is difficult for you to understand, but having your father come here would be a big mistake. He's not a nice man, and he could ruin your career. You'd have to stop singing. You wouldn't want that, would you?"

Shanna didn't know how to answer. Yes, she wanted to see her father. No, she didn't want to stop singing. She didn't understand. "M-maybe we could go see him."

"Absolutely not!" Elizabeth stood again and walked to the window. Gazing at some point in the distant hills, she said, "I didn't want to tell you this before, Shanna. I was afraid it might upset you too much." Her shoulders rose in an exaggerated sigh. Turning back around to face Shanna, she said, "I suppose it's time you knew the truth so you can stop this ridiculous patter about seeing him again. Your father chose alcohol over you and me. He didn't want us around, and now—it's too late."

"What do you mean, too late?" Shanna's heart skittered to a stop.

"He's dead, Shanna. Drank himself to death. He will never be at your parties, and you will never see him again."

Tears welled up in Shanna's eyes.

"It's over, Shanna, and it's for the best." Elizabeth settled an arm around Shanna's shoulders. "We won't ever need to have this discussion again. Now, I want you to go into the bathroom and wash your face. No more tears, OK?"

"Why, Mother? How could you have lied to me like that?"

"It was for your own good." Shanna could almost hear her mother's response.

Was it? Or had Elizabeth just grown tired of Shanna's questions? Had she acted out of love or out of jealousy and anger? Shanna had never thought to question it. Parents, after all, didn't lie.

At the time, Shanna had been devastated. She hadn't wanted to go to her party. But she did because Elizabeth insisted. She dried her tears, washed her face, and never mentioned her father to Elizabeth again.

OK, Shanna rationalized, Elizabeth had lied about his death, but that didn't erase the cold, hard facts. Mike O'Brian had chosen booze over his family. And he hadn't tried to contact Shanna after Elizabeth's death. Once again, she went into the bathroom and washed away the tears.

Shanna was just coming out of the bathroom when she heard the crunch of gravel and a car's engine. Probably Jake with her pickup. She hurried outside, wondering what had possessed her to buy the vehicle in the first place. It had seemed a good idea at the time. But what in the world was she going to do with it when she had to leave?

The car came up over the hill and ground to a halt in her driveway. It wasn't Jake or the periwinkle blue truck. It was a dark green Pacific County Sheriff's car, and the deputy stepping out of it looked like he'd been eating nails. He was about fifty, with graying hair and of medium height and a stocky build. The gun holster rode low around his middle. He straightened and hitched up his holster, sucking in his gut and expanding his chest. When he exhaled, everything settled back to where it had been. His stern expression changed the moment he saw her. Unfortunately, his demeanor did little to calm the anxiety shooting through Shanna's veins.

A wide grin split his face, revealing a perfect set of teeth. "I'm Undersheriff Turner. I take it you're Shanna O'Brian."

"Depends." She heaved an exaggerated sigh. "If you're here on official business, I suppose I have to be, but if it's anything else—you see, Sheriff, I'm on vacation. And I'd just as soon not let anyone know I'm here."

"You don't need to worry none about that. We'll try to respect your privacy." He turned serious again. "I'm sorry to trouble you, ma'am, but I got a call from the police in Portland this morning asking me to track you down."

She frowned. "How did you know to come here? No one has this address."

"Apparently they do. I was just asked to check the place out."

"Why?" Joshua must have gone to the authorities. "Did Joshua Morgan send you?"

"No." His frown deepened. "That name didn't come up."

"Then what are you doing here?"

"I'll get to that. First I need to show you a couple of photos and ask some questions."

"Would you like to come inside?"

"Sure."

Shanna showed him in and pulled out a chair at the kitchen table. "Do you drink coffee?"

"Yeah, that would be great."

Retrieving two clean cups, she poured him coffee and refilled her tea. Sheriff Turner pulled papers out of a manila envelope and placed one on top of the other on the table's oak surface.

Shanna handed him a cup, trying not to let her shaking hands betray her growing unease. Slipping into the chair opposite him, she asked, "Are these the pictures you want me to look at?"

"Yes." He slipped the bottom one out and turned it around so she could see it. "Do you recognize this jewelry?"

Shanna examined the picture. It was a fax and not the best quality, but she recognized it. "Yes, it's mine. The brooch is one my mother left me when she died. It was stolen out of my hotel room in Portland. Did they catch the guy who did it?" Shanna relaxed a little.

"Not exactly. I need to show you another picture—a mug shot, actually." He slid the photo around. "Do you recognize this man?"

She covered her mouth and closed her eyes, but the image of the man remained in her mind. Clearing her throat, she nodded. It was the man she'd seen at the elevators. "H-he was at the hotel where I stayed night before last." She turned the picture over and pushed it back to him. "Is he the one who broke into my room? You said they didn't catch him."

"They didn't—the guy turned up dead in a motel downtown this morning. He'd been murdered. The police found your jewelry and this address in his room."

"My address? What was it doing there?" She clutched her stomach as the realization hit. He must have found it when he searched her room. Her intuition about not getting into the elevator had been right. "I think I'm going to be sick."

Shanna made it to the bathroom and heaved everything she'd eaten that morning. After a few minutes the sheriff rapped on the door. "Ms. O'Brian. You OK in there?"

"Yes—I'm all right," she gasped. "Just give me a minute to clean up."

Shanna washed her face, willing the spasms in her stomach to stop. That horrible man had been in her room and found the address to her house. If someone hadn't killed him, he might have found her here. She'd have been alone. No FBI agent to run to. The thought of what might have happened made her stomach lurch again.

She rinsed out the washcloth with cold water and pressed it to her face. *You're safe now,* Shanna told herself. *He's dead. He can't hurt you anymore.* But was she really safe? If that horrid man knew about her cabin, did others as well?

Chapter Twenty-One

Shanna willed herself to calm down, much as she did before a show. *Deep breaths. Muscles relax.* Rational thought eventually replaced the panic. Finally she was ready to face the sheriff again.

"I'm sorry to have upset you." Sheriff Tucker stood when she entered the room.

"No need to apologize." She sat down at the table again. "I…it's just so frightening to think how close…" No, she wasn't going to think about the horror of what might have been. She needed instead to concentrate on the fact that he was no longer a threat. "You said he'd been murdered?"

"Yes—last night. Shot at close range."

"Do you know who or why?"

"No, I'm afraid I don't have much information yet. I was just asked to check out the address. And ask you some questions."

He knew more than he was letting on, but Shanna let it go. "I'm not sure I can help you. I didn't know the man personally."

"Can you tell me where you were last night?"

So that was it. "Am I a suspect?"

"Not necessarily, but I have to ask."

He was handing her a line, but she flashed him a grateful smile anyway. "I was here. Asleep." Her gaze, steady now, met his. "I didn't kill him."

"You were in Portland recently," he asserted. "And you did have contact with him."

Shanna shuddered. "I wouldn't say I had contact. We were both on the second floor waiting for an elevator—I didn't get on. Um…there was something unnerving about him—the way he looked at me. I…I made an excuse and started to go back to my room."

"Did you see him after that?"

"No. When I came back from dinner, my room had been broken into. I didn't know it was him. After the police left, I couldn't stay there. I was afraid he might come back. All I could think about was getting away from that place and—that room."

He gave her a sympathetic look. "You could have gotten another room."

"Yes, I suppose I could have." Shanna opted not to tell him she was also escaping the FBI agent. Somehow she doubted he'd understand that. "I'm not sure it would have made a difference. I left Portland around midnight Tuesday night—or rather Wednesday morning. I was afraid. When I left the hotel, I drove straight through to Long Beach. Checked into a hotel around 3 A.M., slept a few hours, and came here."

"Which hotel?"

Shanna rubbed her forehead. "Edge or Light something. It was on the beach and there was a restaurant on the top floor."

"That would be the Edgewater Inn. The Lightship restaurant. One of my wife's favorite places to eat."

"Yes, well, they can verify I was there, and Nancy, from next-door, knows I was here. Except—"

"Except…" He waited for her to continue.

"You said he was killed last night?"

"Right."

"I just realized I don't have an alibi after midnight, Sheriff." She picked at the frayed edge of a place mat. "I saw Nancy for a short while yesterday and not again until ten this morning. I dropped my rental car off in Astoria at eight this morning. I have no proof that I didn't drive to Portland last night, kill that awful man, and drive back. I didn't do it, of course, but..."

"Why were you taking your car back so early in the morning?"

"I wanted to get rid of it as quickly as possible. It would be too easy to locate me through the car rental agency. I thought I'd gotten away from the hotel without being seen but wanted to be sure. It never occurred to me the thief might have gotten my address."

"Well, let's hope this guy's death is the end of it. I don't know the details about the investigation. I'll have to let them know I found you and talked to you. The main concern was that you were unharmed. They may have more questions. One thing for sure, you don't need to worry about this guy anymore." Sheriff Tucker picked up the photos and tucked them in the envelope, then pushed back his chair.

"I appreciate your coming by, Sheriff. You'll let me know if you hear anything more about the case, won't you? And maybe find out when I can get my jewelry back?"

"You can count on it." He stepped out onto the porch. "It's been nice meeting you, Ms. O'Brian. You're much prettier in person—not that you aren't on television. My wife will be tickled I got to talk to you."

"Um, Sheriff, tell her not to mention to anyone that I'm here."

"Gotcha."

She waved as he got in his car, then ducked back inside. The encounter had left her weak and shaken. What had she gotten herself into?

"Oh, Lord." She collapsed in the rocker. "All I wanted to do was..." Shanna couldn't finish. The only words that came to mind were *run away.*

Shanna did run, but not far. Still in her sweats, she left the cabin and took the narrow path that wound through the dunes and out onto the beach. The wind had picked up, blowing from the north. Though the sun still shone, the chilling wind seemed to blow right through her. She ran into the wind, racing against its steady force. Lack of regular exercise and aching lungs soon slowed her to a walk. Within minutes what had been a cold wind became a welcoming one as her body heat rose.

With every step, the troubles she'd brought with her faded in their intensity. Caught up in the beauty of the day, the flight of sea gulls, and the swift-footed shore birds racing the waves, Shanna sang of freedom and sunny days. She performed only for the waves, which responded in thunderous applause. She turned back at the Ocean Park beach approach, and with the wind at her back, jogged and walked back toward the cabin. Instead of returning to the house, Shanna left her shoes and socks in the dry sand, pulled up the bottoms of her sweatpants, and headed for the surf. She couldn't remember feeling so unencumbered since before her parents had split up. For the next hour Shanna played, jumped waves, collected sand dollars, and built a forest of sand trees by dribbling watery sand in cone shapes.

Finally, wet, cold, and hungry, Shanna picked up her shoes and socks and made her way back to the cozy little cabin. She could barely make out the roof and blue trim from the shore, but as she crested the first sand dune she could see a number of houses. Just south was Nancy and Henry's place, a two-story angular home with a turquoise tile roof. A short distance away was a large new complex built closer to the ocean. Condominiums maybe. Houses and condos dotted the coastline for as far as she could see. And she owned one of them. A giggle bubbled up from somewhere inside her. Shanna tipped her head back. "Thank You, God. What a wonderful place. I don't know what possessed Mother to keep it all these years, but I'm so glad she did. And thank You, too, for protecting me from that terrible man."

After a leisurely lunch of chicken noodle soup and a salad, Shanna went outside to pull weeds and get reacquainted with the old place she used to call home. By midafternoon Shanna had pulled most of the weeds in the various flower gardens and was sitting on the floor in the middle of the small, dilapidated shed she'd once called a playhouse.

Sunlight filtered in through cracks in the shake ceiling and walls. Shreds of what had once been sheer white curtains still hung around the windows. They fluttered now in the wind, dancing like ghosts. Off to one side stood a small wooden table and chair, covered in cobwebs. Pieces of chipped bone china cups and saucers lay on the dirt floor. In her hands she held a porcelain doll. It stared at Shanna with its one remaining eye. A quarter of her face was broken, leaving a gaping black hole. Shanna covered the hole with her left hand and soothed back the matted brown hair with her right, trying to remember what had happened to it.

"Shanna?" Nancy called from somewhere close-by.

"I'm here—in the playhouse."

A few seconds later Nancy ducked inside the three-foot-high opening. "Oh, there you are. What's wrong, sweetie? Why are you crying?"

"I don't know. This place makes me feel so sad." She held up the doll. "Do you know what happened to her? I found her in the corner against the wall. It looked like someone threw her there and...did I break her, Nancy? I must have been careless or terribly cruel."

Nancy shook her head. "It wasn't you."

"Then who...and why?"

"Do you remember anything about living here, Shanna?"

"Not really. I get feelings, you know. Like this place. I know something awful happened. I came in and felt this overwhelming sadness." Shanna wiped the moisture from her face with her shirt sleeve.

"I can tell you about it if you think you're ready."

Shanna nodded, holding the doll to her chest. "Please."

"Elizabeth and Mike seemed fairly happy the first couple of years they lived here. Mike especially so. But you were around two when Elizabeth began withdrawing. She would leave—sometimes for days on end without telling anyone where she was going. That's when I took care of you. She would often sleep late, and some mornings you'd wander over to my house, still in your pajamas, and ask for breakfast.

"Your dad and mom began arguing, especially after her absences. Mike didn't handle your mother's moodiness well. He eventually stopped trying and began to frequent the local taverns. Broke my heart to see them like that. About all I could do was to make sure you were taken care of. I probably should have turned them in for child abuse—people do that more these days, but somehow I couldn't bring myself to call the authorities. I kept hoping they'd be able to work things out.

"One day a few weeks shy of your fifth birthday," Nancy continued, "your mother announced she was leaving Mike for good. I tried to talk her out of it, but she wouldn't listen. You didn't want to go and ran into the playhouse to hide. Elizabeth went into one of her rages."

"I remember." Shanna closed her eyes as the memory tumbled in. "She grabbed Ellie out of my hands and threw her against the wall. Then she brushed my dishes off the table, grabbed my arm, and pulled me out." The memory burned her heart like a branding iron.

"No, Mommy, no," Shanna had screamed.

"You shut your mouth and do as I say. It's for your own good." Elizabeth slapped her face, put a hand over Shanna's mouth, and dragged her to the car.

"Please, don't go." Shanna's father stood on the porch, his dark eyes glistening with tears. *"We can work this out, Liz, I promise."*

Shanna touched her mouth as if that could now ease the pain of the little girl she had once been. "Mama drove away. I never saw my father again." Her gaze drifted to Nancy, who now knelt beside her.

"I know. And it broke his heart." Nancy placed an arm around Shanna's shoulder.

"Why didn't he try to contact me, Nancy? All those years I thought he didn't want us."

"He did try to find you, but Elizabeth wouldn't allow him near you. Eventually he gave up trying."

"He could have fought for custody."

Nancy hesitated. "It was a long time ago, Shanna. I suppose he thought his chances were slim to none, what with his problem with alcohol."

"Can you contact him? Tell him…tell him I want to see him." Shanna sniffed. "I don't know if I can do this, Nancy, but I feel like I have to. My therapist said if I don't work through these past hurts, I won't be able to grow. She said I was harboring a lot of anger and resentment, and it's stunted my emotional and spiritual growth. I didn't believe her at first. Thought I could just ignore them, but they keep surfacing."

Nancy nodded. "Do you believe in God, sweetie?"

Shanna sighed. "I suppose. I talk to Him, so I guess I believe. It's been awhile since I've gone to church. I...well, to tell the truth, I haven't been too happy with God."

"Most of us have childhood wounds that need to be dealt with. I'm convinced that God gives children the ability to overcome or forget the abuses or traumas they suffer until we're old enough to cope. It's like we stuff the bad things in a garbage bag and hide it in a corner of our minds. But eventually, when we're old enough and mature enough, the garbage starts to ferment. It bubbles to the surface and needs to be sorted through and disposed of in a healthy way."

"And keeping it stuffed down isn't healthy."

"No. The healthy way is to let each issue rise to the surface, examine it from your adult perspective, and hand it to God. He's the Great Physician, Shanna. He's the ultimate healer. It's like if you have a ruptured appendix—if you don't have surgery, the infection will kill you. With surgery and antibiotics, a doctor can restore you to health."

"So you're saying God can make everything better?"

"Only if we let Him. The Bible says cast all your cares on Him."

"Guess I have a lot of garbage to sort through. Where do I start?"

"You already have. You came in here."

"I felt like I needed to. It was calling me, you know. The minute I walked in I felt like I was a little girl again."

"Maybe God drew you here to help you remember."

Shanna thought about that for a moment. "You think? Hmm. Funny. I dreaded coming in here, but I knew I had to. Now I feel—I don't know how to explain it—relieved, I guess. I don't like thinking about what happened, but maybe it was worth the pain to know my father is still alive and that he wasn't the one who left."

"And that he loves you. He never stopped."

Tears filled Shanna's eyes again. "Thank you. Um…" Still holding the broken doll, Shanna stood and brushed the dirt from her behind. "Would you like a soda or iced tea or something?"

"Thanks, but not right now. I need to get cleaned up before Henry comes back. He's due in anytime now."

Shanna nodded and said good-bye, then squatted down to gather the broken pieces of the doll's face and went back to the house. Excitement coursed through her at the thought of being reunited with her father after all those years of thinking he'd abandoned her. Excitement, but anxiety, as well, and anger, and… She took a deep breath. There were too many emotions to name. Her thoughts were a jumbled mess, and Shanna was beginning to wish she hadn't come back. The logical thing to do was get out of there. Find a hotel room where she wouldn't have to think.

No, that wasn't the answer. She couldn't keep running from the past. Nancy was right. If she wanted to live a normal life, she'd have to stay and work it out.

Shanna set the doll and the broken pieces on the table. She'd have to get glue on her next trip into town. After showering, Shanna changed into clean jeans and a sweatshirt. Tossing her dirty clothes in the corner of her closet, she made a mental note to pick up a laundry basket and soap.

She was just finishing up her hair when she heard the rumble of an engine and tires crunching in her driveway. Seeing a flash of periwinkle blue, Shanna hurried out to the porch and waited for the mechanic to shut off the engine.

"Hey." He waved and opened the door.

"I was wondering when you'd show up." Shanna came down the steps.

"Took me a little longer than I thought." Jake jumped out of the truck and headed toward her, keys dangling from his outstretched hand. "Got her fixed up good as new. You have any trouble at all, bring her back."

"I appreciate that." Shanna took the keys. "Do you want me to run you back into town?"

"If you wouldn't mind."

"Not at all—it'll give me a chance to pick up some supplies."

Shanna delivered Jake to his body shop in Ocean Park, then stopped at the store before going home. When she arrived, a rental car with Oregon plates sat in her driveway. Her first impulse was to back out and drive like crazy—to get as far away from Ocean Park as possible.

She gripped the steering wheel and forced herself to pull up beside the car. "You're not running anymore, Shanna O'Brian." It was probably the FBI agent. It didn't occur to her until she'd shut off the engine and climbed out of the truck that Jim Broadman might not have been working alone and that whoever killed him might now be after her.

Chapter Twenty-Two

It was neither. Relieved, Shanna smiled and greeted the familiar figure emerging from the cabin. Though Tom Morgan posed no threat, she made a mental note to lock up next time she left the place.

Joshua's brother met her halfway to the house and hugged her, lifting her off the ground. "Thank God you're OK." He set her down and, still grasping her shoulders, leaned back to look at her. "We've all been worried sick about you. What's the deal, taking off like that?"

She stared at the plaid black-and-red pattern on his wool shirt. "I had to go. There was no way I could stay at Morningsong with Joshua running things. I'm sorry if I..." She stiffened and twisted away, suddenly feeling betrayed and angry. If Tom knew where she was, Joshua would as well. "What are you doing here? How did you find me? Did Joshua send you? If he did—"

"Whoa." Tom raised his hands in surrender. "I'll answer all your questions, but one at a time, please."

He looked sincere, but then, Tom always did. "You weren't all that hard to find. I admit you had us stumped for a while."

"So Joshua knows I'm here, and he sent you to bring me back?"

"Take it easy, Shanna. Joshua's got a lot going on. He'd come himself, but you know how it is."

"Right. He sends you to convince me he has my best interests at heart? No thanks. You can tell him I'll talk to him when I'm good and ready. In the meantime, I'm staying here."

Tom shrugged. "Whatever. Look, I came because I wanted to make sure you were OK. Joshua says you two have a lot of unfinished business, but, hey, that's between you two. Your fighting's got nothing to do with me."

"You're right. I'm sorry." Shanna sighed and invited him in. "I should have known he'd track me down. I guess I was hoping for more time."

"How long do you plan to stay?" Tom sank into the rocker and stretched his long, denim-clad legs out in front of him, crossing his Tony Llama boots at the ankle. To look at Tom, one would never guess the magnitude of his wealth.

Shanna had always liked that about him. He didn't wear his wealth or flaunt it. "Long as it takes, I suppose. I was born here, and coming back has brought up a lot of issues about my childhood." She explained as best she could about dealing with old memories and locating her father.

"It's great that he's alive. I suppose you'll be going to see him."

"Maybe—if he wants me to. Nancy, my neighbor, is going to contact him. In the meantime, I have tons to do here. I had most of my mother's things sent here and eventually need to go through them. I'm dreading that."

"Yeah, I guess that's the tough part of somebody dying—least that's what Nan says. She was getting ready to go through Granddad's closets when I left." Tom looked around. "Doesn't look like you have too much."

"It's all up in the attic. I have stuff my parents left behind when they…um…moved out of here, and all the boxes I shipped here when Mother died."

"Sounds like a lot of work. Why not just give it all to charity?"

"I imagine a lot of it will get tossed, but I can't just leave it."

"Would you like me to help? I could bring the boxes down to

you." The empathy in his gray blue eyes warmed her.

"No, but thanks for the offer. This is something I have to do alone." She glanced upstairs. "When I get the courage. In the meantime, can I get you something to drink?"

"Got any beer?"

"No, but I have root beer and chocolate-chip cookies."

"Guess that'll have to do." He winked and grinned.

Shanna fixed the drinks while Tom opened a bag of cookies and dumped several on a plate. They took their goodies outside and settled into the weathered wooden chairs on the front deck.

"So," she said to cover an awkward stretch of silence, "how is everyone at Morningsong—Max and Nan and Christi?"

"They're fine, I guess. Christi and I broke up the day after you left." His features hardened when he said her name. "She said she's been dating Beau Freemont—her lead guitarist. Can you believe it? The guy's a first-class jerk."

Shanna tipped her head. "I'm sorry."

"No sweat. I was getting tired of her anyway. I'll be moving to L.A. in another week. Soon as I wrap up some loose ends at Morningsong."

"So you'll stay on with the company?"

"Why not? I thought I'd take some evening classes and get my business degree. I'd be a fool to quit now."

"Is it what you really want?"

He gave her a sidelong glance. "What does that matter?"

Shanna shrugged. "Maybe it doesn't."

"You got a nice view. How come you never came here before? Or maybe you did and just didn't tell any of us."

"I haven't been here in years. Didn't even know my mother still had the property until she died. Actually, I'd forgotten all about the place until the lawyer told me it was in her will. I wish I had known. Maybe things could have been different."

His gaze came back to hers. "Sounds as if you like it here. You're not planning to stay, are you?"

"I honestly don't know what I'm going to do. There's nothing for me at Morningsong. Not anymore. I never thought I'd say this, but I should have left years ago."

"What about your music?"

Shanna closed her eyes, feeling wary and unsettled again. "If you're trying to coax me back, I won't go. Joshua put you up to this, didn't he?"

"No, he didn't. I just don't want to see you throw your career away." He leveled an unreadable gaze on her. "Say, why don't you move to L.A. with me? You'd be away from Joshua, if that's what you want."

"Thanks, but I don't think that's an option for me. It'll be better if I break with Morningsong completely. I'll lay low here for a while, find a lawyer who'll get me out of the contract, and start over somewhere else."

"You're nuts. You know that? You could have everything and you're throwing it all away, and for what? A lousy little cabin in the middle of nowhere? Shanna, you could have a mansion on any coast in the world. You own part of the biggest recording business in the country."

"It isn't what I want."

Tom's hand crushed the empty can. "I know what you want, Shanna. You can deny it, but it doesn't change the fact. You want Joshua. But you know what? You stay here and you'll lose him for good. He'll give up pretty soon and go back to Laurie."

"If that's what he wants to do, he should." Shanna stood. Her hands shaking, she picked up the cookie plate. "I think you'd better go now, Tom. You can tell Joshua I'm not coming back."

"What about your contract? I doubt any lawyer's going to be able to get you out of it. And don't forget, you're still married to him. Josh isn't about to let you go."

"As for the contract, sue me. As for still being married—it's a piece of paper, nothing more. I doubt it's even legal. If it is, he can file for a divorce. That way he can marry Laurie. He should, anyway. After all, she did have his baby."

Tom followed her into the house and set his crushed can on the counter. "So you've made up your mind that you don't want anything to do with us." His anger had been replaced with a look of rejection.

Shanna patted his shoulder. "I will always love you and Nan, no matter what happens on a business level or between Joshua and me. You're like a brother to me. I hope that won't change."

His smile reappeared. "In that case, maybe I'll hang around here for a few days. We can have dinner or see the sites. What's your schedule like?"

"I don't have one, really. I like to walk on the beach before breakfast."

"How about dinner tonight?"

"I suppose. Here?"

"Nah, meet me in Long Beach at, say, five-thirty. There's a place called 42nd Street Café. I saw it coming in."

"Where are you staying in case something comes up?"

"Oh no, you don't. I'm not giving you a way out. Nothing's going to come up in the next hour."

"Next hour?" She glanced at her watch and groaned. "My goodness, it's four already and it takes nearly half an hour to get to Long Beach."

"My point exactly." He grinned and winked. "See you at five-thirty."

He gave her a hug before he left and drove away in the rental. Shanna went back inside feeling uneasy. Not with Tom but with the fact that Joshua knew where she was. What would he do when Tom told him he hadn't been able to convince Shanna to return to Morningsong? Would he come himself? She chewed herself out for hoping he would. "I don't want you here, Joshua Morgan," she stated firmly but still didn't manage to convince the part of her that loved him.

Shanna arrived at the restaurant a few minutes early. She'd showered, dressed in jeans and a short-sleeved white shirt, and made it out the door in record time. Her still-damp hair hung in loose curls around her face. She hadn't bothered with makeup except for a touch of mascara. It wouldn't matter to Tom. She had to admit it felt good to see him again—to be in touch with someone from home. Much as she hated to admit it, she still thought of Morningsong as home. She'd lived there too long not to have formed a deep attachment. She missed the lush green hills and flowers. And, of course, the people—Max, Nan, Beth, and some of the others. *But,* she told herself, *you'll get over it. It's time to move on.*

The waitress brought her water. "Can I get you anything while you're waiting?"

"Iced tea, please."

Her tea came and fifteen minutes passed. Shanna was beginning to think she'd been stood up. But when Joshua walked in, Shanna knew she'd been set up. She should have been furious, gotten up, and walked out. Instead, she sat like stone—brainless, speechless, unable to move as he walked toward her.

"Shanna." His warm, deep voice left her staring up at him, yanking her back into an adolescent fantasy. Her heart hammered in her chest, frantic for a way out. She resented the power he seemed to have over her, wished she could remain as cool and aloof with him as she could with other men.

"May I join you?"

"I guess that was the plan, wasn't it?" She swore revenge on Tom Morgan, vowing to tear him limb from limb.

Joshua tossed her a questioning look as he lowered his athletic form into the chair that was almost too small. "I hope I'm not interrupting—"

"Don't bother to make excuses. I should have known you'd show up sooner or later."

"I could go." He pushed back his chair.

"That's not necessary." She'd have to talk with him eventually. The restaurant would be far better than her cabin. Shanna imagined him sitting in the intimate space, his powerful presence draining her of any will power she possessed. No, this was definitely better.

Joshua couldn't believe his good fortune. The minute he'd discovered where she'd disappeared to, he'd wanted to follow her. Max warned him to go slow, and that had been his intention. He planned to leave the initial contact to someone else, but this morning, after talking to Nate at the sheriff's department, he realized he had to come himself. Joshua packed clothes for him and Ryan, and coerced Nan into coming along to care for the boy. They flew to Portland, then chartered a plane to Baker Bay on the south end of the Long Beach Peninsula and arranged for a car to meet them at the small airport. Only a couple of hours before, he had settled Nan and Ryan into the Pacific Palisades Condominium near Shanna's cabin and had gone back into town to talk to the authorities. They hadn't heard from Donovan Hill as of yet, but the local sheriff assured him that Shanna was fine.

He hadn't planned on contacting her until tomorrow or maybe even the next day, but now that she was here… He reached over and gathered her small hand in his, tightening slightly when she pulled away, then releasing her.

"What do you want, Joshua? Whatever it is, let's be done with it so you can leave."

What I want is you. Joshua couldn't bring himself to verbalize his thoughts. It was too soon. "We need to talk, but not here. Let's eat first, then maybe we can walk on the beach later."

"I suppose that would be all right." She tore her gaze from his and looked down at the menu.

The waitress came a few minutes later to take their orders.

"You were born in this area?" He strove for a light, nonthreatening tone, remembering Max's admonition to go easy.

"In the cabin where my parents lived. My neighbor, Nancy, told me about it." Shanna smiled. "I was born during a storm, and Mother couldn't get to a doctor. Nancy delivered me."

"I'd like to see it—the cabin, I mean."

Shanna shrugged. "It's not much. Just a little two-bedroom place.

You'd like Nancy. She took care of me a lot when I was little." Her brown gaze lifted to his as if she were about to say more. When the waitress brought their salads, she studied hers, examining each bite before putting it into her mouth.

"Do you like it here?" Joshua asked, needing her to look at him again to reenter her world.

"Yes. I love it." Her eyes lit up. "There's something almost magical here. It's as though…" She hesitated and tipped her head to one side. "I wish you could experience the freedom I'm feeling here. It's like all my life I've been in a foreign place and now I'm home."

Joshua could hardly breathe. Was it his imagination, or was she becoming more approachable? "I'm glad. Tell me more about it—and Nancy."

Shanna did and found herself relaxing in his presence. Their main course arrived at the same time Tom walked in.

He looked from one to the other, not bothering to sit down. "Sorry I'm late. Had car trouble." Turning to Joshua he said, "I didn't think you were coming."

"I wasn't until this morning."

"How did you know Shanna would be here?" Tom asked.

"I didn't. The manager of the place I'm staying recommended it."

Shanna frowned and looked up at Tom. "Are you saying you didn't set this up?"

Tom shook his head. "I'm hurt that you'd think I'd do something so underhanded." He grinned. "But since you're both here, maybe I should butt out."

Joshua frowned. "I'm confused. You and Shanna were meeting here for dinner? I thought you were going to L.A."

Tom shrugged. "I care about her, too, you know. I was thinking maybe I could talk her into coming back to Morningsong."

"And did you?"

Tom sighed. "'Fraid not. Now that you're here, I'll leave it to you. See ya."

With that, he left. Joshua stared after his brother for a long moment, then shifted his gaze back to Shanna. "I didn't set this up. I didn't even know Tom was coming out. He probably thought he'd have better luck talking to you than I would."

"It doesn't matter."

"No, I don't suppose it does. How long are you planning to stay here?"

"As long as it takes." Shanna speared a piece of sturgeon and brought it to her mouth.

"To do what?"

"Well, I hate to use the old cliché 'to find myself,' but in a way, that's what I'm doing."

He caught her gaze and held it. For a moment it seemed as though the restaurant had pulled up roots and left them sitting alone in some ethereal kingdom. "Maybe while you're looking you can find me too."

Shanna glanced away. "I don't think it works that way." She steered the conversation back to safer things, like asking about Nan and Max and Beth.

Chapter Twenty-Three

Half an hour later, they left the restaurant. Shanna agreed to walk with Joshua but insisted on driving her pickup to their rendezvous point, which was the south end of the boardwalk. She figured she'd be safe enough there. Why safety seemed such a factor, she wasn't certain. She knew Joshua would never hurt her—not physically, anyway. She just didn't want to be entirely alone for fear he'd try to win her over again, and for fear she might say yes.

They walked for a time in silence, listening to the ocean's roar and gulls screeching overhead.

"I'm not sure what more we have to say to each other, Joshua," she said finally. "It will never work for us. You and I both know there's no use pretending our marriage can survive. You have your life; I have mine. There's no middle ground. It would be best if you have your lawyer draw up the divorce papers, and I'll sign them. I don't want anything from you." He visibly winced, and Shanna knew her words had cut him deeply.

"That may be, but I want something from you."

Her gaze met his, challenging. "What could I possibly have that you want?"

He sighed. "I was hoping for love, but I'm beginning to wonder if you're capable of giving that to anyone. Maybe the best I can settle for is that you'll find it in your heart to love Ryan."

"Ryan—your son?"

"*Our son,* Shanna."

She stared at him until he became a blur against the setting sun. "No," she said when the word finally gained the strength to escape. "That's not possible. We gave our baby up for adoption. You signed the papers. Andrew said he gave him to a couple back east. He—"

"To me, Shanna. He gave Ryan to me."

She shook her head. "No. Andrew could never—I trusted him. I don't believe you. I don't know what you're trying to pull or why you'd try to convince me the child you had with that—with Laurie—was mine, but it's not possible."

"Please, let me explain."

"It's too late for that. Just go away. Go back to Morningsong. Ryan needs his real mother. N-not me."

"You *are* his real mother. I know it's a shock, but you have to believe me. I would never lie about a thing like that."

She stared at him and backed away as though he were some sort of monster. "I can't," she whimpered. Taking another step back, she hit the railing, then turned and ran.

Joshua dragged a hand through his hair, trying to decide whether or not to follow her. Max would probably tell him to leave her alone. But he couldn't let her go—not like this.

"Shanna, wait." He caught up to her as she slammed the door of the truck. Joshua reached for the handle.

"Stay away from me." Shanna locked the door, started the truck, and backed out of the parking space, then gunned the engine, spraying gravel and sand in his face.

Exasperated, Joshua trudged back to his car. She'd probably be going back to the cabin. He knew where it was, but he needed to give them both time to calm down before he approached her again. *You're being a fool—an idiot who can't take no for an answer,* he told himself. *Let her go. Forget her.*

God help him, he wished he could. She didn't want him; he supposed he'd eventually have to accept that, but not yet. All he could do now was give her the letters Andrew had written and hope she'd come around. Maybe he would never be able to convince her that he loved her, but at least he'd prove Ryan was her son. Once she knew that, maybe she'd change her mind.

If she didn't, he'd go back to Morningsong and try to get on with his life.

He chided himself for coming in the first place. This wasn't the time, especially with the pirating investigation still going on. He needed to get to the bottom of it. Joshua hated to think any of his employees could be responsible, but he needed to face the facts. Elizabeth may have started it, but the tapes stolen after her death proved she hadn't been working alone. He couldn't bring himself to suspect Shanna, even though the sheriff had mentioned her as a possibility. He had begun to wonder about Max, Debra and her husband, or Beth and Cliff. None of them seemed likely suspects, but they all had access, as did twenty or so other employees.

He hadn't yet located Andrew's notes on the matter. Perhaps he wasn't convinced this was actually a problem. Surely Andrew would have brought something that important to Joshua's and Tom's attention. Tom was as surprised to hear about it as Joshua had been.

"Joshua Morgan?" A lean man with a scar over his left eyebrow stopped him as he opened the door to his car.

"Who wants to know?"

"I'm Agent Hill." He flashed a badge and returned the wallet to his jacket pocket. "Saw you from the restaurant up there and thought this was as good a time as any."

"I wondered when you'd get around to talking to me. Nate told me you were working on the pirating case. What can I do for you?"

"You can start by answering a few questions." He glanced at a couple walking by. "Let's walk; we're less likely to be overheard.

"First of all," Hill said, "what brings you out here?"

"Long story. I came to find my wife. Talk some sense into her."

"That would be Shanna O'Brian." He glanced in the direction she'd gone. "Looks like you didn't get very far."

"That's putting it mildly." Joshua stuffed his hands into his pockets. "Look, could we hurry this up?"

"What size shoe do you wear?" He glanced down at Joshua's expensive leather boots.

"What kind of question is that?"

"Just answer."

Joshua shook his head. "About a twelve."

Donovan stopped at a picnic table on a wide extension of the boardwalk and rested a foot on the bench. Pulling a photo out of his breast pocket, he handed it to Joshua. "You ever seen this guy?"

Joshua winced. "Poor guy. What happened to him?"

"Murdered."

Joshua whistled. "I can see that. He looks familiar. I've seen him before but can't place him."

"He ever work for you?" Donovan started walking again.

"Not me. He may have worked for my grandfather. I've only been back at Morningsong for two weeks. Before that I was in L.A. Who is he?"

"Name's Jim Broadman. Last known address is in Nashville. I suspect he followed Shanna out west. He was on the same plane she and I were."

"You and Shanna were on the same plane?"

"I followed her out. I think I may be looking for the same thing Broadman was."

"Which is?"

"Evidence that could expose whoever is pirating those CDs and videos from you folks. He broke into her hotel room and stole her jewelry, but I don't think that's what he was after."

"I'm not sure I follow. You say someone murdered him? Any idea why?"

"No. He's got a record—the guy might've gotten himself in trouble with someone from the Portland area, as far as that goes. A drug deal gone bad." Donovan plucked a cigarette out of his pocket, started to light it, then put it back. "Trying to quit," he muttered, then told Joshua about the address they'd found. "I'm following a hunch that he's somehow connected with the pirating of Morningsong recordings."

"Well, he wouldn't have been working for us—not with a record. We screen our employees pretty thoroughly. That's why I'm having a hard time thinking of anyone on staff who might be involved." Joshua lifted his shoulders and turned his back to the wind. The temperature had dropped a good ten degrees since he'd arrived. "We check applicants out thoroughly and make it a practice not to hire people with criminal records." He wished the agent would finish up his business so he could get on with his.

Donovan turned with Joshua and headed back the way they'd come. "Shanna came out west thinking she was getting away from her troubles, but it looks like every one of them followed her."

"So what you're saying is, even with this guy dead, Shanna could still be in danger." Joshua had heard only bits and pieces of the story so far, but things were beginning to gel. Yet it was too soon to share his suspicions with the agent.

"Maybe. Though I'm beginning to wonder." Donovan pulled the cigarette out again, this time lighting it and blowing the smoke behind him, where the wind whipped it away. "I thought maybe the guy who killed Broadman might come after Shanna. 'Course, he still might, but if he's worried about what she knows or has in her possession, you'd think he'd kill her before she found the evidence and went to the police. Unless she's in on it."

"Not a chance." Joshua frowned.

Donovan raised his scarred eyebrow. "We'll see. I hope you don't plan on going anywhere for a few days."

"I was thinking about going back to Morningsong tomorrow or the next day."

"So soon?"

"I came here to talk Shanna into coming home. If she refuses, there's nothing more for me to do here." Reaching his car, Joshua opened the door and slid in. "Are we about through?"

"Just a couple more questions. Are you aware your brother is out here?"

"Yes—I just saw him. Knowing Tom, he came out to make sure Shanna was OK. We're all like family, and her leaving was a shock to all of us."

"What about Max?"

Joshua hesitated. "I asked him to fly out yesterday. Thought he might be able to talk some sense into Shanna." He frowned. "Come to think of it, I don't think he's contacted her yet. She didn't say anything."

"Doesn't that seem odd to you?"

Joshua gripped the steering wheel. "Not necessarily. Besides, we don't know that he hasn't tried."

Shanna didn't go home that night in case Joshua had followed her. She checked into a nearby motel under a phony name. Not that she expected to get any sleep. She was running again. Running from the haunting voice that told her Ryan was truly her child.

She kept seeing visions of Joshua's son at the funeral. He was an adorable little boy and did look like Joshua. Could he really be hers? She hadn't seen any resemblance to herself, but then she hadn't gotten a close look at him, either. Ryan was about the right age.

Impossible. She argued against the idea. Elizabeth would never have stood for it. Still, Andrew had defied her on the annulment. Family meant a lot to Andrew. It wouldn't be out of character for him to find a way to keep the child.

"No," Shanna moaned. "It isn't possible. He belongs to Laurie."

The words sounded hollow, and in her heart she knew the truth. No one ever actually said the child was Laurie's, she realized. Shanna had drawn that conclusion. Perhaps that's the way it was supposed to have been.

Still, if Andrew had given her baby to Joshua, wouldn't Nan have known, and Tom? Yet when she'd mentioned Ryan being Laurie's son to Tom, he hadn't corrected her. Had Andrew lied to all of them? And what had he told Joshua?

Shanna spent the next few hours trying to make some sense of it. Part of her wanting to believe Ryan really was hers. The other part refusing to accept it. If Ryan was hers and Joshua's, what then?

~

At 4 A.M. Shanna gave up on the idea of sleep, checked out of the motel, and drove back to her cabin. Joshua would have given up on her long ago. Thankfully, the driveway was empty. Shanna shut off the engine and picked her way in the predawn light to the house. When she stepped into the dark cabin, a chill crept into her bones. The moon illuminated the front room, spilling an eerie light as far as the dining room table. A large white envelope was clearly evident against the dark wood. She flipped on an overhead light and picked up the envelope. It was sealed and addressed to her in Andrew's handwriting.

She stared at it for a long time, then set it back on the table. Joshua must have left it there, but how had he gotten in? She was sure she'd locked the door. As if answering her question, the white cat meowed and wandered out of the bedroom. She must have left the bedroom window open.

"Hey, little fellow, where have you been?" Shanna scooped the kitten into her arms and nestled it against her face and neck.

The cat purred in response. Shanna moved toward the partly closed bedroom door. A cool breeze ruffled the Priscilla curtains. She closed the window and turned around. A scream caught in her throat. Someone was lying in her bed.

Chapter Twenty-Four

Shanna flattened herself against the wall, wishing she'd left the window alone. The figure snored softly. She scanned the room for some sort of clue, but even with the light filtering in from the dining room, see could see nothing clearly. Her gaze caught the familiar shape of a cowboy hat hanging on the bedpost. A pair of boots stood at the end of the bed.

The kitten chose that moment to struggle free. Sinking her claws into Shanna's arm, she yowled, broke free, and landed on the bed.

"What the dickens is going on?" Max's gravelly voice brought Shanna instant relief. He reached for the bedside light, turned back around, and blinked at her, his large, calloused hand going to the kitten who was now curling in circles on his lap. "Shanna, what are you doing here?"

"I think that's my line." Her relief turned to fury. "You scared me half to death."

"I'm sorry." He rubbed his eyes and shook his head as if to clear it. "You weren't here, so I waited. I was reading and fell asleep. What time is it, anyway?" With one eye closed he tried to focus on his watch.

"Five." Shanna moved to the open door and stood against it with her arms crossed.

"And you're just getting in?"

"I didn't want to see Joshua, so I checked into a motel for the night."

"Got news for you, sugar, it's still night. Don't suppose you'd let me catch a couple more winks..."

Shanna folded her arms and glared at him.

"I didn't think so."

"I'll make you some coffee while you get dressed. Then you can tell me why you're here."

Despite her anger, she was glad to see him. Glad it was him in her house and not Joshua. Max, even though she felt he'd betrayed her by siding with Joshua, was much safer.

Minutes later, Max emerged from the room looking a little too much like an aging Marlboro man. His dark, leathery skin had a sallow appearance. He was too thin. She'd noticed that before. "Got that coffee ready, darlin'?"

Shanna set a steaming mug on the table, then made a cup of herbal tea for herself and dropped into the chair across the table from Max.

"How'd you get here?" She looked in the driveway again and saw no sign of a car.

"Walked over."

"You're staying close-by then?"

"You might say that."

"Let's not play games, OK, Max? If Joshua sent you to change my mind, you can forget it."

"Suit yourself. Still think you owe it to yourself to talk to him."

"I did last night."

"Joshua's here?"

"Seems as though all of Morningsong is here. And don't tell me you didn't know. Ganging up on me isn't going to work."

Max took a long sip. "Joshua tell you about the boy?"

Shanna bit her lip. "You knew?"

"He told me after you left."

"I see. And you believe he's mine?"

Max glanced at the papers on the table. "I think it's entirely possible. I suspect you'll find your answer in there."

Shanna forced herself to open the envelope. Inside was a copy of the birth certificate and a letter. The certificate bore the name Ryan Andrew Morgan. The date and the hour Shanna had given birth. Shanna and Joshua were listed as birth parents. The document, with its official seal, seemed authentic.

All night she'd wracked her brain trying to come up with an explanation as to why Joshua would tell her Ryan was hers and not Laurie's. There was none. The only thing that made sense was that Joshua had been telling the truth. They were still married, Ryan was their child, and because of that Joshua felt obligated to work things out with her. He had always had a strong sense of duty—to Andrew and to Morningsong and apparently to his son. *But not to you,* Shanna reminded herself.

Tears glistening in her eyes, she looked at Max. "Why didn't anyone tell me? All these years I thought I'd lost my baby..."

Max covered her hand. "Read the letter, darlin'. Andrew had his reasons. He did what he felt he had to do."

With trembling hands, Shanna unfolded the letter written on Morningsong stationery.

My dearest Shanna,

There are many things I must tell you. I only hope you can forgive me for the pain I caused you. While I'd like to lay the blame fully on Elizabeth, I must bear at least part of the responsibility. Just as your mother felt she was acting in your best interests, I, too, felt I was acting in the best interests of you and my family. My goal was never to hurt you or Joshua but to hold your dreams for you until such a time as you were free to take them back.

When you and Joshua married, Elizabeth insisted on an annulment. I pretended to agree and promised to take care of all the legalities. She threatened to go public with the story that Joshua had abducted and raped you if I didn't. I couldn't let her rip my family apart like that. I had papers drawn up, gave her copies, but knowing how much you and Joshua loved each other, I never filed them, so you are still legally married. I went along with her plan to make you believe that Joshua was unfaithful so you'd forget about him. She hired Laurie Daniels to see that photos of the two of them made it to the gossip rags. Laurie was only too happy to comply. She fell in love with Joshua and made herself indispensable as his secretary.

I thought it was over then. I prayed that eventually you and Joshua would reunite. When we discovered you were pregnant, I was forced to continue the charade. Taking the baby from you was the hardest thing I ever had to do.

Tears blurred the page. Shanna brushed them away and handed the letter to Max. "I can't…read it to me, please."

Max took the letter and cleared his throat. "'Once again,'" he read, "'I pretended to go along with Elizabeth. I had my attorney draw up adoption papers and present them to you to sign and gave her copies. Ryan is my great-grandson. I could not bear to hand him over to strangers.

"'If I could turn back the clock and do it all again, I would have stood up to Elizabeth. I'd have thrown her out instead of allowing her to blackmail me all those years. Now that she's dead, it's easy enough to say.'"

Max stopped reading. He pinched his eyes shut. Letting the paper drift to the floor, he buried his face in his hands. "If anyone is to blame in all of this, darlin', it's me. I never should have let her take you away."

Shanna lifted her tearful gaze to stare at him. "What did you say?"

He hauled in a ragged breath, resting his elbows on his knees.

"You knew my mother before she died?" Shanna wasn't certain how many more surprises she could endure.

"I kept hoping she'd change. I should have made her see a psychiatrist when she got so bad."

Her mind soaked up his words. "You... You're my father..." Shock, denial, betrayal, and anger warred for first place in her mind, squeezing out the sliver of hope—of joy. She ran her hands through her hair and bounced to her feet. "This is crazy!" Pushing the chair aside, Shanna paced into the living room and back as the realization sank in. "I don't believe this. Why didn't you tell me?"

"I wanted to. I'd been in touch with Andrew off and on since I found out you were recording with them." He wagged his head from side to side. "Heard you on the radio and went out and bought your first album. He kept me posted on what you were doing, where you were going to be—sent me pictures. I went to your concerts when I could. When Elizabeth died, I figured I'd see if you were up to a visit from me. Andrew advised me to wait until things settled down before I told you who I really was. In the meantime we figured I could work for you."

"You should have told me."

"Like I said, I wanted to, but I could never bring myself to do it. Whenever I tried talking to you about your father, you closed me out. I knew Elizabeth had poisoned your mind against me. I was afraid if I told you who I really was, you'd send me away. At least as your manager I could be close to you. Sometimes you even treated me like a dad."

Shanna's lips curled in a half smile. "Sometimes you acted like one. Maybe that's why I cared so much about you."

"I'm hoping you still care. Can you forgive me? I know you have cause to hate me, but..."

"I never hated you—not really. I felt hurt and angry that you'd abandoned me. It hurt too much to talk about you. And Elizabeth didn't want me to." Shanna spotted the broken doll lying in the rocker. Someone had glued in the missing pieces. She scooped the bedraggled thing up and held it close. "Did you do this?"

He nodded. "While I was waiting for you to come home."

"Thank you." Shanna sank into the chair and rocked, staring out at the waves.

"Shanna, I...I don't know what to say." Max moved into the living room and stood in front of the window. "I wish I could have told you sooner. I was afraid you wouldn't want me around."

Shanna brushed the moisture from her cheeks.

"I love you, darlin'. I tried to see you for a long time after Elizabeth took you away, once I found out where you were, but she wouldn't let me near you." He stopped. His Adam's apple shifted up and down. "She threatened to…let's just say Elizabeth had to have things her way."

"Why? What could she possibly have had against you?"

"She told me she'd bring me up on charges of child abuse." He leaned forward and settled a callused hand on Shanna's arm. "I never hurt you, but I knew I'd never stand a chance against her. She could turn things around and make people believe anything. For a long time I thought I was the one to blame for all the trouble. I'd been accused of it often enough. By the time I straightened out my own life, it was too late."

Shanna stroked the doll's hair. "How could it have been too late?"

"She thought seeing me would upset you too much and hinder your performances. She didn't want me to destroy your career like I'd done hers. There wasn't much I could do about it. I would never have won in a custody case—not with my record of drinking. And no one would have believed me over her. All I could do was keep track of you. I didn't want to interfere."

"She told me you were dead."

"I know. In a way I was. Leastwise there were days I wish I had been. That story I told the other night at the dinner party—about Andrew getting me into a treatment center—that was true. I'm a different man now. God worked a miracle in my life, helping me stay sober and then letting me be with you these last few months."

"What about the ranch? You seemed pretty eager to quit being my manager."

"I thought it might be a good idea to distance myself for a while. Besides, I haven't changed my mind about you taking a long vacation. I was hoping you'd take me up on the offer to visit me there. I had this idea it would be easier to talk to you there and maybe tell you who I really was."

"You took Joshua's side against me. I felt like you were throwing me to the wolves."

"Joshua told me about his plans to bring you into the business. He wants to make a go of your marriage. I couldn't fault that." Max lowered himself onto the window seat.

Shanna brushed his words aside. "Why didn't you stop her? If you were watching me like you said, why didn't you do something? If you and Andrew are telling the truth, my mother called all the shots. How could you let her hurt me like that?"

"Your mother had ways of making sure people did what she wanted. Besides, you always seemed so happy when I saw you. Andrew never told me any of the details about your marriage. I figured you'd just changed your mind. I didn't know about the baby until you mentioned it the other day. It wasn't until after Elizabeth died and I came to Morningsong that I began to realize how much she'd hurt you."

"So you sent me to a counselor and tried to get me straightened out." Shanna stopped the rocker. She was tired. Overwhelmed. Numb. Her thoughts and feelings suspended in some kind of vacuum, waiting until she could sort through them. "I…I'd like you to go now." She settled her gaze on him. "Or m-maybe I should be the one to leave. It's your house, isn't it?"

"Stay. I'm bunking over at Henry and Nancy's." He threw back the last of his coffee and smashed his hat on his head. Turning at the door, he said, "I'm sorry, darlin'. I never wanted to hurt you."

Max—Mike—Dad, whoever he was, walked away. The sun was just rising, turning the clouds on the horizon a soft rose-petal pink.

Shanna showered, slipped on clean sweats, then shrugged into a jacket and went outside. She needed to clear her head. She wanted all the confusion to go away and wondered if it ever would. The air felt fresh and cool against her skin. The day promised sunshine, while rain—or a storm—would have better suited her mood.

Chapter Twenty-Five

Nancy intercepted her on the path where it forked off to the two houses. "I was just coming over to check on you. Mike said you seemed pretty upset."

"That's an understatement. I thought maybe a walk would help."

"Would you like company? Sometimes it helps to have a neutral person to talk to."

"Somehow I don't see you as all that neutral. You're my *father's* friend."

Nancy smiled. "Maybe neutral was the wrong word. But I can promise to listen, and I won't give you any advice unless you ask for it."

"Why didn't you tell me Max was my father?"

"I didn't make the connection until last night. I told him to tell you right away. I don't much believe in keeping that kind of thing secret."

"He should have told me before."

"Yes, he should have. I hope you'll be able to forgive him. I really do think he was afraid of how you'd respond."

"And I'm not responding very well, am I?"

Nancy looped an arm through Shanna's and pulled her along. "As well as can be expected. You've had quite a shock."

"That's putting it mildly. I don't know what to think. Part of me is angry and hurt, but I'm glad he's alive."

"That's understandable. I suspect you'll need some time to adjust."

They walked in silence for the next few minutes, Nancy staying true to her promise not to give advice and Shanna not asking. Near the water's edge, Shanna pulled off her shoes, stuffed her socks into them, and tied the shoes together, letting them dangle from her hand as she waded into the surf. "What happened to her, Nancy?"

"Elizabeth?"

Shanna nodded. "I don't remember her hating me, but when I think about what she did to me and to Max—my father—she seems almost evil."

"Not so much evil as misguided. And not everything she did was hurtful to you. You are a sweet young woman and a successful performer."

"Thank you." Shanna ducked her head. She was successful but felt undeserving of the compliment. "Most of the time Elizabeth was good to me. I loved singing, and she paved the way for me. I'm not sure I would have been able to get there on my own. She was right about that. I never wanted to be anything else."

"You used to put on shows for us." Nancy smiled. "Oh, Shanna, I wish you could have seen yourself. Two years old and you were belting out songs like 'Jesus Loves Me' and 'Twinkle, Twinkle Little Star.' You were born to it. And look at you now."

"I guess I should be happy. She devoted her entire life to my career. I'd probably be a fat, lazy housewife with a dozen kids and no life of my own if she hadn't..."

Nancy looked stricken.

"Oh, Nancy. Did I say that? I sounded just like her."

"That's what she thought of me, you know." Nancy stepped around the ragged remains of a crab. "Back then I had two kids, with my third on the way. I weighed about two hundred pounds. She thought I was wasting my talents. One day she said to me, 'How can you live like this? You could be doing something so much more important—painting, showing your work in galleries all over the world, studying in France, but instead you live here in a lost corner of the world in a beach shack.'"

"Your house doesn't look much like a shack."

"Not now. We remodeled a few years ago. Before that it was about the size yours is. It wasn't easy to raise four kids in a little place like that, but we managed." Her thoughtful gaze scanned the horizon. "Elizabeth asked me once if I ever wished I hadn't married Henry."

"What did you tell her?"

Nancy stooped to pick up a sand dollar and brushed the sand away. "I never regretted it for a minute. Henry and I are as committed to each other today as we were when we married—maybe even more so. I guess I'm an old-fashioned sort, but I happen to believe marriage is forever."

"I did, too, but it takes two to make it work." Shanna back-pedaled to a safer topic. She didn't want to talk or even think about Joshua. The time would come all too soon when she would have to. "What about your art? Didn't you miss it?"

"Not really. I just refocused my talents in other directions for a few years. It takes a lot of creative energy to rear four children." She chuckled. "Ecclesiastes says there is a time to reap, a time to sow..."

"'A time for every purpose under heaven...'" Shanna began to sing the old folk song based on that portion of Scripture. Nancy joined her and they finished the verse together.

"It's true, you know. For me there was a time to paint, a time to be married and have babies, a time to be a mother and to watch my children grow. And now life has gone full circle. It's time for me to paint again. I have a showing of my watercolors at the art fair next weekend."

"That's wonderful! I'd like to see your paintings."

"C'mon over—I'll give you one if you'd like."

"I would like that very much." Shanna's smile faded. "My mother hated being married, didn't she? She must have hated having me too."

"Elizabeth didn't hate you. Like a lot of young couples, your parents fell in love, got married, and had all sorts of wonderful dreams. Your mother's dream was to become a singer."

"I know. She blamed Dad—and me—for holding her back... Well, not in so many words. She just made sure I knew that marriage and a family would ruin my career."

"Did you ever wonder why she didn't go on to become a singer after she left him?"

"I guess she was too busy taking care of me." Shanna stood still as a wave rolled in and sloshed around her ankles.

"No, Shanna. It wasn't the lack of time. Your mother never made it as a singer because she couldn't sing. Oh, she had a pleasant enough voice, but she didn't have that extra spark or the personality, the charisma. Not like you. She was turned down by one record company after the next. Instead of facing her own inadequacies, she started blaming Mike, then motherhood. She became terribly depressed and bitter. Eventually, she began to see you as a way to obtain the glory she'd always wanted for herself. That's why she turned you into a child star. When your father objected to her obsession to get you on the stage, she took you away."

"I still don't understand why he didn't come after us."

"We all wanted to, but we had no idea where she'd taken you. It wasn't until you had been picked up by Morningsong and started recording that we knew where you were. Mike wrote to you at Morningsong, but the letters were all returned unopened. Finally Elizabeth wrote back and threatened to turn him in to the authorities for child abuse if he didn't leave you alone."

"What am I going to do, Nancy?" Shanna wandered into the dry sand and sat down. "A week ago I was a performer. I was just starting to take control of my life. I'd managed to put all the awful things that had happened in the past behind me."

Nancy plopped down beside her, brushing sand from her hands. "And now?"

"I feel like everything has come crashing down on top of me. I'm almost afraid to breathe in case there's more." Shanna told her about her marriage and the baby, about Andrew's will and how Joshua had tried to manipulate her into staying at Morningsong. And about Ryan. "I don't know what's real anymore. Maybe I never did. I feel like a puppet, and everyone has hold of the strings but me." Shanna jerked one arm up. "You're a singer, Shanna." She held up her other arm, hand and fingers dangling lifelessly. "No, no, Shanna, you're a wife." Sticking her right leg out, she said, "Now you have to be a mother, Shanna." Pushing her other leg out, she said, "Time to go back to Morningsong, Shanna. Now I'm supposed to accept my father with open arms."

Nancy laughed. "I'm sorry. I know it isn't funny, but you look so comical."

Shanna lay back on the sand, her arms outstretched. "Do you know you're the only one who isn't trying to yank my strings?"

Nancy leaned back, propping herself up with her elbows. "Then I guess you can just be yourself."

"Maybe that's the scariest of all." She swallowed past the lump forming in her throat. "I don't know who that is."

Nancy rolled over onto her stomach and let the sand sift through her hands. "Maybe a little of each. Are you a singer?"

"Of course."

"And you are Mike's daughter."

"So he says."

"Trust me on that one, Shanna. Mike is definitely your father, and he loves you dearly. His deception was dishonest, but he felt it was the only way to be with you."

"OK, so I'm a daughter. I guess I'm a wife and mother, too, but I have no idea how to be either."

"You can learn."

"I'm not sure I want to."

"You could walk away."

Shanna sat up and shook the sand out of her hair. "I'm not sure I want to do that, either."

"Sounds like you could do with some prayer." Nancy cast her a wary glance. "Sometimes when we don't know where to go or what to do, it helps to set the whole complicated mess on God's shoulders. The Bible gives us permission to do just that. 'Cast your cares upon Him.' "

" 'Let go and let God.' I've heard that before." Shanna grimaced at the sarcasm in her voice. "I'm sorry. I tried trusting God with my marriage and my baby, but He ignored my prayers."

"Our prayers aren't always answered in the way we want them to be. And often God's timing is different than ours. God sees the big picture, where we only see small pieces at a time."

"So you're saying I should give God another chance?"

"Something like that."

"I'm not very good at praying anymore. Would you?"

"Sure." Nancy wrapped a comforting arm around Shanna's shoulders and began to pray. "Heavenly Father, You know our needs. You understand our sorrows and our burdens even better than we do. You see clearly, while we see only through the mist of our tears. We know that You can work all things for good if we will only believe." Nancy went on to ask God to give Shanna wisdom to choose wisely in the days and weeks ahead, to heal her past wounds, and give her a time of rejoicing. "And, Lord," Nancy concluded, "I pray You'll allow Shanna to sense Your love and grace and peace even in the center of the storm she's experiencing now."

With her eyes closed, focused on Nancy's words, Shanna felt something akin to peace and an assurance that the storm would eventually end.

"Thank you." Shanna sniffed and reached into her pocket for a tissue to blow her nose.

Nancy squeezed her hand. "You're welcome." Standing, she brushed the sand from her backside. "I need to be heading back. Henry and Mike will be wanting breakfast. Would you like to join us?"

"I'm not sure I'm up to seeing him right now."

Nancy nodded in understanding. By the time they reached the fork in the path, Shanna had changed her mind. "Maybe I will have breakfast with you. I'll have to face him sooner or later."

"Are you sure?"

"Yes. I realized as we were walking that God did answer one of my prayers. It took long enough, but every night after Mother and I left here I prayed that I'd be able to see my father again. When she told me he'd died, I gave up. Now that he's here and alive, it seems silly to waste the time we could be together fussing about what he should or shouldn't have done. And like you said, he did try to see me."

Nancy hugged her. "And he never gave up hope. You won't be sorry." Grabbing Shanna's hand, she pulled her to her house. "Let's go rustle up some grub."

The "grub," or at least part of it, had already been rustled up by Henry and Mike, who were seated at a large table drinking coffee. The distinct scent of bacon filled the house and drifted outside. The table, placed in front of one of two bay windows, offered a view similar to hers. Both men rose when they entered. "It's about time you got here." Henry, a large man with a full beard, chuckled. "We got tired of waiting for you."

Nancy stepped into his arms for a kiss. "Smells wonderful. Hope you made enough for both of us. I don't know about Shanna, but I'm famished."

"Cooked up a whole slab of bacon, and Mike made enough blueberry pancakes to feed an army. You two have a seat and tell me how you want your eggs."

"Any way you want to fix them," Nancy said.

Shanna slipped off her jacket and draped it over the back of a dark green recliner. The house was roomy and light. The living room wall held an eclectic assortment of paintings from various artists. It had been modernized so the living and dining rooms and kitchen had a high ceiling. A fan hummed above her head, ruffling her hair. A fire burned behind a glassed-in fireplace.

"Come on in and make yourself comfortable," Nancy said. "Do you remember Henry?"

"Sure she does." Henry gathered her in his arms. His beard tickled her forehead. "It's good to see you, Shanna."

She didn't remember him, but there was something warm and kind and familiar about him. She hugged him back. "Good to see you too."

She followed Nancy to the table and held her breath. Her father looked tense, as though their meeting as father and daughter rather than manager and performer was as unnerving to him as it was to her. She felt no sense of betrayal now, only relief that they had found each other. He'd been as much a victim of Elizabeth's actions as she had. And he loved her.

"Hi, Daddy." Shanna came around behind him, placed a hand on each shoulder, and bent to kiss his cheek.

He clasped her left hand with his right and held it. "I'm glad you're here, darlin'."

When he released her, she slipped into the chair next to him. "You must have been expecting me. You have the table set for four, and you fixed my favorite pancakes."

"Wishful thinking. I…uh…sent Nancy over, thinking maybe she could convince you to talk to me."

"Shanna convinced herself, Mike. I just listened." Nancy set a pitcher of orange juice in the center of the table.

The eggs sizzled as Henry broke them into the frying pan. "Any preferences? If not, they're all over easy."

"That sounds fine to me," Mike said.

"Me too. Can I help you with anything?" Shanna asked.

"You can pour the juice." Nancy brought the platters of bacon and pancakes.

"I'm feeling kind of awkward with this reunion thing." Shanna took her father's glass and filled it, then her own.

"I reckon it'll take you awhile to get used to the idea."

"What do I call you?" She poured juice into the other two glasses and set the pitcher down. "I keep thinking of you as Max, but I know your name is Mike."

"Daddy sounded just fine to me."

"I suppose now you'll expect a Father's Day card every June," Shanna teased, growing more at ease.

"Nope. Not *a* card, nineteen of them. One for every year I missed." He reached up to flick away a tear that had dripped to his cheek.

The sun poured through the kitchen window and skylight,

warming the room and Shanna's spirit. She had always felt comfortable with Max, and now that he was Mike, her father, she was beginning to feel the same camaraderie.

Henry brought the eggs, which looked more scrambled than over easy. He and Nancy sat down, and the four joined hands for prayer. Henry asked the blessing, thanking God for friends and food and fathers and daughters. Saying their amens, they followed Henry in picking up their orange juice glasses and clinking them together in a toast. "To families and friends," Henry said.

"To families and friends," the others echoed.

For the first time in as long as she could remember, Shanna felt loved and accepted. Henry regaled them with his fishing stories, and Mike talked about the ranch and the new horses he'd acquired.

After breakfast Henry and Mike went fishing. They'd asked Shanna to go along, but she declined, choosing instead to look at Nancy's collection of watercolors and oils. Her father had hugged her before he left, an awkward but sincere gesture. The hugs and their relationship would get better with time. They would have the rest of their lives to be a family.

Chapter Twenty-Six

"They're so beautiful, but I don't feel right about you giving me one." Shanna's gaze drifted over the watercolors, moving time and again back to the one of a woman on the beach. She wore a long pink ruffled dress of the 1800s. She held a kite string with one hand and her skirts with the other. Her hair had been swept up in a chignon and loosened by the wind. On the ground lay a parasol, and at her side was a laughing child, pointing to the box kite that hovered overhead. Shanna loved the soft pastel shades, but more than that, she was awed by the look of sheer joy on the woman's face.

"It's yours if you want it," Nancy said.

"I couldn't—it must be worth a fortune. Let me buy it from you."

"It's not for sale." Nancy lifted the painting and handed it to Shanna. "I've already given it to a very dear young woman who's like a daughter to me."

"I don't know what to say."

"A simple thank-you will suffice. Let's go hang it in your cabin."

Shanna thanked her several times on the way to the cabin. They hung it on the bare wall opposite the fireplace, where Shanna could see it when she entered the house.

"Want to help me take the paintings to the art show?"

"I'd love to, but I'm out of clothes. I need to find a Laundromat."

"No problem. Grab your things and we'll wash them at my house. Then you can help me pack up my paintings."

By eleven the paintings were ready to go and Shanna had clean clothes. She took her clothes back to the cabin; changed into jeans, a peach-colored T-shirt, and a jean jacket; then met Nancy in the driveway.

After delivering the paintings in Long Beach, they ate lunch at Pastimes, a unique restaurant situated behind a gift shop. They ate egg salad sandwiches on hazelnut bread and drank iced almond lattes. When they'd finished lunch, they wandered through the store, delighting in the scent of spicy potpourri, the music of a harpist, and the enchanting array of books and gifts. Shanna bought a pale blue throw in a thick, soft weave. On the way to the car, Shanna stopped at an apparel store to pick up a pair of jeans and a couple of long-sleeved cotton shirts.

"I don't know when I've ever enjoyed myself so much," Shanna said as Nancy dropped her off at the cabin and helped her take her purchases inside.

"It was fun. I don't want to see it end. And I don't want to waste this glorious sunshine." She set the bag down on the table and tipped her head to one side. "Want to go for a walk?"

"Sure. Let me put my stuff away and I'll meet you on the path."

Shanna tossed her new throw over the rocking chair and hung up her clothes, then changed into shorts. She jogged down the path where Nancy was already waiting.

"The guys are back," Nancy announced. "They wanted me to stay and help them clean their sea perch."

"Oh well, if you'd rather, we could walk later."

"Are you kidding?" She chuckled. "I told them they needed the practice."

They headed out toward the breakers and walked into the wind, the afternoon sun still warm and bright.

They'd gone only a short distance when Shanna saw a small child running on the beach a couple hundred yards away. "Nancy, look." She pointed in the child's direction. "There's a little kid out there all by himself."

Nancy shaded her eyes with her hand. "I'm sure his parents are around somewhere, but let's head over there just in case. The tide is going out. Sometimes visitors to our coast don't realize how dangerous the surf can be."

They were still a couple hundred yards away when Shanna thought she recognized him. "Remember what I said this morning about something else falling on top of me?"

"Hmm?" Nancy tossed her a puzzled look.

"Well, this is it. I'm not positive, but I think that's Ryan—Joshua's little boy." Shanna stopped. "Maybe you should go ahead, make sure he's not alone. I don't think I'm ready for this."

"I understand." She glanced around. "I still don't see an adult. Do you know where Joshua's staying?"

"Um—Sand...Surf...no. I can't remember."

"Oh no." Nancy shot down the beach. Shanna watched in horror as the little boy ran straight into the surf, jumping waves and laughing, completely unaware of the towering waves crashing toward him.

Shanna raced ahead of Nancy. Before she could reach him, a wall of water crashed down on him. It knocked him over and dragged him into deeper water.

She frantically searched the surface for a trace of the blue swimsuit he was wearing. "There. I think I see him." The women dove into the now chest-high water. Shanna grabbed a handful of material, then groping around in the murky water, managed to snag his leg and pull the struggling child tight against her.

Her chest ached. She needed air. Using her right arm to propel herself around, she struggled to stand on the ocean floor. Her foot touched the sand, but the churning water lifted her up. Her head bobbed to the surface. She gasped for air. Another wave pulled her under. Her foot struck the sand again. She pressed against it, concentrating on pushing herself into shallow water, praying as she did. She touched down again, and this time her head and chest cleared the water.

Nancy grabbed her arm and drew her forward. Shanna wrapped

both arms around Ryan's lifeless body and stumbled into the shallow water. "Help me," Shanna panted. "I don't think he's breathing."

"Let me have a look." Nancy took the child from her arms. She tipped him over her arm and slapped his back. Water spurted out of his mouth.

"God, please let him be all right," Shanna sobbed. "You can't take him away from me now."

Nancy placed him on his back and breathed into his mouth, watching his chest rise and fall. "He has a pulse," she said.

After a couple more breaths, he coughed and started to cry. "Daddy."

Shanna gathered him close. "It's going to be OK, baby. Everything is going to be all right."

"Come on, sweetie," Nancy said to Shanna. "We need to get him inside."

"No," he wailed. "My bucket and my shovel."

Nancy shook her head. "Kids."

"Let's give those to the ocean," Shanna said. "We'll buy a new set for you."

Ryan seemed satisfied with that solution and settled against her, resting his head on her shoulder while she carried him to her cabin.

The cold northerly wind pierced through her wet clothes like a million tiny needles. Yet as chilling as the wind was, Shanna felt an odd and unfamiliar warmth settling somewhere in the vicinity of her heart.

Shanna set two cups of hot chocolate on the table. "This should warm us up."

Even though she and Nancy had gotten Ryan out of the wet clothes and wrapped him in a warm blanket, his quivering lips were still purple. She and Nancy had taken turns getting into dry clothes themselves. Nancy had suggested hot chocolate, then had gone home to see if Mike knew where Joshua was staying.

Ryan eyed Shanna warily over the rim of the cup, took several sips, and set it back on the table, then wiped the chocolate mustache away with the back of his hand. "I shouldn't a gone in the water, huh."

"No, and you shouldn't have been out there all by yourself." Shanna suppressed the growing anger she felt at Joshua for allowing Ryan out on the beach without supervision.

"Yeah. I was s'posed to be takin' a nap. Nana and Dad will be mad."

Shanna's anger abated some. She supposed a five-year-old could be a handful.

The door swung open. Shanna stiffened, half expecting to turn and see Joshua.

"Uncle Max!" Ryan scooted off his chair and ran to him.

"Hey, buckaroo, what the dickens are you doing in that getup?"

Ryan giggled. "My clothes were all wet. We gotta find my dad so's I can get dry ones."

"He's right down the road." He turned to Shanna. "No one answered the phone. My guess is they're out looking for Ryan. Henry and I'll head out and see if we can find them."

"Shouldn't we take him to the hospital? I mean, he seems all right now, but…"

"Sounds like a good plan. Ask Nancy—she's on her way over."

Mike settled Ryan back on the stool, tucked the blanket around him, then left, passing Nancy as she entered the doorway.

"I called the doctor and they want to see him," Nancy said. "Also brought some clothes my kids have outgrown. They'll be a little large, but he'll be more comfortable. Mike, if you find Joshua, tell him to meet us at the hospital."

~

Shanna and Joshua stood shoulder to shoulder next to a stretcher, watching a doctor examine Ryan. "He's a very lucky little boy." The doctor peered into Ryan's ear. Ryan, his head tipped to one side, sat statue still except for his big blue eyes. His curious gaze darted from one to the other, his hand still gripping Shanna's. He'd let go of her only once, when the technician asked her to wait in the lobby while they did a chest X-ray.

Shanna felt uncomfortable standing there beside Joshua as if they were both Ryan's parents. They were, but she felt like an intruder. She wouldn't have been there at all if Ryan hadn't insisted she stay. Nancy and Mike had already gone, so Joshua had offered to take her home and she'd accepted.

"There's some fluid in his lungs, but not enough to cause alarm. I'm prescribing an antibiotic to deal with possible infection and—" The doctor glanced up at them. "How long are you staying in the area?"

Shanna mumbled that she didn't know at the same time Joshua said, "We're leaving in the morning."

"Well, whatever you decide, he'll need to be checked again in a week. If he starts acting sick—runs a fever—bring him in."

Except for thanking her several times, Joshua didn't have much to say on the way back up the peninsula. Ryan sat between them, resting his head on Shanna's lap. The quiet grew and spread through her like air in an overinflated balloon. While she ached to say something, nothing seemed appropriate. "Where's Nan?" Shanna finally managed.

Joshua's gaze left the road and lingered on her a long time before he answered, "She's not feeling well. I shouldn't have asked her to come so soon after the funeral. Now she's upset about..." He looked down at Ryan. "Gets to be too much for her sometimes. I forget how old she is."

Shanna absently stroked Ryan's silky hair. His deep, steady breathing told her he'd fallen asleep. "He needs a mother." The words slipped out before she could stop them. She glanced at Joshua, hoping he hadn't heard.

"He has one."

After a long silence, he said, "You did get the birth certificate and the letter, didn't you?"

She nodded. "I saw them."

"And…?"

"I don't think this is a good time."

He patted Ryan's leg. "You're right. We'll put him to bed, then we'll talk. Your place or mine?"

Shanna frowned, feeling manipulated again. She didn't want to talk to Joshua just yet. Being around him set her heart and mind on some strange, nonsensical course where she couldn't tell up from down. But he was right. They did need to sort through their troubled life and put things together in some kind of logical format they could both live with. For Ryan's sake, if nothing else.

No more running. Shanna reminded herself of the promise to stand her ground and face her fears. "My place."

He was losing her. The fear he read in her eyes told him as much. Joshua had no more game plans left. He couldn't force her, couldn't coerce her. In a way he was glad about that. It showed she was developing some backbone. She wasn't going to let herself be pushed around by anyone. Years ago he'd prayed for her to become stronger, more self-sufficient. He just hadn't expected the answer to that prayer to result in her turning against him. *God, help me say the right things. Make her listen to reason. All I want is to do what's right for all of us.*

When Shanna moved her hand to cup Ryan's shoulder, Joshua placed his on top of hers. Shanna carefully slipped her hand from beneath his. His touch left her too mushy to think, and she needed desperately to have a clear head. Joshua pulled into the driveway and carried the still-sleeping child into the small bedroom where Shanna drew back the covers. Her heart constricted at the sight of Joshua kissing his son's cheek and tucking him in. Looking around at the dainty pinks and ruffles, she entertained thoughts of changing it to blues and greens with dolphins printed on the sheets and pillow slips.

No, part of her screamed. She hurried out of the room. *What are you thinking? He's not yours—not really. You may have given birth to him, but he belongs to Joshua. He doesn't even know you're his mother.* And if she had anything to say about it, he never would. Ryan deserved a mother like Nancy. Someone strong and nurturing who would devote herself to caring for him. Not someone like her whose only real love was the stage.

Shanna leaned against the counter feeling dizzy. Her head hurt. She struggled for air. Her knees, weak and unable to hold her, collapsed. She slid to the floor, feeling hot and cold, shaky, and nauseous all at once. She struggled to hold on to consciousness, but it slipped away.

Chapter Twenty-Seven

Shanna smelled the sweet, warm scent of mangos and passion fruit. She floated in a tropical dream, sunlight glistening on the water, Joshua holding her. She felt the bed beneath her. Heard a gentle voice nudging her out of paradise. She didn't want to leave.

"Shanna? Come on, honey, wake up." Someone held a cup of herbal tea to her lips and lifted her shoulders off the pillow so she could sip it.

She opened her eyes, but the dream was still there, Joshua gazing down at her. His eyes filled with compassion and love.

"Where…?" She rubbed her forehead, pulling away a cool, damp cloth.

"You fainted. Probably from shock of all the excitement this afternoon." He released her and set the cup on the nightstand.

Shanna closed her eyes. So much for being strong and standing her ground. At the moment, she doubted she could even sit up. "Go away, Joshua. I can't deal with you right now."

"You've been through a lot. I understand. Try to get some rest. I'll be here."

Shanna closed her eyes. The afternoon's ordeal and the fact that she hadn't slept the night before must have caught up with her. It took very little time before she drifted off.

When she next opened her eyes it was dark. Wind slammed raindrops the size of marbles against the bedroom window. She heard a fire crackling in the living room. Light from the blaze danced and skipped through the foot-wide opening of the door. Snowball lay pressed against her leg, purring. "I suppose Joshua is still here," she murmured to the dozing animal.

Shanna moved her covers aside, careful not to disturb the cat. She was hot and perspiring, still dressed in the sweats she'd put on earlier. She shuddered as she thought about how close they'd come to losing Ryan. Taking clean clothes into the bathroom, Shanna stripped and stepped into the shower. The cold spray shocked her fully awake.

When the water warmed, she stood under it a long time, hoping it would wash away the confusion and help her come to terms with what she knew she had to do. She pulled on jeans and an oversized green reverse fleece shirt over her head, towel-dried her hair, combed out the snarls, and fluffed up her curls.

She took her time, not wanting to talk to Joshua, yet knowing she had to. When she'd stalled as long as she could, Shanna took several deep breaths to prepare herself for the showdown.

"Hi." Shanna padded barefoot across the wood floor, ending up in the window seat.

"Hi, yourself." Joshua stilled the rocker and watched her pass.

"Where's Ryan?"

"He woke up right after you fell asleep. I took him back to the condo, gave him a bath, and put him down for the night."

"Do you think he'll be OK?"

"Yeah. I had Nan bolt the front door. He can't reach that."

Shanna curled her legs up under her. She watched the rain hammer on the window and wondered how the panes managed to keep from breaking. "Well," she said, "I guess we'd better have that talk."

"I've come to a conclusion." Joshua stared into the fire. The hard tone in his voice surprised her.

"And that is?"

"I've decided not to try to talk you into staying married. If you really want a divorce, I'll start drawing up the papers."

"I see." He'd done it again. Picked her up and spun her around, setting her off course. She'd been ready for battle, meaning to tell him in no uncertain terms that she had no intention of staying married. That he'd be better off without her. Now, hearing him say it, she wasn't at all sure she liked the finality of it. But that was crazy, wasn't it?

"Don't tell me you've changed your mind?"

"No," she said quickly. "It's just that I—never mind." She'd wanted to be in control for a change—to have the upper hand.

"What do you think of him?"

"What? Oh, you mean Ryan? He's adorable, bright. You've done a good job raising him."

"You were right, you know."

"About what?"

"What you said in the car—about him needing a mother."

"Oh, I…I didn't mean—"

"Laurie helped me a lot when we were in California, and Nan is wonderful about taking him when I ask her to, but Ryan needs his real mother. I saw you with him today and…um…I decided that even if we can't work things out between us, we should have joint custody of Ryan. I'm willing to have you take him half the time."

Shanna shook her head. "I don't think that's possible. He doesn't know me and…you didn't tell him I was his mother, did you?"

"No, but I assumed you'd want me to."

"Well, don't. I—" Shanna swallowed back the painful lump forming in her throat. "Joshua, please understand. I love that little boy. But I gave him up because Elizabeth convinced me I wouldn't be able to care for a child and still have my music."

"That's insane."

"The music isn't the only problem now." Shanna reached over to pick up the patched-up doll her mother had broken. "Now that I know more about my parents and the way my mother treated me, I'm more convinced than ever Elizabeth was right. I would never subject Ryan to the kinds of things I went through."

"You can't be serious." Joshua stood. "What does Elizabeth have to do with any of this? You're not at all like her."

"How do you know that? Children who have been abused grow up to abuse their children. I don't want to take the chance. Ryan doesn't know I'm his mother, and he's better off never knowing."

Joshua stared down at her, disgust written on his face. "I feel sorry for you, Shanna. Maybe you're more like your mother than I thought."

She didn't answer. Joshua pushed himself out of the rocker and strode to the door. Without another word, he stepped outside, slamming the door behind him with such finality that she felt the retort sink into her chest like a bullet.

"It's better this way." Shanna stared at the flames. She'd cried for a long time after Joshua left and had just spent the last five minutes telling Nancy why she'd made the right decision.

"Is it?" Nancy came around behind her and massaged Shanna's shoulders. "Seems to me you're making some assumptions that may not be true."

"I don't think so. You knew my mother. She loved me, but that didn't stop her from…from doing those horrible things."

"Elizabeth was obsessed, Shanna. All she could think about was becoming a star. When that didn't work for her, she sank her dreams into you."

"I…I know, but"—Shanna pushed herself out of the chair—"look, Nancy, I don't mean to be rude, but I really don't need this. I don't want your pity or your advice."

Nancy sighed. "All right. I'll leave. But since you're so sure that being reared by Elizabeth turned you into her clone, think about this. For six years, I was more a mother to you than she was. I nurtured you, fed and bathed you, read you stories, and when I couldn't be there for you, your father and Henry were. Since you seem so intent on remaking yourself in the image of your mother, maybe you should think about the influence Mike and Henry and I had on you during those years as well."

Nancy opened the kitchen door and turned back around. "One more thing, Shanna. Instead of settling for being the person Elizabeth created you to be, maybe you should think about being the person *God* created you to be. I'll be around, honey—if you need me." She softly closed the door and walked away.

Shanna dropped onto the window seat. "Oh, God, what am I going to do?"

All of the hurts in her past seemed to meld into one huge, heavy blob that enveloped her, drawing the life out of her like some alien being. She struggled to find an answer, but nothing came. All she could hear was her mother's incessant voice. *"You are an entertainer, Shanna. Marriage and a career like yours do not mix. You are not the motherly type. You're better off without Joshua and the child."*

"Am I, Mother? Am I really?"

Joshua slammed the door to the condo. "Let's get packed. We're leaving tomorrow morning so we can catch an early flight out of Portland in the morning."

"I take it your talk with Shanna didn't go well." Nan rose from the sofa.

"It didn't go at all." Joshua drew both hands through his hair. "I wanted to give her room. Told her if she wanted a divorce I wouldn't stand in her way."

"You did the right thing. She needs to be free to make the decision on her own."

"Yes, well, she made it."

"What about Ryan?"

"She doesn't want him, either. Kept giving me some lame-brained excuse about not wanting to hurt him. She's convinced he'd be better off not knowing about her." He sank into the chair. "Maybe she's right."

"I'm afraid it's too late for that. Ryan knows. He won't stay in bed because he's so excited about his day with Shanna. He's been drawing pictures for her. Says he's going to go over and see her later."

"That's just great. How did he find out?"

"I'm not sure." She poured coffee and brought it to Joshua, setting it on the oak end table beside him. "Children sometimes sense these things"—she hesitated—"or he may have heard us talking."

"What in the world am I going to tell him?"

Nan placed a hand on his shoulder. "I'm sorry. Would it help if I talked to her?"

"I doubt it." Elbows resting on his knees, he held his head in his hands. "It's over. Shanna is out of our lives forever, and the sooner I face that fact, the sooner Ryan and I can move on. I haven't been doing him any favors chasing after her. Just wish I didn't love her so much."

"I know. The sad thing is that she loves you too. And I know if she'd give herself half a chance, she'd love Ryan as well."

"That's what makes this whole thing insane. She does love him. At least that's what she says. She's afraid she might do the same things to Ryan that her mother did to her."

"That poor child. I wish there were something we could do. It's like Elizabeth is still very much in control."

"You're right about that. Shanna keeps saying she doesn't want to be controlled. But she's letting a dead woman dictate her life. Doesn't make much sense, does it?"

"No. No sense at all." Nan took hold of his hand. "Come on in the kitchen. I'll fix us another cup of coffee. Maybe we can figure out some way to bring her back to us. At the very least we can pray."

"That sounds good, Nan, but if you don't mind, I'd just as soon not talk about Shanna anymore. I'm tired of praying. For whatever reason, God seems to have other plans."

"Don't be too sure. I don't believe for a minute God is leading Shanna away from her husband and son. She's listening to the wrong voices. We need to keep praying she'll hear God over and above Elizabeth."

The door to the bedroom opened, and Ryan rushed out. "Look at the pictures I made for Shanna."

Joshua rubbed the back of his neck. There was no easy way to say it. "They're very nice Ryan, and I'm sure Shanna will appreciate them. Maybe we can mail them to her."

"No, I want to give them to her. She helped me out of the water."

"You can't, Ryan. We have to go home."

"No, Daddy. Shanna's my mommy. I have to see her. Nan, tell him we have to stay."

Joshua hunkered down, took hold of Ryan's shoulders, and turned the boy to face him. "Where did you get the idea that Shanna was your mother?"

Tears welled in his eyes. His shoulders lifted and sagged. "I just know."

Joshua pulled the boy close. As much as he wanted to tell Ryan he was wrong, he couldn't. But he couldn't bear to tell him he was right. "Remember when I told you your mother couldn't be with us?"

Ryan nodded.

"Well, that's still true. She loves you, but she has to live in a different place."

Ryan stared at the drawings still clutched in his hand, a frown knitting his forehead. "She likes me, I can tell. I could tell her to come live with us. She would."

"No. We need to pack now."

"But, Dad, Jesus helped me find her. He wouldn't want her to go away." His pleading brown eyes were almost too large for his face.

Joshua sighed. "Sometimes things don't turn out the way we want, Ryan. I'm sorry."

Ryan pushed away from his dad and went to the door. "I want to go see her." He pulled the door open.

Joshua shook his head, picking Ryan up around the waist and slamming the door shut. "You aren't going anywhere. Now, just settle down."

"No, I don't want to go home. I want my mom."

"You can't."

Ryan kicked, struggling to break free. The child was heading into a full-blown tantrum. Joshua secured his legs and headed for Ryan's bedroom. Setting Ryan on the bed, he said, "I know you're upset, but I won't have you acting like that. Now stay in here until you can settle down."

Ryan turned his face into the pillow and began kicking the bed. Joshua closed the door.

Anger stirred inside him. "This is Shanna's fault," he fumed at Nan. "I should take Ryan over there and let her straighten it out. Let her tell him the truth. It would serve her right."

Chapter Twenty-Eight

Donovan studied the results of the fingerprint screening he'd had done on the thumbprint they'd discovered at the murder scene. They had a match from the comparison prints they'd taken at the Morgan estate after Elizabeth's death. He knew who had killed Broadman, but he didn't know why. And he didn't know if the killer was working alone. He doubted it. He'd need more information before making an arrest. "After all this time," he mumbled, picking up the phone, "I don't want anyone slipping out of the noose."

A firm plan in mind, Donovan punched out the numbers to Joshua Morgan's condo.

Shanna, tired of weeping and feeling sorry for herself, climbed the stairs to the attic. She'd put off the task long enough, and nothing hidden in those boxes could bring her more pain than what she was already feeling. Besides, she needed to see if Agent Hill was right in his assertion that Elizabeth had been involved in pirating Morningsong recordings. If she found anything, she'd turn it over to Donovan. Problem was, she had no idea what to look for or where to look.

The boxes were not stacked neatly as Shanna had remembered, but haphazardly, with lids askew. Someone had already gone through them. Her heart raced. Nancy? She was a bit on the nosy side. Maybe Mike. According to Nancy, he'd come here quite often over the last few years. They were the only two people who knew about the boxes—unless she'd told Beth. She did remember mentioning it to Tom. Shanna shivered. Maybe it wasn't as big a secret as she thought. She remembered the horrible man at the hotel. And whoever had killed him. Had that same person killed her mother? Would he kill her next?

Shanna shoved her fears aside and climbed the rest of the way up. She pulled on the light switch and sat down in the dust. Not everything was dusty, she noticed. There were footprints. Made with pointed toes—cowboy boots. Mike wore them. So did Tom. And Joshua on occasion. For that matter, so did thousands of other people.

Someone knocked on the door. Shanna swallowed back her fear, crept to the small attic window, and peered through the water-stained, dusty panes. There was no car, which meant it was probably Nancy.

The door opened. "Shanna?" It was Mike. "You in here?"

Her heart hammering, she waited, battling with the voices raging in her head. *He's your father. He wouldn't do anything to hurt you. But he came to Morningsong right after your mother died. Maybe he got tired of Elizabeth and you having all the money in the family. Maybe he wanted his cut, so he finagled his way into Morningsong Productions and started pirating your records. Elizabeth found out, and he killed her. After all those years, he decided to seek revenge.* No. Not Mike. If she hadn't been so wrapped up in herself, she might have recognized him as her father. The man she'd come to know and love was not a killer.

"I'm up here, Dad, in the attic. I was just getting ready to go through Mother's things." Shanna walked over to the opening. He mumbled something Shanna couldn't understand. She heard a thud and a scraping noise, then a click. "Dad?"

When he didn't answer, Shanna wished she could take back her greeting. She moved away from the stairs, hearing his approaching footsteps. Why hadn't he answered her? He must have been closing the door. "Dad?" she called again. His silence bore witness to her intuition's warning that something was terribly wrong and she was in danger.

Terror clung to her like the sticky cobwebs hanging from the ceiling of the tiny room. She needed to find something heavy. She could hit him as he came up. Shanna opened one of the boxes and grabbed a vase. Raising it over her head, she moved toward the opening again. When the head appeared, Shanna closed her eyes and slammed her weapon against the back of his skull. The vase shattered. She opened her eyes, expecting to see Mike lying on the floor at the foot of the steps.

What she saw was far more frightening.

"Tom! What…" Shanna's voice died in her throat.

Tom Morgan stumbled, regained his footing, and climbed onto the loft. "How'd you know, Shanna? How'd you know it was me?"

"I…I didn't." Shanna clasped a hand over her mouth. Shocked more by the menacing look in his eyes than the gun in his hand, Shanna moved away from him.

"I didn't want to kill you. That's why I had to get rid of that creep who worked for us."

"Us?" Shanna bit her lip.

He smiled. "Oh no, you don't. You're not going to pull the same thing your mother did. You wired too? Elizabeth thought she was so smart. Pretending she wanted in on the deal when all she really wanted was to get the evidence to turn us in. Well, she didn't pull it off, and you won't, either. What did you do, find the tape?"

"No, I—you were up here, weren't you? That night when I was supposed to meet you for dinner."

He shrugged. "That doesn't matter. I couldn't find it. Been back a couple of times, but—I know it's here. Unless you already found it. Is that it? You want a cut of the action? I know you haven't taken it to the police."

Shanna gulped back rising panic. "What did you do to Mike?"

"Who's Mike? You mean Max?"

"His real name is Mike O'Brian. He's my father. You didn't hurt him, did you?"

"I didn't have any choice, Shanna. He knew about me. I don't know how—maybe it was him. Maybe he found the tape."

"What did you do to him?" It was all Shanna could do to keep from screaming.

"Same thing I'm going to do to you."

"You killed him?" Shanna dropped to her knees. "No..."

"You think I wanted to? No one was supposed to get hurt in all of this, but it's too late for that."

"He was my father." Tears blurred her vision as she gazed up at the figure towering over her.

"Shanna, don't cry. I hate when you do that. Look, it's going to be over soon. Maybe I could just..." He shook his head. "No, that won't work. I have to kill you."

Shanna pressed her fist against her mouth. "Who else is in on this? Nan? Joshua? Beth? Laurie? Did Andrew know too?"

"I'm not saying any more. Get downstairs—now. I gotta make your death look like a break-in."

Shanna reached the main floor and would have tried to run, but Tom was too quick. He jabbed a gun in her side. "Go over there next to..."

Shanna followed his gaze to the bloodstained rug in the kitchen.

"He's gone."

Thank God. If he is strong enough to crawl away, maybe... "He's gone for the police, Tom. You may as well give up right now."

"Shut up. I need to think." Tom glanced around the room, his gaze settling on the table and on the keys she'd placed there earlier.

"Get the keys, Shanna. We're out of here."

"Where you goin'?" Ryan rounded the corner of the porch and stepped inside, carrying two pieces of paper. "Can I come too?" His gaze shifted to his uncle's hand. "How come you got a gun?"

"Run, Ryan—run to your daddy," Shanna urged. Her words may as well have been drops of rain on an already soggy ground.

Tom scooped him up. "Hey, little man. That's not a bad idea. You and me and Shanna can take a little ride in Shanna's pickup. What do you say, Shanna. You game?"

Shanna clutched her throat. She needed to stay calm. "S-sure."

Ryan handed her the pictures he'd brought. "These are for you," he said. "I made 'em myself."

Shanna's heart nearly crumbled when she saw what he'd written on the top one. *To my mom. I love you.*

"Do you like 'em?"

"Oh yes, Ryan, very much." Her hands trembling, she set the drawings on the table and picked up her keys. She hoped the pictures would let Joshua or Mike know Ryan had been there. Though she might have fought Tom had she been alone, now she had no choice but to follow his instructions to the letter. A few minutes ago, she'd never have dreamed her charming brother-in-law capable of any crime. Now she had no doubt he'd kill his own nephew to keep from going to prison.

"Her truck's gone. Let's hope we're not too late." Joshua opened the door to Agent Hill's rental car before it ground to a stop in Shanna's driveway. He hit the porch running. "Shanna! Ryan!" Panic filled his voice as he flung open the door, his eyes drawn to the blood-stained carpet.

Sirens screamed as two deputy sheriffs pulled their cars in behind Hill.

Joshua felt as if he'd been transported to some outer world where chaos reigned. He'd gotten an unexpected visit from Agent Hill with news that nearly pinned him to the wall. They were about to head out the door to Shanna's when Nancy called to say Mike had been shot and she and Henry were on their way to the hospital with him.

"It's your brother," Nancy had said. *"He shot Mike and was planning on killing Shanna as well."* It took him awhile to figure out that Mike

and Max were the same person. Shanna's father. Another of Andrew's secrets.

About the same time, Nan discovered Ryan had disappeared again. The missing pictures he'd drawn for his mother had given Joshua a pretty good notion of where the boy had gone. While Nan and a couple of volunteers from the sheriff's department were searching the beach, Joshua went with the FBI agent in hopes of stopping Tom before he got to Shanna.

Joshua still couldn't believe it. Agent Hill had told him about Tom's involvement as well. Only his story involved the murder of some thug in a Portland hotel and Elizabeth's murder. He only hoped his son hadn't been at the cabin when Tom showed up and that he was still on some sandy path somewhere between. The drawings on the table tossed his hopes to the wind.

"Any sign of them?" Agent Hill came up behind him.

"Ryan's been here." He reached for the drawings.

"Don't touch anything," Hill ordered. "We'll get fingerprints."

The catch in Joshua's throat gave his voice a strange raspy sound. "You think Tom took them somewhere?"

"That would be my guess—maybe as hostages to help him get out of the country. On the other hand, Shanna's pickup is gone. She might have escaped and he went after her. Or he may have left her and the boy and run. If Tom was as fond of the two of them as you say, he probably won't kill them. Maybe Shanna's on her way back to your place with Ryan."

Donovan called in the state patrol and gave them a description of Shanna's vehicle and a license number. "If you find them, let me know. Don't try to approach them. We don't want the guy getting antsy. There may be a kid with them. Just keep an eye on them and keep us informed as to their position."

He turned to Joshua. "We'll find them," he said, wishing he could believe his own reassurances. Logic and experience told him otherwise. Tom Morgan was on the run. There was a good chance he'd hook up with his partner or boss, as the case might be. Judging from the long-reaching effects of the crime, Hill guessed they were talking organized crime. That meant all three of them—Tom, Shanna, and Ryan—were expendable.

~

"Sing to us, Shanna." Tom raised his left arm and rested it on the seat back. He picked up strands of her hair and twisted them around his fingers.

She leaned back. "Don't. You're hurting me."

"Am I?" He released her hair and massaged her neck. "I'm like that, you know. Hurting the people I love the most. I'm a lot like my father was—Nan told me that once."

She eased up on the gas pedal, flexing the muscles in her leg. Ryan had fallen asleep on it over an hour ago. Prior to that he'd gone on about how he and his dad needed her to come home and be their mom. "Daddy cries sometimes 'cause he misses you so much. He doesn't think I know. But I do. I used to cry sometimes, too, but not anymore 'cause I know you're my mom and Jesus found you."

"What are you talking about, Ryan?" Tom had asked. "Laurie's your mom."

"No, she ain't. Shanna is."

"Humph. That true? You're Ryan's real mom?"

Shanna didn't answer.

"I should have guessed. Joshua having a kid so soon after you and he split up. How did he end up with him?"

"I don't think this is the right time to talk about it."

Tom examined the gun, then set it on the floor in front of him. "Don't tell me, Elizabeth made you give him up and Andrew took him. Why didn't you tell me?"

"You were gone. In boarding school, as I recall. There was nothing you could have done."

"Seems like there's a lot of things the family never told me." He turned to look out the window at the darkness.

Ryan yawned. "When are we going back home?"

"Soon, darling. Just rest."

"Will you come to live with my dad and me?"

Shanna didn't have the heart to tell him no. She was his mother and he knew it. "I'll think about it," she finally said. "Why don't you lay your head against me and go to sleep."

He had. She reached down now and stroked his silken hair, brushing it off his forehead. *How cruel you are, God. How very cruel. You gave me a son and took him away. Now You've given him back, and it looks as though You're planning to take him away again.*

No, it wasn't fair to blame God. God hadn't taken Ryan from her. Elizabeth and Andrew had. And now Tom was in the process. Shanna took a deep breath to still the fluttering butterflies in her stomach. She had an idea. "I'm going to need to stop for gas soon," she said.

Tom had directed her to the beach approach where he had left his rental car. They'd transferred to it and driven south, crossing the Columbia River to Astoria, then traveling south again, crossing the river at Longview, where they took Interstate 5 toward Portland. Tom hadn't told her where they were going. She didn't want to know.

He squeezed her shoulder and lowered his arm. "There's a place not far from here—before we hit Portland. Pull in there. I'll drive for a while. You can sleep." He grimaced at her. "Stay in the car. I don't want anybody to recognize you."

"I'll need to use the rest room."

"Yeah—no doubt." He picked up the gun again as she exited the freeway and drove the short distance to the gas station. "You go ahead. I'll stay here with the kid, so don't be getting any ideas about running or calling the cops."

He didn't have to say it. Shanna got the message loud and clear. Nevertheless, Shanna walked back to the rest rooms, found a pay phone, and dialed 9-1-1.

"Stay on the line, ma'am. We'll be right there."

"I can't. He'll miss me. I have to go. He's got my son."

"Ma'am, please—"

Shanna hung up and walked back into the main part of the store, stopping at the glass door. She stepped outside. Maybe while Tom gassed up and paid she could get Ryan to safety.

She stared at the empty space near the pumps.

Shanna's heart felt like it had been yanked out of her chest. The car was gone.

Chapter Twenty-Nine

"Joshua." Shanna ran into his open arms. "I'm so sorry. I tried to get him away, but he…Tom…"

"Shh." Joshua stroked her hair. "I know. It's all right."

She hadn't meant to cry again, but a fresh reservoir of tears fell despite her efforts to stop them. Nothing that had happened in the past could have prepared her for the crushing pain she'd experienced that terrible moment she realized Tom had left her behind. No hurt could compare to the agony she felt now. Her baby was no longer a nameless, faceless entity that made her arms ache with longing. He was a real little boy. He was Ryan Morgan, and he'd drawn her a picture that said, *To my mom. I love you.*

Joshua guided her to a sofa and settled her down beside him. "The FBI is working on the case, honey. They'll find him."

"I shouldn't have let him out of my sight."

"You did the right thing, Shanna." Donovan Hill hunkered down in front of her. "You were able to give us a description of the car. We've traced the plates. It's just a matter of time."

"He's right, you know." Nancy leaned down and gave her a hug. "They'll find him. We need to have faith."

Their reassurances did little to assuage her guilt or make her any less miserable. Shanna glanced around the room. Besides Nancy,

Joshua, and Donovan, there was Nan, Nancy's husband, and the sheriff she'd talked to the other day.

Shanna's gaze drifted back to Nancy. "Mike—I mean Dad. Is he—?"

"He's doing much better. The bullet missed any vital organs, thank goodness. Broke a rib and punctured a lung, though. He'll be out of the hospital soon, I'm sure."

"Thank God. When Tom said he'd killed him, I—" She couldn't finish.

Exhausted, Shanna leaned back in the crook of Joshua's arm. She shouldn't be sitting so close or letting him comfort her. Things were too unsettled between them. But his arms felt so good and warm. Funny how tragedies made people forget their differences. Even for a short time.

Shanna must have slept. When she awoke she found herself lying in bed looking into the beautiful sky-blue gaze of her son. She closed her eyes, then opened them again, expecting the vision to vanish. "Ryan?"

"Yep. It's me."

"I thought…" She reached for him. Ryan jumped onto the bed, wrapping his thin arms around her neck. She held him close. If this was a dream, she never wanted to wake up. Never had her arms felt so full and right.

Releasing him, she asked, "What are you doing here?"

"Dad and me was watching you sleep. You sure are pretty, Dad says so, but I think so too."

She rubbed her eyes. She was in her cabin at the beach. Snowball was curled up alongside her thigh. The last thing she remembered was leaning against Joshua waiting for word about Tom and Ryan.

"How did you…? What happened?"

"Hey, sleepyhead." Joshua came into the bedroom with a tray, which he settled on her lap. "I'll answer all your questions in a few minutes. Right now it's time to eat. And don't tell me you're not hungry."

"Yeah, don't tell us that, 'cause I fixed the toast."

"I must be dreaming." She smiled. "Otherwise how could two handsome guys like you be fixing me breakfast?" Despite the questions she longed to ask, Shanna felt herself relax. Ryan was here and safe, and for the moment that was all that mattered. She sensed Joshua didn't want to talk in front of the boy. She'd respect that. Ryan seemed as happy and content as if nothing had happened.

After breakfast, Joshua suggested a walk on the beach. He set Ryan up in the sand with a kettle and spoons for building sandcastles and led Shanna a few feet away, where he set up beach chairs. "Funny how such small things can make children happy."

"Yes, it is." She lowered herself into the chair, thinking of the doll her father had repaired. It had only been a few days ago, and she'd barely acknowledged it. But the kind act had nudged itself deep into her soul and settled into the spirit of the little girl she used to be. Her daddy had fixed her doll. Her heavenly Father had done some fixing too. Her heart had somehow been pieced together, and Shanna felt something akin to joy.

"I know you've been anxious to hear what happened," he said finally. "I'm afraid the story is a bit anticlimactic after all you've been through."

"In what way?" She shifted her gaze from Ryan to his father. Her heart skipped like a rock over water. Oh, how she loved him—perhaps more now than she had as a teenager.

"Tom got as far as Salem, Oregon. He left Ryan sleeping in the car while he went into a Safeway store to get groceries. Ryan woke up and saw you weren't there. He went into the store and told the manager he was looking for his mommy." Joshua chuckled. "The man asked who his mommy was, and when he said Shanna O'Brian the guy went nuts. He'd heard about the abduction on the radio just minutes before. Of course, he recognized your name and called the police.

"About the time Tom got back to the car, the cops were there to meet him. Ryan doesn't have a clue how much danger you two were in. All he knows is that Uncle Tom did something naughty and will have to go to jail for a while." Joshua wasn't smiling now. His gaze drifted toward the ocean.

"I'm sorry, Josh. This must be terrible for you."

"It's harder on Nan. You think you know someone." Joshua shook his head. "It still doesn't seem possible. In some ways I must have known all along something wasn't right with Tom. There was a hard edge around all that charm of his. I just never expected him to be a killer. I don't think in the end he would have hurt either you or Ryan."

"But he killed the man who followed me."

"Broadman. Tom told me he did that to protect you. Broadman had killed Elizabeth on orders from the crime syndicate they were both involved with. He was planning to come after you as well. Tom couldn't let that happen."

"What will happen to him?"

"I'm not sure. He'll serve time. The tape Donovan found proves he was stealing the originals from Morningsong."

"Tape? The evidence everyone was looking for? You found it?"

"Donovan and his men did."

"When? Where? Was it in one of the boxes?"

"No. Remember the music box you were always so crazy about? Elizabeth had tucked one of those tiny cassettes inside, between the two bottom layers. One of the officers discovered it."

Shanna shuddered. "So I had it all along. I wonder why she put it there or how she thought I'd find it."

"I don't know. Maybe she left something else—a clue or something in one of her journals. On the other hand, it may be one of those unsolved mysteries."

"Why did she make the tape, Joshua? Was she in on it?"

"No. She was trying to protect your interests. She must have found out what was going on and figured the best way to deal with it was to implicate them. She did, but they got to her before she could turn them in."

"I'm glad she wasn't involved in the pirating. It's so sad about Tom."

"Hmm. He's my brother, Shanna. I keep wondering what I did wrong to have him turn out like that. It wasn't Nan and Andrew—they brought us both up. 'Course, I suppose it could have been my parents. Life was pretty rough for us when Dad got to drinking."

"You shouldn't blame yourself or your parents. Tom made his own choices. He didn't have to steal from Morningsong. And just because our parents make the wrong choices doesn't mean we have to..." Shanna lifted up a handful of sand and let it run through her fingers.

"Did you hear what you just said?"

Tears gathered in her eyes. "Yes. I did. Nancy was right. I don't have to emulate the hurtful things Elizabeth did. When Tom forced Ryan and me to go with him, I knew I'd have done anything to keep Ryan from getting hurt. I would have given up my life—my music—everything. Nothing in the world mattered other than keeping him safe.

"Being here with Nancy and my father has given me a new perspective on that. I guess the singing isn't as important to me as I had once thought. It's not anywhere near as important as our son."

Joshua reached for her hand, cradling it in his.

"Oh, Joshua, when Tom left me at that gas station, I thought my heart would break."

"I know. I don't think I've ever felt so terrified."

"I love him so much, Joshua."

"That's good, because like it or not, you and I have been given an ultimatum."

Shanna frowned and pulled her hand free. "From whom?"

He nodded toward Ryan. "The boss."

"What?"

He smiled. "Ryan says he won't go back to Morningsong until I can talk you into coming with us. I'm inclined to agree with him."

Shanna's heart somersaulted. What only a few days ago seemed like a curse suddenly sounded like a dream come true. "He may have a bit of a wait. I'm not going back."

Joshua nodded. He looked away, disappointment evident in his eyes. "So you want me to go ahead with the divorce. I guess I understand—"

"No, I don't think you do." She placed a hand on his arm. "I want to stay here at the cabin for another week or two, at least. I need to steep myself in this place—talk to my father and get to know who I am outside of who Elizabeth taught me to be. And I want to get to know my little boy." She looked away, unable to meet his gaze. "And I want to get reacquainted with my husband—that is, if he still wants to."

Joshua became still, and for a moment Shanna feared he'd say no. When he finally spoke, it was with difficulty. "I do. More than anything in the world." Joshua stood and offered her a hand up. He took something out of his pocket. "Remember this?"

She nodded. It was the gold band he'd given her years before. "I thought Elizabeth threw it away."

"She did. Andrew rescued it, just like he did everything else—our marriage, our baby. He gave it back to me before he died." Joshua lifted up her hand and slipped the band on her finger, then brought her hand to his lips.

Shanna wrapped her arms around his neck and stretched up for a kiss. He didn't disappoint her.

TO BE CONTINUED

GET ACQUAINTED.

Shoofly Pie
—*Tim Downs*

Get to know Kathryn Guilford, from a remote North Carolina county, and Nick Polchak—a.k.a. the Bug Man. When Kathryn receives news that her long-time friend and one-time suitor is dead, she refuses to accept the coroner's finding that his death was by his own hand. Although she has a pathological fear of insects, she turns in desperation to Polchak, a forensic entomologist, to help her learn the truth. Gold Medallion award–winning author Tim Downs takes you on a thrill ride as Kathryn confronts her darkest fears to unearth a decade-long conspiracy that threatens to turn her entire world upside down.

ISBN: 1-58229-308-2

BECOME FRIENDS.

Betrayal in Paris
—Doris Elaine Fell

Get acquainted with twenty-seven-year-old Adrienne Winters, as Christy Award finalist Doris Elaine Fell weaves a tale of mystery and intrigue. Headstrong Ms. Winters is relentless in her pursuit to clear the names of her brother and father who were victims of a double betrayal on foreign soil. Travel along as Adrienne's adventure takes her from the streets of Paris to the hot sands of the Kuwaiti desert. Set on the backdrop of the September 11 Pentagon tragedy, Adrienne discovers a gentle romance as she sorts out her family's history and her faith in God.

ISBN: 1-58229-314-7

Other Books by Patricia H. Rushford

Fiction:

The McAllister Files:

Secrets, Lies, and Alibis (with Harrison Ford)

The Helen Bradley Mysteries:

Now I Lay Me Down to Sleep
Red Sky in Mourning
A Haunting Refrain
When Shadows Fall

The Jennie McGrady Mystery Series: (ages 10 and up)

Too Many Secrets
Silent Witness
Pursued
Deceived
Without a Trace
Dying to Win
Betrayed
In Too Deep
Over the Edge
From the Ashes
Desperate Measures
Abandoned
Forgotten
Stranded
Grave Matters

Nonfiction:

It Shouldn't Hurt to Be a Kid
Have You Hugged Your Teenager Today
What Kids Need Most in a Mom
Emotional Phases of a Woman's Life

ENJOYMENT GUARANTEE

If you are not totally satisfied with this book, simply return it to us along with your receipt, a statement of what you didn't like about the book, and your name and address within 60 days of purchase to Howard Publishing, 3117 North 7th Street, West Monroe, LA 71291-2227, and we will gladly reimburse you for the cost of the book.